THE VAMPIRE CURSE

THE VAMPIRE CURSE

THE VAMPIRE DEBT: BOOK TWO

USA TODAY BESTSELLING AUTHOR

ALI WINTERS

Second Edition
Paperback ISBN-13: 978-1-945238-12-3
Hardcover ISBN-13: 978-1-945238-13-0

This is a work of fiction. Names, characters, businesses, places, events, incidents, and time periods are the products of the author's imagination or used in a fictitious manner. The views and beliefs of the characters do not necessarily reflect that of the author's. Any resemblance to actual persons, living or dead, or actual events is purely coincidental. No AI was used in the creation, editing, production, of this book or on the official associated art. All aspects were created with human hands.

www.aliwinters.com
www.thevampiredebt.com

ALSO BY ALI WINTERS

ADULT ROMANTASY

Shadow World: The Vampire Debt

The Vampire Debt

The Vampire Curse

The Vampire Court

The Vampire Oath

The Vampire Crown

Shadow World: Standalones

The Vampire Trap

Wicked Prince of Frost

Stand Alone Titles

High Stakes

YOUNG ADULT

The Hunted Series

The Reapers

The Exodus

The Moirai

The Fallen

Flirting with Death (a short story)

The Hunted series Omnibus

In The End duology

Sound of Silence

Light in Darkness

In The End Omnibus

Stand Alone Titles

Cast In Moonlight

Favor of the Gods

Shadow World
SUNFA
Nightwich
CASTLE
Progsdale
Durford
Littlemire
Valeburn

MOUNTAINS
Sangate
Gloamfarrow
Windbury
Galeport
Murhelm
Crescent Isle
Stormvale
N

For Alexis

CHAPTER ONE

ALARIC

"Shall we go greet our guests?" Lawrence says, striding toward the door. Any lingering emotion over my refusal to mark Clara has vanished from his demeanor.

I clench my fists at my sides. The empty glass in my hand shatters. The shards fall to the floor at my feet, crunching underfoot. I don't even feel the sting of cuts along my palm, though they are entirely healed before I'm halfway across the room.

From their perch on the mantle of the fireplace, Cherno lifts their small head and cocks it to the side in silent question. I jerk my chin in the direction of Clara's room in answer, then I am out of the office and at the front door of the manor two seconds later, Lawrence following close at my heels.

Mr. Steward waits by the door for me to give him orders. Normally, he greets the guests and brings them into the drawing room to await my arrival. Tonight, I dismiss him. I'd rather not have these visitors get any ideas about his purpose in this household.

Once he is safely away, I open the door.

Three vampires stride from the black carriage. Their attire is equally dark and without a shred of any other color. The female—though the weakest of the lot—ascends the steps, preceding the two men.

"Della," I say, infusing as much cheer into my voice as possible. "I was beginning to think you would never grace Windbury with your radiance."

"You are full of demon shit, Mr. Devereaux," she says, but a smile still graces her lips as she enters. Della runs a finger along the edge of my jaw, her long nail scratching at my skin. I feel small beads of blood well up before my skin heals.

Della's eyes remain locked on Lawrence. She doesn't pause until she stands before him, her chest pressed to his. She reaches up to the back of his head to pull him down to place a kiss on his mouth. He doesn't return the kiss, but he doesn't fight it either, he just allows it to happen.

A pale white and gold rat scurries from her

shoulder to his, flicking Della's chin length black hair with the pink whip-like tail.

Lawrence left his demon with Della. It was his way of keeping an eye on the others. His distrust in such a seemingly ordinary gesture tells me all I need to know.

"I missed you too, Arinah," Lawrence whispers as the demon nuzzles him with their little pink nose.

I face the two vampires standing just outside the threshold.

Cassius, as always, wears his white blond hair loose. Though now it has grown more than halfway down his back from the shoulder length it was the last time we crossed paths.

The other man? *Him,* I do not know.

"It has been a long time, friend," I say greeting only Cassius, though he is anything but a friend.

"Are you not going to invite us in?" he asks. His expression is passive, the only hint of his true thoughts show in a singularly, raised brow.

A breeze picks up, bringing with it the bite of an early winter chill—another reminder that in two months' time, Clara and I will be forced to venture north and face Elizabeth. But if I have any say in the matter, we will avoid it all together.

The demons in the forest beyond the property line howl. They are louder than normal—closer.

I hold in a curse. Their presence has been an ever-increasing problem lately, demanding more and more of my attention. And I must go out again soon to chase them back.

However, with my newly arrived guests to keep me occupied, I don't know how or when I will be able to take care of the encroaching demons or find the cause, let alone keep any one of these vampires from draining every drop of blood from Clara's veins.

"Yes, please come in, Cassius… and," I pause, finally turning to the unknown man.

Red rings his irises. It is not an uncommon sight for a vampire who needs to feed, but he is the only one showing that trait at this moment. He would have fed with the others. Which only means one thing—his bloodlust is barely contained.

My blood boils. Upon hearing I claimed a human for the first time, Elizabeth has deemed fit to send a newly created vampire to my home.

"I don't think we have had the pleasure of meeting yet," I say with false pleasantries. "I am Alaric Devereaux."

His hair is short and is a mix of blond and light brown. His clothes are neatly pressed without a single stitch out of place—exactly how Elizabeth prefers us. In his left hand, he carries a fat toad, thick with warts.

Charming.

"Victor Connors." He holds out his hand.

It takes a long moment to understand what the reptile's presence means.

Rather than taking his hand, I step back and gesture for them to enter.

"Did you drive the horses with demons?" Lawrence asks. "I only arrived a few hours ago myself. You were a good two days behind me."

The door clicks shut, silencing the night song of demons.

I walk through the manor, knowing they will all follow. I don't trust the lot behind me with my life— or anyone else's for that matter—but it would be a show of weakness to watch them. So, I keep my head forward.

Cassius lets out a hearty laugh. "We did find some minor demons to possess them," he admits with hubris. "We didn't want to miss anything... *interesting.*"

Fifty years spent as Elizabeth's lap dog has done nothing for his arrogance.

The next few days will be long and tedious.

Mrs. Westfield hurries out of the drawing room as we near, careful to keep her eyes downcast and hands clasped before her.

Once we have all settled, I serve each a glass of blood. Not enough to be considered a meal. Being several hours old it has lost its warmth and is not up to my standards. I do not pour myself a glass, but it is enough to tell them—you are not welcome here.

Lawrence sits in one of the two wingback chairs while Della lies spread across the chaise lounge, looking as though she awaits many servants to cater to her every whim and desire.

Victor glares down at his glass, wrinkling his nose in distaste. That doesn't stop him from throwing his head back and drinking it in one swallow. His tongue darts out to lick up a stray drop lingering in the corner of his mouth. He runs a finger along the inside of his glass and sucks the last bits of blood.

I will need to test his weaknesses. How far can he be pushed before he nears his breaking point?

"We should have brought our own humans with us," Della whispers to Lawrence loud enough for everyone to hear. She sips from her glass, the blood staining her lips. We all hear her, though no one acknowledges her words. She walks a thin line of disrespect for a lesser vampire.

Cassius stands stoically before the fire, drinking his glass like it is a finely aged brandy.

"Where is the fresh blood?" Victor asks.

Della and Lawrence stare at him in horror, or perhaps they are just surprised that anyone would voice such an insulting question to someone who could rip him apart with little effort. He is indeed newly sired if simple games are beyond him. Elizabeth was a fool to send him.

"If you are not pleased," I say, straightening my cuffs and infusing as much disinterest into my voice as possible, "you are free to stay at one of the local inns instead or leave and return to Nightwich."

Cassius crosses the room to stand by my side and throws an arm over my shoulder. I want to push him off, but doing so would be a direct insult to Elizabeth. And she is already causing me enough of a headache all the way from her miserable castle in the Sunfall mountains. She is not even here, but she is in everything that is said and done since Lawrence arrived on my doorstep.

"Do not be upset, Victor didn't mean anything by it," Cassius says.

Lawrence watches on, silently sipping his drink and looking amused. He is of no help, so I walk to the window to remove Cassius's arm from me, unable to stand this man's false attempts at niceties. It is a favor to us both, as neither of us would pass up the chance to rip the other's throat out if the chance were given.

The wind picks up, whipping through the forest trees. Above, the moon is bright in the cloudless sky, splattered with stars.

"What possessed Elizabeth to send all of you?

Surely Lawrence is more than capable of bringing any news she could want to send?" I turn my head slightly to eye Lawrence meaningfully.

Cassius sneers, but the expression vanishes just as quickly as it appeared, replaced by a predator's smile.

"We were all eager to meet this delightful human snack of yours." He looks around as if she has been in the room, hiding the entire time. "Where *is* the little morsel anyway?"

I narrow my eyes at his transparent attempt at speeding up protocol.

"I am afraid that she is retired for the evening."

Victor growls, drawing our attention to him. He sits cross legged on the floor before the fire, dragging his finger along the inside of his glass. *Fuck.* He is still *very* new, and his blood lust is stronger than I could have anticipated.

It has been some time since Elizabeth has sired a new vampire, nearly a century ago if memory serves.

Why him? Why now? And why send him here where there is a newly claimed human?

Cassius joins my side at the window, but he doesn't look out. Instead, his reflection shows that his gaze is locked on my face.

"Winter solstice is in two months' time," he says quietly as he reaches into the pocket of his vest to pull out a large envelope, then hands it to me. The black wax seal on the back holds the symbol of the waning crescent moon with a raven's feather cutting through it.

The paper is thick and heavy. Not a single word is written on the outside, not even my name. I break the seal and open it.

A formal invitation to the Solstice masquerade on the last day of the year and to the festivities that will last for two weeks. It is the same invitation as every other year to celebrate a successful claiming season.

Except this time, the script does not belong to any servant or scribe. It belongs to none other than Elizabeth herself. The faint scent of iron rises up, and I inhale. This invitation was not written in ink but in human blood.

There is so much more meaning behind this than a quick glance could tell.

After a moment, I raise my eyes to meet Cassius's. "The post could have delivered this just as easily as one of you. I fail to see the point of this gathering."

A wicked smile spreads across his lips, but there is no humor in it. "Oh, but we have all come to make sure you and your little pet make it there this time."

Dread turns my blood cold, but I manage to keep my voice calm. "Message received. You may all leave in the morning." I start to turn away, stopping after two steps, when he chuckles.

"Oh no, my friend. We will be here with you, and we shall personally escort the both of you to Nightwich for the celebration. Elizabeth will be thrilled you have finally decided to act like a real vampire." He comes around to stand in front of me, he fidgets with my cravat as if to straighten it.

My fists clench at my sides, crumpling the edge of the invitation.

"In fact," he says quietly. "We are *all* anxious to meet the human who has managed to capture your interest after all these years."

CHAPTER TWO

CLARA

A FLUTTERING NEAR MY HEAD HAS MY EYES SNAPPING open. My heart thunders in my chest. It takes me a moment to blink the bleariness of sleep from my vision, but when I do, perched inches from my face is a small black bat watching me sleep.

I suck in a breath to give the beastie a piece of my mind, but a single, loud knock on my door halts my tongue.

Sending a glare in Cherno's direction, I throw my blankets off hoping to scare the creature away.

It doesn't work. Even as I open the door, I don't take my eyes off the little intruder.

"Miss," Mr. Steward says quietly. There is an unidentifiable note to his voice that is out of place.

I take him in—from his downcast gaze to the

slump of his posture, which looks uncomfortable and unnatural. In his hands, he holds out a thick bundle.

I step back and motion for him to enter.

Wordlessly, he sets the clothes on the bench at the foot of my bed, then crosses the room to stoke the dying fire in the hearth.

Mr. Steward sets the iron poker aside. He stays crouched for a long moment, staring into the flames. "Mrs. Westfield has finished fixing the last of your pockets."

I start at the words and eye the clothes he'd brought. I suppose my attempts at sewing were even worse than I'd originally assumed.

He stands and heads to the door, where he pauses, keeping his back to me. He hasn't looked at me once since he came in. The avoidance bothers me, though I'm not sure why.

"Three more guests arrived late last night. I suggest you keep to your rooms until the sun is high." And then he leaves, closing the door with a soft click.

I face Cherno, who is still watching me with those large, dark eyes. So many thoughts race through my mind. It has been at least a week since I've seen the butler, and now, he wakes me up, delivering clothes and a cryptic message.

Then there are these guests...

"They are vampires, aren't they?" I ask, feeling the

need to say something, even if it's a question I know the answer to.

Cherno lets out a soft squeak as if confirming. Taken aback at the seemingly intelligent reply, I tilt my head. It could be a coincidence.

"Is that why Alaric sent you to my rooms?"

Another squeak.

I smile and shake my head. Awake for less than ten minutes, and I am having an imaginary conversation with a vampire's pet bat. I must still be half asleep.

Glancing out the window, I sigh. It will be several hours before the sun will be at its zenith and already I feel trapped. I've stayed in my rooms for entire days before, but it was always my choice. I had known I could leave any time I wanted.

Outside the window, the sky is a dreary gray. Thick clouds, heavy with rain, swallow up every inch of blue in the early morning haze.

I untie the string holding my clothes together. Embarrassment washes over me after examining the newly redone pockets. They are more hidden and reenforced. The seams are straight and sturdy and it's only by looking at these that I realize how terrible my sewing skills truly are.

There is no point in dwelling on it, so I reach back to untie my nightgown and stop, aware of a set of eyes watching my every move.

"Turn around," I say to the bat, moving my finger in a circle. My jaw drops when Cherno does as instructed.

I snap my mouth shut. *Just a coincidence.* Or maybe Alaric took the time to train the creature with basic gestures and commands?

That must be it.

I dress quickly. This has been a strange morning, and I'm not sure what to make of it.

I take my book from my night table, sit in the chair near the fire, and try to read. It's only after a dozen pages that I realize I haven't paid attention to a single word. I sigh, giving up, and close the book.

Tapping a finger on my chin, I mull over what Mr. Steward said.

Three more guests, plus Mr. Harkstead and Alaric, make five vampires under one roof. Alaric is one thing. I have spent enough time with him to know he won't come for me in the middle of the night to end my life. I know what to expect from him.

A chill skitters down my spine. Mr. Harkstead terrifies me. He is a predator in a way Alaric never was, even when I thought he might still kill me.

How different could they be to visit Alaric? Then again, he did warn me... he even offered me an easy way out. I am a fool... a damned fool for not taking the opening Alaric had given me last night.

I set the book down and pace. It is not late in the afternoon yet, but it is close, and I am crawling in my skin with nothing but my thoughts.

It's close enough to noon, and the sun is now peeking through the clouds, burning away the morning gloom. I wonder why it was so important to wait until midday. Are vampires unable to stand the bright light?

"I'm going to the stables," I say.

Cherno's head pops up. I hurry to the bed and snatch the dagger from under my pillow and place it into my pocket before striding out of the room. The sound of flapping leather wings follows me down the hall.

Once I am outside, Cherno disappears. The air is chilly, but the day is bright. The sky is a clear, bright blue that stretches on endlessly.

Though I've never been to the stables during my time here, I find my way to them effortlessly. Behind the barn is a large fenced in field. Two large, black horses graze. One has white covering the bottom portion of its two hind legs, the other has a spot of white between its eyes. While they are roughly the same size as other horses I have seen, they are sturdier. They look as if they were built to be powerful rather than fast.

A twig snaps underfoot, and the horses lift their

massive heads, their nostrils flaring. I am glad there is a fence between us, I'm not sure they wouldn't trample me.

After a moment, they resume grazing, and I cautiously approach the fence. The one closest seems to watch me warily. They must decide I pose no threat because they eventually ignore me.

Their thick manes nearly brush the ground every time they reach for another bite of grass.

I fold my arms on the top rung of the fence and rest my chin, content to watch them. I have only seen horses tethered to wagons and carriages, laden with straps and equipment, and often their coats would be patchy, their legs coated in mud. This pair gleams. It is clear they are well cared for.

The horse with the mark on its forehead meanders near me. Its coat gleams in the sunlight and it looks softer than velvet. I wonder if it would mind if I reached out to pet it?

"Do you ride?" a rich, deep voice asks, warm breath brushing over my ear.

I spin, nearly losing my balance, and catch myself on the fence.

Alaric takes a step back. The sun guilds his black hair, bringing out hints of blue in the shining strands.

"What are you doing out right now? I thought the sun…" I trail off, not entirely sure what I thought. I only know that Mr. Steward told me to wait until midday before leaving my rooms.

Alaric inches closer, then dips his head as if he will whisper a secret to me. "The sun doesn't kill us—if that's what you thought. It weakens our powers, so most vampires prefer to sleep during the height of day. We are demon cursed and bound, but we are not demons ourselves."

"You don't sleep during the day?" I ask.

He smiles. "Sometimes, but I wanted to talk with you in private." He moves closer, caging me in with his arms, though it's hardly necessary with his body pinning me to the fence.

We have been more intimate than this before, but there's also something different about this moment.

"What are you doing?"

Alaric pulls in a breath, then offers a rueful smile. "Ah, yes." He pulls back slightly. "You see, my guests are watching from the window. They believe you have been marked, so if we keep our distance from each other it would seem odd, and they might guess the truth. So, unless you wish to be marked…"

In answer, I lift a hand and tuck a strand of hair behind his ear. This feels awkward, and I'm not sure what to do with my other hand, so I rest it on his bicep.

"Good girl," he says, but there is no joy in his tone or his expression.

If I didn't know better, I would say he is disappointed.

Pretending for others feels wrong. Every time we've been close in the past, it just *happened*. But that doesn't stop my heart from hammering at his nearness.

"So, do you?" he asks.

I lick my lips and try to remember what we are talking about. "Do I what?"

"Ride." Alaric nods his head in the direction of the horses.

I have never touched one, let alone ridden one. In Littlemire, they are beasts of burden, tools for people to use. One or two of the more well-off farms owned one. Only the more affluent families can afford to keep more than that to use for leisure and sport, such as going on staged hunts as part of their celebrations.

"No, I have never had occasion to."

"Then," he says, moving to the side and leaping over the fence in a fluid motion. The horse with the white mark on its forehead trots up to him the moment his feet land. "Perhaps, this is a perfect opportunity."

Alaric mounts the horse without a saddle or reins.

But when he holds a hand out, beckoning me to

him, I have no choice but to squeeze my way between the gaps in the fence boards and go to him.

I stop beside him. He towers over me from his seat, and I have to crane my neck back to look up at him. Sitting astride the horse, he towers over me.

The animal is massive and made of solid muscle. He sits with his legs straddling the beast. However, I am wearing a dress. I'm not sure how this will work.

I take a deep breath and slip my hand into his. He pulls me up effortlessly in front of him.

My eyes widen. This is so high off the ground, and sitting as I am, I feel as though I could slip and fall off at any moment.

The horse shifts impatiently. I let out a small squeak.

"Are you all right?"

"I—yes, but won't it hurt if I fall?"

"I would never let you fall," he says. At first, I think he's teasing me, but his face is serious. "You can put one leg on either side of the horse if that would make you more comfortable."

"I'm wearing a dress," I say through clenched teeth.

He shrugs and urges the horse to begin walking.

"Fine," I say.

When his arm tightens around my waist, I indelicately move one leg to the other side, causing my skirt to bunch up and show the lower half of my legs. I should be embarrassed but there is only Alaric and nature for as far as the eye can see as we move away from the manor.

The horse walks at a leisurely pace. I hold my breath waiting for the horse to take off at a tooth jarring run. But the ride is smooth and steady. At my back, Alaric holds me against him. With his arm around me, I feel safe. My breathing evens and I lean back into him without thinking.

We ride in silence for the first lap around the pasture.

"What did you mean by you being demon cursed?" I ask.

I know he heard me because every muscle in his body goes rigid at my back, but Alaric says nothing for so long, I begin to think he won't answer.

"It is a figure of speech—nothing more," he says in a clipped tone. His fingers twitch as if he's calculating his thoughts and unaware of this tick.

It's a lie. If that were true, he would have replied immediately. I twist to face him and find his mouth mere inches from my own. My heart thumps against my ribs, remembering the feel of his full lips. *Demons and saints...*

I swallow those thoughts and meet his gaze. "No, I don't think so," I say sharply. He frowns, his sapphire eyes darkening. This time, I speak in a kinder tone.

"You don't need to lie to me, I should think we were past all that… whatever it is, you *can* trust me."

I'm not sure why I say that. I've never given him a reason to trust me. I've spent weeks attempting to stab him… but things feel different between us. I'm not sure when they changed. Maybe the night he was injured, or the night when I would have given him *everything* had he not stopped us, or two nights ago when Elise tried to kill me.

Or some other moment, or perhaps all of them combined.

There's a heavy pause hovering between us as I realize those words are true. Alaric must also realize it because his features soften.

"I have said too much already, and we have other matters we must discuss."

As much as I want to push the issue, I decide it's better to let it go for now.

With his free hand he reaches up and pulls my hair over one shoulder. And then his mouth rests against my skin. My pulse jumps, and I know he can feel it as he places slow kisses along the space between my neck and shoulder.

Between his kisses, the hand holding me to him, and the other resting on my upper thigh, a haze settles over my thoughts, clouding my mind. Warmth pools low in my belly and it takes everything in me to keep from shaking my head in an attempt to clear it. I am thankful his hands aren't wandering freely—then thinking would be impossible.

"This visit will be dangerous for you," he whispers between kisses.

And with those words, icy adrenaline floods my veins.

"But I will do everything in my power to protect you. They are not to be trusted, so don't let your guard down, even for a second." Another kiss. "And always carry the dagger."

I swallow. Were it not for his words keeping me somewhat grounded, I might almost believe this moment is real.

"What about *this*," I ask, pressing my back against him to indicate how intimate he is when we are seemingly alone.

He breathes a heavy sigh. "We must make them believe you have been marked. I will touch you as if you are really mine." My heart thumps and lodges itself between my ribs. He smiles against my shoulder. "And not just when you attempt to kill me—which, forgive me, my dear Clara, that bargain must be put on hold for the time being. We cannot have them knowing the truth if you wish to live."

"Then how am I to earn my freedom?"

"For now, let's concentrate on keeping you alive. You can have your freedom when it is safe."

My head swims. I am glad he stopped kissing me, but now my stomach is in knots. He had offered me an escape last night, but like a fool, I had refused.

"I want to get down," I say, my voice is soft and desperate.

When the horse finally comes to a stop, I open my eyes, unaware of when I had closed them. We are in the exact spot where we mounted.

Alaric dismounts quickly, then reaches up to take me by the waist and guides me down. My legs shake, and I think he can sense it because he hasn't released me yet. Instead of doing so he pulls me in close and wraps his arms around me.

"When I touch you, understand that I am doing so to protect you." There is hesitation in his voice. "Do you trust me on this?"

Do I trust him?

It's a strange thing to consider. I have been trying to kill him, to draw blood in order to win my freedom and leave… He is a vampire—a monstrous beast that rips families apart—and I'm only human. He hates me for killing his sister, and I hate him *because* of what he is.

Yet he is asking if I trust him with my life.

I pull back to look him in the eye and say, "Yes."

CHAPTER THREE

CLARA

NEITHER OF US SPEAKS AS WE WALK BACK INTO THE house, arm in arm. This is a game—one that could be deadly for me for reasons I don't yet fully understand. Why would other vampires care what he does with me? He claimed me. That should be the only thing that matters.

But there is so much more to this than I ever anticipated. All I wanted to do was keep my sister safe and alive. I have spent the last month and a half trying to get back to her.

Once inside, I blink to adjust my eyes to the dim light. Standing in the doorway of the drawing room is the vampire from last night. He holds a goblet full of what I can only assume is blood. He is the one from last night in the library.

"Run little human. Hide. The others are coming, and they are far more dangerous than even I..."

His hazel eyes follow us. Nerves crawl up my spine.

Alaric guides my chin up with one finger. He gives me a tight smile and pulls me a little closer into his side.

The walk to my rooms has never felt so long. I can practically feel the gazes of all four of the vampire guests following us. Though I don't see them, I know they are there.

I enter, and when I turn to close the door, he is already inside.

Alaric raises a brow as if he knew I'd intended to shut him out.

"Clara," he starts, and there's something in the way he says my name that makes me bristle. "If I mark you—"

"No," I say, not even letting him finish. "We have been over this before. You know why I don't want the mark."

He looks distraught, which makes me feel terrible for snapping. I step up to him and see genuine worry in his eyes. I reach up and brush my fingers along his brow to smooth away the frown lines. He is worried for my safety.

"I do not know what to do with you," he says.

From someone else's mouth, it would border on insulting, but he doesn't mean it in the way a human would, or even the way another vampire would.

"It will be all right." I have no idea if that is true. We both see it for what it is—a flimsy platitude. But it's all I have to give.

He steps back and nods. "I will continue to ask you to reconsider the mark until you change your mind or you are safe."

I grit my teeth until my jaw aches. He knows my answer will always be no.

"You know the laws, Clara. You have always known them. Once a human is claimed, they are at the whims of their vampire master until their death."

My eye twitches. *Master.* My heart races for the second time today, but now it is for an entirely different reason.

I am not a thing to be owned.

"Then what is the point of this charade?" I hiss, motioning between us. "If you are my master and I must fall to your will, then why not bite me now and be done with it? If what I want means so little, *why pretend* you are giving me a choice at all? Just force the mark on me already and be done with it. Or better yet, kill me."

Baiting a vampire… not exactly a smart move on my part. One might actually believe that I *want* to die.

His eyes narrow as he lets out a low snarl, fangs bared. I take an involuntary step back, but he advances, closing the distance between us until his chest is flush with mine.

"The point, dear Clara, is that the last thing *I* want is to have a human unwillingly tied to me for the remainder of their life."

My eyes widen at the venom of his words. I open my mouth to speak but he holds up a hand, staying me.

"I continue to ask," he says, his voice is soft and low. He looks exhausted. "Because I do not know of a better way to keep the others away from you."

I'm not ready to let go of this yet. Though there is little point in fighting for the sake of fighting, and he does not seem willing to continue.

"Fine," I say, throwing my hands in the air. "Keep asking me if you must, but I can only promise to *think* about it. I just don't understand why you are pushing this. We've already agreed to—" Now it's my turn to hesitate. "To-to make them believe I am yours."

My heart pounds when I hear myself say those last three words. They are words I can't mean, and they are not something I can want. *Xander is still waiting for me.*

I turn to face the window, wrapping my arms around my middle.

The view of the front of the property and the tangled forest beyond is one that has become more familiar to me than the one outside of my home in Littlemire.

"At least it won't be for too long," I say. There is a silence at my back that has me turning on him, eyes wide. My voice raises an octave, "*Will* it be long?"

The answer is in his unwillingness to look me in the eye. "There is more to the situation than I said earlier."

My hand bumps against the blade at my hip when I lower my arms to my sides. I have half a mind to run him through with it right now.

"Why did you withhold information you knew I would want? You say you need me to trust you but then you do this. But how can I trust you if you keep things from me?"

He is not cowed by my anger, but neither is he upset. "Trust me to tell you what you need to know, when you need to know, is part of the trust I need from you," Alaric says evenly. "This is a lot to take in and I wanted to ease you into it, to give you the chance to process it all."

It irritates me that his reasoning does make sense. I can't help the part of me that wants to fight. I know it isn't about him or whatever information he held back, but rather everything I am struggling to hold on to and come to grips with.

"Well, out with it then," I demand.

"They will be staying here through the end of the season."

Black spots form across my vision. *Two months...* "That's... that's..."

He continues on as if what he said wasn't anything to worry about. "Then they will escort us both to Nightwich."

"Go to Nightwich," I sputter. "What about—"

Alaric holds up his hand. "Our stay will only be a week or two at most."

I press my hand to my head. My vision wavers and I stumble slightly as my legs threaten to go out from under me. I might as well walk downstairs with open veins and offer myself up for dinner.

Alaric steps forward and grips my elbows, keeping me upright. I cling to his forearms unable to stand without his support because this ruse of ours might as well be for an eternity.

I've never been skilled in the art of lying, always wearing my heart on my sleeve. I don't know if I can pretend for so long.

Now, his insistence on marking me makes sense. Finding my legs again, I take a step back.

"This is impossible," I say. The freedom he promised me slips from my fingers like smoke from a doused fire.

"Perhaps it is, but without the mark, it is our only option." He straightens his back and looks almost regal. "There will be several tasks the first of which will be presenting you to my guests tonight."

"Present me?"

"It is a simple matter and one of the things we must do to avoid their suspicions. Otherwise, they will wonder why I am trying to hide you." His lips draw into a tight line.

I take a long, deep breath, then release it slowly.

"Tell me what being marked entails," I say, then hold up a hand. "Not because I want it, but knowing will help me do what I need to do."

Alaric's eyes darken a shade. In a blink, he is a hair's breadth away. His hands come up to cup my face, bringing his face closer. My eyes slide shut, ready for the kiss I'm sure will come.

"First," he whispers, his breath brushing my lips. "There can be no attempts on my life." One hand tangles in my hair, the other moves around my waist to pull me flush against him. "And second, you would not pull away."

Alaric kisses along my jaw and down my neck. I

try not to move or react, but my damned body has a mind of its own, pressing even closer to his.

"Yes, like that," he says. "And it ends with you *needing* to obey my every word."

He releases me. The cold air contrasts with his embrace. My eyes snap open and he stands halfway across the room.

I nearly gasp from the sudden loss of his warmth and the last thing he said. *Shit... He manipulated me so easily.*

I narrow my eyes.

"I am not your puppet," I snap.

"This is not for me, my dear Clara, but so the others believe. You are—" he shakes his head. "I would never want you to be a mindless puppet. This is nothing more than a part we must play."

"I hate this... it makes me feel like... like..."

"A possession?" he offers, with a hint of bitterness in his voice.

I nod.

"Then you must remember, my dear Clara, that you are not."

I clench my fists in the folds of my skirt. "You could always let me go."

"I'm sorry, that is no longer an option. You have been claimed they know you live and who you are."

It isn't the answer I wanted, but in truth, I did not

expect anything else. Still, knowing that does nothing to ease the ache in my heart.

Alaric backs away to leave. "Mrs. Westfield will be in shortly to help you prepare for the night."

I nod. There is nothing else I can do.

He pauses long enough to say, "Remember to obey."

CHAPTER FOUR

CLARA

I DON'T MISS THE FACT THAT MY DRESS IS THE EXACT shade of blue as Alaric's eyes. I tilt my head, contemplating how much time and effort it must have taken to make sure the material ended up this particular shade.

Reaching up to run a hand through my hair, I barely manage to stop myself in time from ruining the long and painful hour Mrs. Westfield had spent arranging it into intricate knots and curls. Whether it was more painful for her or me is still up for debate.

My neck and shoulders are bare, and the neckline is low in the current fashion for extravagant parties. My arms are covered in long, gloves that match the dress and halfway past my elbows to hide the thin wrapping on my healing arms.

I worry my bottom lip between my teeth. Alaric had said he was going to present me to the four vampires. I'm not ready for that many eyes on me, let alone the possibility of more than being watched.

I pluck at the material of the skirt. It's lighter than any other material I've worn before. The built in corset is tied so tight I can hardly move naturally.

No pockets and the material is too thin for me to strap my dagger to my thigh, let alone hide it anywhere else on my person. *I wonder where Alaric meant for me to hide it while wearing this...*

It seems I have no choice but to leave it behind. He will be with me, and I have to hope that his presence will be enough.

Obey. Obey. Obey... the thought of doing everything someone else demands twists my stomach into knots. I've never obeyed anyone before in my life and I survived well enough. Of course, survival has always meant doing what is necessary, and this is necessary.

But dealing with humans is not the same. This is akin to walking into the forest in the dead of night, challenging a demon to possess me just to see how it would rip me apart.

I wring my hands. The longer I have to stand here and wait until I am summoned, the more I begin to doubt my ability to pull this off.

A knock sounds, and I nearly jump out of my skin.

"Come in," I call.

Mr. Steward enters and looks me up and down appraisingly. He tsks and stalks over to the foot of my bed, where the thick choker necklace still sits.

"Turn around," he says.

I do. He clasps it around my neck, and I have to resist the urge to rip it off. It's like being strangled.

"They will see you do not have the marks without it," Mr. Steward admonishes. "You haven't touched your food either."

I shrug. Who in my position could eat? "I'm ready," I say.

Without another word between us, he motions for me to follow. I take a deep breath and blow it out, focusing on calming my heartbeat, and then I follow the butler through the halls.

Mr. Steward stops abruptly when we reach the library. "You will do just fine, Mrs. Valmont."

I blink up at him. For someone who isn't fond of me or my presence here, he is being strangely encouraging. I would say almost fatherly with his concern, making sure I'm ready, but I don't know what to expect from a father.

My father has only ever demanded I do whatever was necessary to bring home money for his gambling and to put food on the table.

Of course, it hadn't started out that way. At first, I had done so willingly at his request as he struggled to save the floundering trade business. But after Mother was claimed and reported dead, his addiction to spirits overwhelmed him. Within a few short years, the entirety of the responsibility of keeping the roof over our heads had fallen to me. My thoughts turn to my sister...

I miss Kitty. I wonder if she is well. With these guests here, I do not know how I can safely leave and return to her.

I don't trust Father to make sure she gets the medication she needs to be well. I can only hope she has used the money I stashed to secure herself a decent marriage with one of the younger men in town. But she mentioned nothing of the money or her medicine in the single letter I received.

She still expects me home soon, and I can only guess that is why this is the only letter I've received since coming here.

We turn down a hall, away from the drawing room near the front of the manor and the dim lighting pulls me from my thoughts of home.

"Are we not going to the drawing room?"

Mr. Steward lists his head to the side. "No, the music room is more suitable for this occasion."

The doors to the music room are closed. I scrunch my brows together.

He motions for me to stay, then opens one door and takes a single step inside, waiting for a long moment.

I can hear voices from within, though I can't make out what is being said. Then Alaric's warm timbre silences the room with a single word.

Mr. Steward clears his throat and bows. Then from his mouth comes, "Introducing, the lady Clara."

I swear my heart freezes in my chest. *Lady?* I am no lady. Why didn't he tell me I also had to act like a *lady* on top of everything else? I would have asked for a lesson at the very least … the Otherworld knows I need it.

The butler backs up and motions to me. I take a shaky step forward, and steeling my spine, I focus on slowing my pounding pulse.

My feet move forward. Slow and steady. My mind races wildly, too fast to take everything in. Somehow, I manage to keep my features placid and emotionless.

The closest vampire is the one from last night—Mr. Harkstead. His blond hair is tied back by a leather cord at the nape of his neck. It's odd how human he looks. He nods in my direction, and I'm shocked at the lack of intimidation in his demeanor. From the short conversation we had in the library I had expected him to try.

Behind him on one of the sofas is a woman with black hair cut into a chin-length bob. Her cream silk gown is accented by red jewels around the neckline.

She doesn't bother looking up. A man, barefoot and shirtless, kneels on the floor before her, arm raised, her mouth pressed to his wrist. She strokes his cheek as she opens her mouth and bites down.

My stomach churns.

The other two male vampires stare at me as though they can see straight through me.

The man with silver blond hair holds a woman to him. She is nearly limp in his arms, her head lulled to the side, neck exposed.

The last vampire is a man with short hair that is a mix of gold and umber. Two women sit at his feet, grasping at his legs. That one looks weak and sickly pale. Blood streaks down her neck, soaking the collar of her dress. The other has several puncture marks along her arms. Neither seem to notice anything else, they only want his attention… his touch. Their desperation is nearly palpable.

But he is looking at me like he has yet to drink his fill. The red rings around his irises are so thick they almost seem to glow even from across the room.

Demons and saints what in the Otherworld have I walked into?

I have to wonder if any of the humans in this room will make it out alive or if they will all be dead long before the sun rises.

The door closes behind me with a soft click, leaving me locked inside a veritable viper's nest.

"Clara," Alaric's voice drawls to my right.

My gaze drifts to him. One second, he is standing beside the piano, then the next, he is closing the distance with long strides. His arm wraps around my waist, and his mouth crashes down on mine. My first instinct is to pull away, but I can't…

I let myself melt into him, returning the embrace as if I mean it.

He ends the kiss then he offers me a glass filled with a red liquid. I take it without hesitation.

Obey… obey…

A quick sniff of the contents tells me it's wine. I take a sip, watching Alaric through my eyelashes. Then I take a longer drink and another until my glass is empty.

The murmuring that quieted before resumes once again. Though I can feel them watching us and I know they are looking for any small sign of weakness.

Alaric snaps his fingers and a woman with bite marks along her wrists hurries over, carrying a silver platter with several more filled glasses. He takes my empty cup and sets it down, retrieving a full one then handing that to me.

His fingers stay on mine a second longer than necessary, then he bends his head down, nuzzling my ear, and whispers, "You will want to pace yourself, my dear Clara. There are still the introductions to be made."

He leads me to a settee. Despite his warning I empty my second glass before we are halfway across the room.

Alaric turns me around to face the room, and there is already a vampire standing before us.

"Mr. Harkstead," I say. His name escapes my lips unbidden. Too much wine? Maybe Alaric was right about slowing down.

I have absolutely no idea if I should have spoken or if I am expected to only speak when given permission. There are so many unknowns to this night.

"Please," he says with a genuine smile. "Call me Lawrence. It is a pleasure to finally meet you, *lady* Valmont." He emphasizes the false title with a surprising lack of mockery.

Then the three of us make small talk. I am stupefied at how normal this feels. Alaric's fingers press into my waist in a comforting gesture.

"I look forward to seeing you around, Clara," Lawrence says.

He takes a step back but stops when the female hooks her arm through his and leans her head on his shoulder. It occurs to me that out of the five vampires in this room, she is the only female among them.

"Don't be ill-mannered, Lawrence," she admonishes.

She is draped on him as if she could be his wife, but there is a coldness to her stare, and his posture has stiffened. It is obvious that things are not quite so simple between them.

"You are right, how intolerably rude of me," he says without the slightest shred of sincerity. "Lady Valmont, this is Della Moore."

The red jewels that adorn her glint like dark drops of fresh blood against her pale skin. Della extends her hand as if she… expects me to kiss her knuckles? Yeah, that is not going to happen.

"It is good to meet you, Mrs. Moore," I say, ignoring her hand.

Lawrence's lips tick up at the corners. Della looks insulted, and for a moment, I think I've messed up and they have all figured out the truth. But Alaric gives me no corrective hints, no looks, no words, no gestures or warnings.

Before I can think on it further, Lawrence leads

her away. The short-haired vampire approaches. He still wears an expression that borders on contemplating taking my blood, even with Alaric at my side.

"Good evening, lady," he says. "I am Victor Conners."

We exchange greetings and speak about the view of the grounds. All the while, Victor watches me with his unwavering brown eyes.

A shiver works its way down my spine. Perhaps it's because he doesn't blink often enough, or maybe it's the emptiness in his eyes, or how he intentionally shows me his fangs each time he smiles or speaks.

I drink another glass of wine during the time we talk.

By the time he leaves, my shoulders and back ache from the tension that has been building since I walked into the room.

The woman with the tray walks by, and Alaric goes to wave her off, but I take another glass before she moves out of reach.

The last vampire has yet to approach, he talks to Lawrence and Della near the fire. He hasn't looked in my direction since the moment I walked in.

Alaric and I sit on the settee, and he pulls me into his side. I try to relax as best I can—which is nearly impossible with this cursed corset squeezing me. So, I focus on the glass in my hand. My cheeks are warm, and a buzz fills my head. Even my body tingles in a strange but not unpleasant way.

"Are you not hungry tonight, Alaric?" a voice like warm velvet croons from the side.

I freeze before looking up into the emerald eyes of the one vampire I have yet to meet.

"You have not had a single drop of blood tonight, and yet your pet is right here." Unlike the others, he does not introduce himself to me, nor does he speak to me, though his gaze does not leave my face. "She looks about ready to fly away... like a little bird," he muses quietly, more to himself.

I dislike the way he says *little bird* like a cat waiting to pounce. His eyes linger on my neck as if he can see the vein pulsing under the necklace.

I can't think straight. I don't know what to say, or what to do... I can barely remember how to breathe. Alaric will be forced to feed on me right here.

Against my will, my heart races. The vampire cants his head to the side, listening, a pleased smile forming.

I tip my head back and finish my third glass... Or is it my fourth? Or...

Alaric's hand glides down my waist to my hip, then pulls me tighter into his side. He dips his head and nips gently at my jaw. His fangs brush my skin, eliciting a sigh.

"I had my fill earlier today," he says, not taking his eyes off me.

He doesn't insist on the two of us introducing ourselves. Instead, he keeps his entire attention on me until we are alone again.

Alaric's hand comes up to cup my cheek and turns me to face him. Then he kisses me, and everything falls away, everything except the feel of his mouth on mine. He breaks away to nip at my ear.

Softly, he whispers, "I think the drink has gone to your head. Perhaps it is time for you to retire."

I nod, understanding his meaning. He helps me to stand. He remains in place as I walk out of the room, my legs surprisingly steady even though my head is swimming from all the wine.

That wasn't so bad after all.

CHAPTER FIVE

CLARA

THE TREE BRANCHES ARE NEARLY BARE. IN THE DARK OF the night, they look like demons rising to take shape, reaching up through the forests. Silver moonlight glints off the still lake making it look as if it is made of glass.

I rub my temples, massaging the dull ache behind my eyes. I'm not sure how long I have been standing in the middle of my room looking out over the grounds.

I don't know what I was doing before. The wine must have gone to my head more than I realized. I have never had so much before at one time.

The open window lets in a soft breeze that flutters the curtain and chills the floor beneath my bare feet.

The fire in the hearth is little more than small flames and embers. It must be sometime near dawn.

My thoughts are muddles, my limbs slow to respond, sluggish as if I am underwater.

I make my way toward the window, wondering what could have possessed me to open it in the first place. Every muscle in my body is stiff and it takes all the focus I can muster to make them obey.

A motion below stills my hands as I reach for the window. Instead of closing it, I pull it wide open. I blink to clear my vision, but there isn't enough light. Whoever, or whatever, shifts in stilted and uneven movements, then appears several yards ahead of where it was.

I press my cold hand to my forehead, attempting to stop my mind from spinning.

The figure, both human and shapeless in form, stops in its tracks. I am not sure how I know—it's far too dark to make out any details—but they are looking straight at me.

Two pinpoints of red form where the eyes should be. For a long moment, neither of us move.

A shiver runs over every inch of my skin, and my breath forms soft white puffs in the air before me.

There is a noise... like softly spoken words, though they sound jumbled to my ears. I lean forward until my upper half is hanging out of the window, straining to make out what is being said. My hands brace against the ledge, nails biting into the damp wood, made soft by the recent rains.

Get back inside. If my hand slips, I will topple forward and fall out. And it is a long way down.

Whoever… or whatever it is repeats the same string of words. Over and over and over.

The features begin to take shape. The eyes flash bright and there is a wicked smile that forms across the mouth that wasn't there a second ago.

Demon.

Run… run… My mind screams the command, but I remain rooted in place, a prisoner in my body. *Run!*

I suck in a lungful of icy night air. I'm released, stumbling backward several steps before managing to catch myself.

As I back away, black smoky plumes rise up to my window, blotting out the world on the other side. It hovers, growing impossibly thick.

Demons cannot enter homes unless invited.

Hoarfrost forms on the windowsill with a slow crackle, then spreads down the wall to the floorboards. The black mass outside continues to condense.

I take a single step back, and my heart nearly stops as the demon slides through the open window like a heavy fog. It pours inside through the opening. Within, a lightning storm flashes in a series of snaps.

The demon swirls in concentric circles over the floor, surrounding me, drawing nearer with each rotation.

I can't move without stepping into it. It swirls over my feet, then slithers its way up my body.

"Sssweeet huuuumannn..." they hiss. "I will conssssuumme yooou... possessss yooou."

My head thunders and each beat of my pulse makes the world quake. Then everything is dark, and I can't see. I try to scream, but my mouth, my throat, my voice, all fail me.

My breathing comes faster as I wait for the demon to rip me apart and consume me. Then points of light, like distant stars form, dim at first, then brightening until I can see again. Tallow candles in sconces along the walls, though only a few are lit. I don't stop to look around, I run as fast as my shaking legs will carry me.

My feet pad down the hall, muffled by the thick runner. I don't know where I'm going, but I know I can't stop.

A man ascends the top of the stairs at the end of the hall. The upper half of his body is shrouded in shadow.

I reach out a hand.

"A—" I start, but nothing more than a strangled sound makes it past my lips.

The icy cold has traveled up my body, numbing my muscles. I fall but don't feel the ground as I hit. The dark mass stalking me rushes over me and swallows up my consciousness.

Warm fingers brush the side of my face. It feels good. I try to say as much, but all that comes out is a groan.

After a few tries I manage to open my eyes. A face hovers before me, surrounded by night.

I blink. The face comes into focus. The white-haired vampire crouches before me, pale eyebrows raised. His mouth quirks to the side.

"It is not safe for a human to wander the halls at night in a house filled with vampires." There is too much humor in his voice for his words to be a threat.

I try to recall the details of the last few hours… the last few minutes, but everything is muddled. My head pounds the harder I try to remember.

"I… You—" I try to scramble away, but he places his hands on my shoulders.

"Be still," he says quietly.

"Who…" I begin.

He smiles and presses his palm over my forehead as if I have a fever.

Without the look of contempt on his face, he is quite handsome. The way the corners of his lips tilt up in a secretive smile. His green eyes glitter, even in the dim light.

"That's right, we were never formally introduced." He speaks softly. "Forgive my rudeness, my *lady*. I am Cassius Wellington."

"Oh," I say. I've never before been introduced to anyone while lying on the floor.

I'm—"

"You are the lady Clara Valmont," he says. "We all know who *you* are."

"I'm sorry, Mr. Wellington."

"Please, call me Cassius."

I press my elbows into the floor, lifting myself up a fraction. "I must have been sleepwalking… it must have been a nightmare. That's never happened before."

Cassius hums, nodding as if such a thing were an everyday occurrence. "Being in the presence of so many demons can do that to a human."

The details of my dream come back in a wave when I hear the word *demons*. I lick my suddenly dry lips. How could he know? "Demons?"

"Yes," he says, taking me by the hand and elbow and helping me to sit. "Allow me to walk you back to your rooms."

I shake my head and push to my feet. My legs are weak, and my body aches. "Thank you, but no, Mr. Wellington."

He only says, "Call me Cassius."

I smile demurely, too tired for pleasantries, and take two steps before my knees buckle. Cassius is at my side in an instant, supporting me against his side.

He is nothing like the man I thought he was earlier. The hostility in his demeanor has become friendly…

"You're much nicer than you were earlier," I say before I can think better of it.

Rather than lashing out or being offended, he laughs. "You are quite fascinating, my lady—and observant even when you are drinking your weight in wine."

My face flushes.

"Let us simply say that Alaric and I haven't always been the… closest of friends."

I frown. I'm not sure I want to know what he means by that, and something tells me that I shouldn't ask.

Finally reaching my door I pull my arm from his and smile. "Thank you, Cassius."

He beams at my use of his name.

I open the door and freeze. The fire in the hearth has died completely, but the windows are closed, and there is no sign of the frost that covered the walls or floors earlier.

"Is something wrong?" he asks.

I turn back around. "No, it's nothing. I'm just tired." The nightmare felt so real that I expected the room to be out of sorts.

Cassius steps closer and takes my hand, bringing it to his mouth and placing a kiss on the inside of my wrist.

"Goodnight," I say when he doesn't let go.

His eyes darken, fingers wrapping tighter around my wrist. "He might have claimed you, but it is clear he does not care for tradition."

I swallow delicately. "What do you mean?"

His words send fear through me even though nothing about him is threatening.

"It means, that even if he has started the process to mark you, so long as it is not complete—and I can tell that it is not—then you can choose to be marked by another. You do not need to be forced to take on the mark of the one who claimed you."

I try to pull my hand from his, but his grip tightens. Not painfully, but enough to keep me from moving away as he leans in.

Cassius places his mouth close to my ear. My heart skips a beat. If he tries to compel me, there is nothing I can do.

But he doesn't.

"You could choose a vampire who knows how to use their demon." He pauses. "I could give you anything you wanted. I could turn you into one of us if you wish it. I could give you a life you've never been able to dream of; endless pleasure. I would teach you how to live… you would have everything you could ever want and more, including a home with such opulence that this place will look like a graveyard in comparison."

Finally managing to get my lungs to work again, I step back, slipping my hand free from his. I want to get as far from him as possible, even though there's no way I could outrun him. Instead, I give him my best smile.

"Thank you for your assistance. You have surely given me a lot to think about," I say evenly, fighting to keep my heart slow and steady. "If you'll forgive me, my head is pounding from the wine and I'm afraid I'm not in the best place to make such an important decision."

"Of course," he says, giving me a slight bow. "Sleep well, lady Clara. Sweet dreams." He turns and walks back down the hall.

I close the door softly between us and lock it.

54

CHAPTER SIX

CLARA

The pulse of my heart hammers in my skull, and my entire body aches. Beams of morning light drift through the windows of the library as I pass, sending a sharp pain through my temples. I squint, wanting to avoid that room for the first time since coming here.

My nerves got the better of me last night. It was foolish to drink so much. I have only had the occasional glass of wine or mead in town with Xander. But it was never anything as fine as what Alaric served last night. Who knew drinking could lead to fitful bouts of nightmares?

I shudder at remembering the demon that haunted me throughout the night, lurking in the shadows as I tried to sleep.

Meandering my way through the manor to the

dining area, I look forward to a nice, hot cup of tea to clear my head. First, I must focus on setting one foot in front of the other and making it downstairs without stumbling. Thoughts of monsters and demons can wait for another time.

The softest sound of breathing seems to follow behind me. A chill skitters down my spine, and I spin around.

Silence and an empty hall stretch out behind me. Nothing is out of place, nothing moving. The windows are closed off to the cold morning air as winter creeps its way into being.

I scoff at myself. It is nothing more than my sleep-deprived mind and remnants of nightmares playing tricks on me.

When I finally make it to the dining room, nothing is waiting for me. I've grown accustomed to a large breakfast laid out. I walk in and take a seat at my usual spot anyway, too drained to go back to my room.

The kitchen is through the door at the far end of the room, but right now I want a large glass of water before I go any further.

Flittering leather wings swoop through the room, then Cherno lands on the table several feet in front of me. I don't have the energy to be bothered by those tiny feet on the table.

The pounding in my head intensifies. I bury my face in my hands—a poor attempt at escaping this relentless pain.

The bump of the serving cart against the door as it pushes it open, rattling the dishes on top. The sound is like several hundred needles prodding at my brain.

I wince at every sound Mrs. Westfield makes as she sets a cup in front of me before pouring the tea. Then a plate piled with food—the scent that would usually make my mouth water now churns my stomach.

She leaves without so much as a single word or glance in my direction.

The food that normally makes my mouth water churns my stomach today. Pushing away the plate, I wrap my hands around the hot cup, letting the heat seep into my chilled fingers. I take a sip, and the warmth fills my belly and spreads.

Cherno stares at me with those large brown eyes that almost seem to glow a soft red in the dim light. For a second, I wonder if I am still drunk because it looks as though Cherno is *smiling* at me.

But that's silly. Bats don't smile.

With that expression and those pointed ears, there is nothing threatening about this little beastie.

"You know," I mutter more to myself. "You're kind of cute."

Cherno squeaks and shuffles within reach.

A bat is a strange choice for a pet. However, Alaric obviously adores this tiny thing… I saw it in clearly on the creature's face when I had called Cherno "that."

I hold my breath and slowly reach out my hand, hovering over Cherno's tiny head. Then when the creature doesn't move, I stroke its head right between the two large ears. The simple gesture is almost enough to make the pounding in my head abate.

"Good morning," I say.

Cherno squeaks twice, but the third sounds like my name.

"You can understand me?" I ask, and then I freeze. The absurdity of the question is glossed over as my brain catches up. I pull my hand back. "Did you just speak?"

Cherno blinks once. Twice. Those large eyes seemingly getting bigger. Then a small and quiet voice answers, "Yes."

I straighten my back and clasp my hands together in my lap. There's a long silence. I have so many questions, but all words seem to have evanesced from my mind.

Cherno inches forward, head canted to the side.

"H-how is that possible? You're a bat."

Cherno's expression falls, then a single squeak followed by, "Not a bat."

I take a breath in, and let it out slowly. Then again. My thoughts are racing, and over everything, the word *impossible* screams the loudest.

Animals don't talk. This creature—this *bat*—is not an animal. If Cherno isn't an animal... *then what?*

Trying to keep my hands from shaking, I lift them slowly, then place them palms down on the table and lean in to bring myself eye to eye with Cherno.

"What are you, if not an animal? I thought you were a vampire's strange pet..."

Cherno's eyes flash red.

Those eyes are not brown but... a deep, deep red. The pieces click into place. Cherno isn't a pet—but a *demon. Cherno...* is a *demon.*

Is this what Alaric meant when he said vampires were demon cursed? Is this small, unassuming creature his master? Are they holding Alaric prisoner?

Their interactions certainly never came across as such. There must be more to this... then again, it could be a figure of speech.

I don't get the chance to ask.

"What a pleasant surprise," Lawrence croons from the doorway. "Just the human I was hoping to run into."

Why would he be looking for me? My blood runs cold. Lawrence walks leisurely around the table, taking a seat across from me.

His blond hair is tousled, the collar of his shirt is undone in a way that would be nearly indecent if he were human. He wears a deep green vest with a black brocade pattern—the same one he wore last night. He looks like he just stumbled out of bed after barely sleeping.

"Are you going to drink that?" He nods toward my teacup but doesn't wait for an answer before he snatches it and drinks the remainder in a single gulp.

I narrow my eyes. "No, please, help yourself to my tea. There is a worldwide shortage, and I would hate to selfishly drink it all," I say flatly.

Lawrence chuckles.

I barely stifle a scream as a small white and pink face with whiskers pokes out from inside his collar.

The *rat* sniffs the air, then scurries down his arm to the table and over to where Cherno sits.

Demons and saints. What is wrong with vampires that they have such… creepy little pets? But I suppose they *aren't* actually pets. I don't know if I should find that comforting or more disconcerting.

The two demons sniff each other. Cherno speaks words, the rat only squeaks, but they don't seem to have any trouble understanding each other.

Lawrence runs a finger along the brim of the teacup and studies me. I resist the urge to squirm in my chair.

His attention is finally pulled away when Mr. Steward comes in with a goblet on a silver tray. Blood, if the red around the vampire's irises slowly swallowing up the hazel is any indication.

Once we are alone again, Lawrence looks from the cup to me, then back. "This will never be as good as it is fresh from the source."

I grip the sides of my chair until my fingers ache.

He sniffs at the blood and throws back his head, swallowing the contents in a single gulp. His eyes open slowly, and he gives me a wicked grin, his blood-stained fangs on display.

"Do not worry yourself, *lady* Clara. I will not bite you. After all, you *are* marked by Alaric," he says.

His tone is mocking as he recites the lies Alaric and I have told. I can't tell if he knows the truth or is guessing at it.

I dip my chin, aware I do not have Alaric's mark. The skin on my neck is untouched by a vampire's fangs. Loose strands of my hair fall over my shoulders to hide the evidence.

I give him a tight smile, shrugging a shoulder. Not the truth, but not a lie either.

He snorts. "Was the title of lady your idea, or his? Because I think the three of us all know you are not of any notable birth—I saw the hovel you lived in."

My heart stutters, my head jerking up to meet his

narrowed gaze. I refuse to confirm or deny any of his suspicions.

He could be trying to trick me into revealing too much. And I'm sure he'd know a lie if I dared to utter one, so I stay silent.

"You are curious, little human," he says, then waits as if expecting me to ask him to continue.

I press my lips into a tight line but raise a single eyebrow.

Apparently, that is all the prompting he needs. "What is it you want?"

"What do you mean?" I ask before I can stop myself.

"I mean. If you could go anywhere, be anywhere without obligation where would you choose?"

"At home taking care of my sister." It's an easy question. I would always choose her. She needs me.

Lawrence tsks and wags a finger. "I said without obligation. Where would you go if no one wanted or needed you or decided for you?"

His question stings in a way I wouldn't have expected. I open my mouth. Close it. Finally, I say, "I don't know."

Lawrence stands, and in a blink, he rounds the table to stand next to me. With another quick movement, he has my chair turned to face him. He leans forward, looking down his nose.

I swallow my heart back down.

He reaches up and brushes my hair back from my shoulder. "Strange though, how you don't have a bite mark on your neck where our dear Alaric had his mouth all over you for a good amount of time during your little joy ride around the field yesterday."

My hand shoots up to clamp around the area. The memory of Alaric's mouth on my skin comes back. Heat works its way up my neck to my cheeks. "That's... he didn't... he didn't bite me then. That's—" I stop talking, not sure what I am even trying to say.

A pleased smile stretches across his face as he straightens. "I suppose," he says, rubbing a hand along his jaw. "There are far more... *delicious* places to bite, besides the neck."

My mouth parts to deny I have been bitten at all, but he is already walking away. Which is good because I almost said far more than I should. Not even a day, and I'm already putting our plan in jeopardy. Yet somehow, we are supposed to do this for two months?

Just as he's leaving through the open door, Alaric enters. They exchange a brief greeting. Alaric's eyes drift to me, and I turn my face away. My cheeks still burn from my exchange with Lawrence.

I keep my focus on Cherno. Alaric's reflection is mirrored in the demon's large eyes. Alaric walks through the room, stopping only when he stands before me.

Both Cherno and the rat move to my discarded plate and begin picking at the food.

"I need to speak with you," he says, his words clipped.

I bite down on the inside of my cheek and raise my chin to look him in the eye. His expression is unreadable.

Knots form in my stomach instantly. I must have failed last night. Lawrence's visit a moment ago was proof enough of that. I drank too much. I was careless.

The worst thing is that I have no idea what kind of punishment I will have to face.

Alaric holds out his hand to me, and I slip my hand into his.

A sense of foreboding twists at my heart as his long fingers wrap around my hand.

CHAPTER SEVEN

ALARIC

"Is everything all right?" I ask Lawrence. Clara's flushed cheeks, the way she avoids meeting my gaze, and the demon shit eating grin on his face sparks my suspicion.

"I was just leaving," he says lazily. The scent of blood lingers on his breath, and I look again to Clara.

A low growl rumbles in my throat. Lawrence raises a brow, then raises his hands before walking away.

I approach Clara slowly. Everything about her posture says she is ready to bolt.

"I need to speak to you," I say.

If Lawrence has so much as laid a finger on her, he will live to regret it.

I offer my hand, and after a moment's hesitation,

Clara looks up at me, then slips hers into mine. I lead her from the dining room and down the hall toward the music room.

She keeps her head straight forward, chewing on her bottom lip, a movement that draws my eye.

I take her wrist and stop her. She avoids looking at me.

"Did something happen?" I ask. "Did he touch or threaten you?"

Color stains her cheeks, but she shakes her head no.

"If that were true, then why won't you look at me?"

Silence.

"Clara, tell me. What happened?"

She purses her lips and finally meets my gaze. Her cheeks redden further. Her gaze wavers until she looks away. "He implied that you bit me... *elsewhere.*"

That had not been the answer I'd expected. The tightness in my chest that had formed, vanishes.

I want to pry more words from her lips, but she still seems uncomfortable. I let it go, content in knowing Lawrence hadn't laid a fang on her or threatened her.

"Why didn't you tell me how to act? What to do? How should I talk to them?" Clara asks a barrage of questions.

Holding back my amusement, I clasp her shoulders. "Because I wanted you to be yourself. You knew the important parts of what you must do. No one would believe I claimed some timid girl who fawns over any vampire that comes near. You are strong and fearless—there is a fire in you, and I wanted them to see that."

Clara inhales sharply and holds her breath for several heartbeats as she contemplates my words.

"Oh," she breathes.

We resume walking. I reach into my breast pocket and pull out the invitation then hand it to her. She takes it, hopelessly attempting to smooth out the wrinkled edges before reading it.

"We have been invited to the winter Solstice Masquerade at Nightwich in just under two months' time," I say.

She remains silent and passes the invitation back.

"Where are we going?" she says, finally raising her head to look around instead of at the floor.

"To the music room, so I can teach you to dance."

Clara scrunches her nose. "Teach me to dance? Why?"

"We must prepare you for the masquerade as much as possible."

I look at Clara, her head held high and her sights trained straight ahead. I fight the smile that threatens to form. That expression hasn't left her face since I found her in the dining room.

Did Lawrence's words affect her that much?

My smile slips as my amusement fades. The masquerade… two months. It is longer than Clara has been here, but it is not as long as we need.

I don't know if I can keep her safe. Though I will do my best, there is only so much that even I can do.

Clara stops walking at the threshold of the room. She takes it in, her brows pinching.

I make my way to the phonograph and turn it on. Soft music flows and crackles through the funnel.

"I don't understand," she says.

I only hold out my hand, beckoning her. She doesn't hesitate—which is unusual for her. She is always absorbing information and questioning everything before acting.

"How can we dance in here? Won't the furniture get in the way?"

I hold back a laugh. "Normally, yes, but I assume you have no prior experience with dancing at formal parties?"

She glares.

"That is not an insult, my dear Clara."

"You saw how I lived… we both know there are no parties for people like me."

"We will start from the beginning, but you need to

practice moving about while paying attention to your surroundings. We have much to cover and too little time."

She slips her hand into my outstretched one. Uncertainty is written across her face as I take her other hand and place it on my shoulder before settling mine on her waist, pulling her close.

Catching the rhythm of the music, I take one step, then on the second step, Clara runs into my chest.

"Let me guide you," I say.

She huffs and drops her chin to watch our feet. A few more steps into the dance, and she is trying to lead me. I barely suppress another laugh.

"It's no use, I was not made for this sort of thing."

Removing my hand from her waist, I take her chin between my thumb and forefinger and lift her head. Her eyes go no further than my throat, her frustration with herself is apparent.

"You are doing fine, Clara. We have only been at this for a few minutes." I release her and reposition our hands. "Follow me—don't try to lead and keep your chin up."

Clara blows out a breath, and finally, she meets my gaze.

For a third time, we begin. She steps on my feet a few times before catching the rhythm.

The song ends, but our dance continues. It feels

strange, the two of us touching in such a mundane way… and her *not* attempting to stab me for once.

Her eyes dart to the phonograph, and finally, I stop, releasing her to restart the music.

"Again," I say.

Wordlessly and dutifully, Clara repositions herself.

"You are doing better," I say.

Though the tilt of her brows suggests she doesn't entirely believe me, we manage to make it through an entire song without her turning away or averting her eyes. The moment is more intimate than any kiss or touch we have shared.

We slow to a stop along with the music. Neither of us pulls away.

Uncertainty fills her features, replacing the determination and focus she had as we moved together.

Can this really be the woman I hunted down? The murderer I claimed and intended on making her pay for taking Rosalie's life. Because Clara is a killer… the reason my heart has been rent in two.

And here I am, dancing with her, doing everything in my power to protect her.

I grieve for Rosalie, and yet part of me wants the woman before me. I am doing everything in my power to honor the fact that Clara would rather die than bear my mark. And I am risking everything for her.

My heart is a twisted thing. This is a sick joke played on me by the powers of the Otherworld. I should hate her. I should want to kill her. Instead, everything about her calls to me, and I am powerless to fight it.

She killed my only reason for living... but she has also told me why. A vampire had already claimed and killed her mother. She only wanted to protect her sister from the threat she had been raised to see us as.

I would be lying if I said I wouldn't have done the same for Rosalie.

Clara's mouth parts then closes. Her tongue darts out between her lips, then she swallows. The movement of her delicate throat catches my eye.

"I..." she starts.

As if choreographed, I cup her face with both hands, sliding my fingers into her hair as she pushes up onto her toes. I lean down, guiding her closer. We have kissed countless times before, but this is something different.

Clara's eyes slide shut. She sighs. Her warm breath brushes my lips.

"Pardon me, Master, but a letter has just arrived for the Miss," Mrs. Westfield says.

Clara pulls back as if she were caught doing

something she ought not to do and expects to be punished.

I release her and retrieve the letter from the head housekeeper. She bows her head, then takes her leave. I return to Clara and hand her the envelope.

She stares at it for a long moment, then her eyes brighten. Clara sits on the nearest sofa and crosses her legs then rips open the letter. Her eyes scan the words on the pages, then again a second time, slower.

Clara places the letter in her lap and looks up, eyes glazed.

"What is it?" I ask. Tendrils of dread work their way through my bones.

"Kitty... she," Clara pauses, looking at the letter again. "She's getting married in a month."

"There you are," Lawrence says as he strides into the room, having pulled himself together since breakfast.

If only I could send the lot of them away. They offer nothing but inconvenience and bad timing.

"Clara," I say, keeping my eyes locked on Lawrence. "Why don't you finish reading your letter in your rooms? I will come see you later."

She uncurls from the couch and stands, too wrapped up in the news she received to pay any attention to how the mood has shifted.

Clara trails a hand down my arm as she passes but

doesn't look up. To my amusement, she doesn't even acknowledge Lawrence's presence.

He watches Clara until she is gone. Then he is at my side, his expression of intrigue and humor replaced with a stony seriousness.

"What are you doing with her?" he hisses.

I raise a single brow. "Teaching her to dance."

Lawrence throws his hands up and paces. "Demon shit, you know what I mean."

I walk around him and turn off the phonograph.

"She is still unmarked," he says quietly. "You haven't even started the process. She barely has your scent on her and only because you touch her. Any vampire that comes within a foot of her will know."

I keep my back to him. This again. He's done nothing but hound me since the moment he arrived.

Looking down at my hands, I flex my fingers. The feel of her hand in mine still lingers.

"You must mark her before the ball. I don't care if she agrees or not, not unless you'd rather see her ripped to shreds and feasted on."

"No," I snarl, rounding on him. My voice echoes off the walls, filling the room.

"Then mark her, even if you must compel her into agreeing. Fuck, I will compel her myself if I must so you can keep your hands clean."

His offer is tempting but pointless. I would have

compelled her myself if the thought of doing that to anyone didn't disgust me.

"That will not be necessary," I say.

And now it truly won't. She will not need my mark.

"I will not be able to keep this a secret from Elizabeth. You know that. She would have my head on a pike if I even tried."

"I know."

"Then you'll do it?"

"I will make sure that Clara is taken care of," I say.

It is not a lie. I have every intention of making sure she is safe long before I must leave for Nightwich. It will be tricky, but it will work.

There is no other choice.

CHAPTER EIGHT

CLARA

Kitty is getting married to a young man named Abraham Morgan. It's a good, strong name, and he comes from a good family.

I am stunned, but I couldn't be happier for her. I don't know how she managed to secure the engagement. Perhaps they fell in love, and his family overlooked the meager dowery I managed to gather.

I clutch the letter to my chest and hurry down the hall, eager to write back, congratulating her. I round the corner that will lead to my rooms and stop short when I nearly run into Della. Cassius and Victor are a few paces behind her. Contrasting with the utter lack of emotion on Victor's face, Cassius's smile borders on sensual in an unnerving way.

Della's eyes narrow, glancing from my face to the

letter I hold to my chest. I smile demurely and move to walk along the wall, almost expecting one of them to stop me, but they don't.

Once I'm back in my room, I leap onto my bed and read the letter a dozen times. Abraham, her fiancé, is completely enamored with her. When she mentions him, her handwriting swoops more and has a hurried look to it. I can tell she is just as infatuated with him.

Soon, Kitty will have everything I've ever wanted for her.

Yet, under all my happiness, I can feel my heart trying not to break because I will not be there for the happiest day of her life.

A knock on the door startles me. Looking up for the first time since I sat down, I realize several hours have passed. The door opens before I can get up to answer it, and Alaric steps in, closing it quietly behind him.

"Are you all right, Clara?" he asks.

I nod and he is at my side in a second. I flinch. I don't know if I will ever get used to his ability to move so fast.

"Kitty is to be married in one month," I say.

"Does that upset you?"

I grab one of his hands. "Not at all. I couldn't be happier for her."

He cups my cheek, a thumb brushing along my lower lashes. "Then why are you crying?"

I pull back and wipe the backs of my hands over my eyes. "I *am* happy for her, but I am sad I won't be there," I say.

There is no chance for me to draw blood and win my freedom now. We already went over that yesterday. Drawing his blood would be a death sentence. The other vampires' presence means our bargain is on hold until… until we return here after the Solstice Masquerade, I suppose.

I pull in a breath and hold it as I look into his midnight blue eyes. He quirks a brow as if he already knows what I wish to ask.

"Alaric, I know I have to stay here… but, if I could go home, just for the wedding and return, then…" I trail off, entirely unsure of how to end my request. *Then what? I will behave like a good human pet?*

That is not something I can promise. I still want my freedom. I want to return to Xander, to be near my sister… to live the life I always strove for.

The two of us might have an agreement to appear as though we are bound together, to act as if I belong to him, but that doesn't change the reality—I would never choose to be here, and he wants me alive to pay for killing his sister.

Alaric's expression darkens. He looks as though he

is trying to find the words to gently let me down. The thought of him refusing already makes my heart ache. My emotions bubble over in hot tears that prick my eyes.

And why would he grant this? He doesn't owe me any favors, nor does he have any reason to trust me, regardless of what was said yesterday.

"Clara..."

"Alaric, please." I hadn't intended on begging.

"Of course you may go, Clara." He slides off the edge of the bed and stands. "I will send you first thing in the morning. You can expect to be there within a day and a half. Mrs. Westfield will make you some food for your journey."

It takes a minute for his words to register, but when they do, I leap off the bed and throw myself at him, wrapping my arms around his waist as I press my face to his chest. He stumbles back two steps before steadying himself.

"Thank you. Thank you, thank you, *thank you*! You have no idea how much this means to me."

At first, he doesn't move, then slowly, he returns the hug. "I think I have some idea."

My mind races with all the things Kitty and I will have to catch up on. I start to pull away, mentally listing off everything I will need to pack, but the arm around my waist doesn't budge. Alaric crushes me to his chest and dips his head, resting it in the crook of my neck.

I hold my breath, not sure what he is doing. His breath glides over my collarbone. There's nothing possessive in him right now, and with every passing second, the feeling of melancholy grows until it surrounds us. I cannot put a finger on what it is about this embrace that gives me that impression, only that the longer he holds me, the more I feel as if I am losing him.

But he isn't mine, and I am not his. And you can't lose what never belonged to you. Besides, he is a vampire, and I want to end them all....

Except I don't think I can.

I wrap my arms around his neck and rest my head on his shoulder.

When was the last time we were truly enemies? Though if we aren't, I'm not entirely sure what we have become.

Vampire or not, he means something to me... It's difficult to hate him. He is kind and gentle.

Upon meeting, I would have gladly killed him, and though he claimed the same, I don't think he has it in him to hate—to feel anger and pain, yes—but not hate. He is a better person than I am.

Alaric moves his head slightly. His mouth brushes across my skin. Demons and saints... I could drown in him. But I can't... I can't allow that to happen. I will be going home to Kitty and Xander.

His mouth hasn't moved from my neck, and I can't tell what he is thinking, if he might bite me, ensuring I have his mark before I leave so he can force me to return.

"You promised," I whisper.

Alaric stills. I am afraid he might still mark me... but mostly, it scares me that I'm not repulsed by the idea.

He pulls away, his face an emotionless mask. His eyes darken with what looks like hurt.

"Alaric..."

"Let me look at your arms," he says, stopping me from saying whatever excuse I would offer.

If he wanted to mark me without my permission, he would have done so already. There was no reason to mistrust him... in truth, I think I did not trust myself.

Alaric takes one arm and pulls up my sleeve, then the other. The marks on my skin are still bright pink and tender. The skin puckers where it has knit together, and I know they will scar. But I am alive, so I will take it.

"They are healing nicely, but you should keep them wrapped for the next week."

With how deep the cuts had felt, how much blood

I lost, I thought for sure it would take weeks to heal. Though he used all the power he could, the night-forged silver's magic fought his attempts to mend my wounds.

He rebandages my arms, doing a better job than I had.

"Don't worry," I say as I pull my sleeves back down. "I will keep them wrapped."

He nods once, still closed off to me. I hate it. I don't want to leave things like this between us.

I made him feel untrusted... *Demon shit.* It shouldn't bother me. But it does.

Friend... the word tumbles through my mind, and Otherworld damnit, he is. I don't know how or when became so, but he is.

"I will have Mr. Steward include bandages and an ointment to aid healing." And then, he strides across the room and leaves without looking back.

A gentle hand rests on my shoulder, shaking me awake. I force my eyes open and blink away the blur of sleep to see Mrs. Westfield standing over me, a tallow candle set in a wrought iron holder.

"Wake up, Miss, it is almost time for you to leave."

My eyes fly open, adjusting to the watery gray light of morning. It's not yet dawn but blood reds and bruising purples are smeared across the sky. Soon the sun will guild the edges of the clouds and burn away the night's lingering mist.

I dress quickly with Mrs. Westfield's assistance. A simple, dark green dress with long sleeves and a modest collar, unlike the majority of the clothes I have here, designed to keep my neck exposed.

We walk down the halls of the manor. An eerie silence fills the house. It seems unusual when there is a house full of vampires and at least two demons.

The carriage waits directly in front of the steps of the manor. The footman sits atop the carriage, keeping his head facing forward as if he were carved from stone. My trunk is already tied to the back.

While I'm glad I haven't crossed paths with the visiting vampires, I had expected Alaric to see me off. My gut clenches in disappointment.

"I have prepared a basket for you with individually wrapped meals, and a few bottles of cider and water. It will be enough to get you to your destination," Mrs. Westfield says. "Happy travels."

Then she turns and walks away.

Alaric gave me permission to go, but it still feels like I'm sneaking away during the middle of the night.

Pulling in a deep breath of cool morning air, I walk down the steps toward the carriage. I don't even know how long I have before I must return, though I assume at least a month.

My nerves hum as I lift a foot, preparing to haul myself inside. I look over my shoulder, expecting Alaric to show up any second now... but there is only the footman and myself outside at this early hour.

I don't want to leave like this. I don't want to leave things strained between the two of us. Guilt clings like the stench of stagnant water over what I implied last night.

I finish climbing in, resigned to waiting until after I return before setting things right.

As soon as I sit down on the cushioned bench, Alaric is standing just outside. One hand holding the door open, the other resting on the frame.

"I didn't think you would come to see me off," I say. My posture wilts in relief.

He smiles at that, but there is no joy in it. I bite down on the inside of my cheek. Did my implication that he would bite me without permission hurt him that much?

"I—"

He motions for me to lean forward. I do without hesitation.

Alaric places a kiss on my cheek then turns his head so his mouth brushes against the shell of my ear.

"Your debt to me is paid—do not return to this place."

I gasp lightly as he pulls away. My mouth hangs open. I can't seem to wrap my mind around what he said. I haven't drawn a drop of blood yet, he can't mean...

"I don't understand," I say.

But the carriage door slams shut. Alaric knocks twice on the side, and the horses break out into a jolting run.

I barely have time to turn and look out the window to see Alaric walking up the steps toward Lawrence, waiting for him at the door. Then, the trees lining the edge of the property close in, blocking my view.

CHAPTER NINE

CLARA

By the time the carriage finally comes to a halt, my back aches beyond anything I could have imagined. My bottom is sore from feeling every bump and dip along the way. But I suppose a day and a half of traveling without stopping will do that.

Once, I thought travel like this was impossible. But I suspect those were not ordinary horses driving this carriage, and I am beginning to doubt the footman is just a man. How else could he have survived all night, exposed to demons as we passed through the forests?

Pulling the curtain back a sliver, I look out, then all the way to take everything in. The midday sun glares down through a gap between thick gray clouds.

I don't know this manor. When Kitty said they

were well off, I assumed she meant in the same way Xander's family is. However, this manor is far larger than anything I've seen in the main area of Littlemire. Then again, I have never been to the north end.

Even I could never sneak my way into that part without being sent away by the local law enforcement and treated like the thief I was—not that they had any proof.

This manor pales in comparison to Alaric's, it must be the largest in Littlemire.

Two older servants, both with mostly gray hair, open the front doors, and several long seconds pass before a man and woman exit the house. They are Father's age but their eyes are bright, as if life has not weighed so heavily on them.

Following a few steps behind is a young man with a beautiful woman on his arm, her wavy brown hair is pulled up, and she is adorned in a long, yellow dress the color of buttercups in the spring.

Another young man follows them out, but my attention is drawn back to the girl. It takes me too long to understand that she is not just any girl—but my sister. She looks so vibrant and healthy, she practically glows.

They all stop at the top step, except for Kitty and the man, who must be the illustrious Abraham she wrote about in her letter.

The footman finally descends from his seat and opens my door as Kitty and Abraham draw near.

February

I step out and before I have time to adjust to the light of day, Kitty engulfs me in her arms, hugging me tight.

"Oh Clara, I hardly recognize you! I have missed you so much," she says, pulling back to take me in.

She is clean and I am suddenly aware that I have been stuck in a carriage for nearly two days straight and am in desperate need of a bath and an unwrinkled dress.

"Me?" I say with a laugh. "You are looking well, I barely recognize you either."

"We just got your letter this morning saying that you would be arriving, but we didn't expect you so soon," she says, looping her arm in mine.

Letter? I know I hadn't thought to send a letter. Alaric must have sent one for me. I let out a stuttering breath just thinking his name.

The footman sets my trunk down, and the two servants hurry to pick it up and take it into the house.

"This is Abraham," Kitty beams up at him, "And this is my sister, Clara."

He smiles, his deep brown eyes glinting with what I can only describe as pure happiness. There is a smattering of dark freckles across his cheeks and nose. He extends a hand. "It's nice to finally meet you, your sister has told me so much about you, I feel as though we are already family."

The other son loops an arm around his shoulders and beams as well. He is about an inch shorter, and the same dark brown skin. I blink, surprised to see twins. Though, unlike Abraham, he doesn't have freckles, and his frame is leaner.

"Hello sister," he says, then wraps me up in a hug, lifting me off my feet before plopping me back down.

"Watson!" Kitty admonishes. "Behave yourself. Can't you see she has been through enough?"

"It's fine, Kitty," I say, though I'm not entirely sure she hears me as she drags me up the steps to introduce me to her fiancé's parents. The boys are a perfect match for their parents, taking their height and strong jawlines from their father and their eyes and smiles from their mother.

I am surprised at how this family welcomes me into their home... how they have welcomed Kitty. All four of them radiate love and kindness.

I am so happy for my sister. I don't know how she managed it, but they will be a good match for her. She deserves to be part of a loving family for once in her life.

My eyes water. This is how I've always imagined family to be. And now Kitty will have this.

"Oh Clara, can you believe it?" Kitty gushes throwing herself atop the bed of the room I will be staying in.

"The room is beautiful," I say.

Kneeling down in front of my open trunk, I pull out the last of my clothes to store in the beautifully carved armoire. I pause.

A small thin package, wrapped in thick, black velvet, rests at the bottom of the trunk. I reach in and lift it just enough to feel its familiar weight. But I know I hadn't packed it.

My heart jumps into my throat, and I swallow it back down. Alaric must have put it in here… though I can't imagine when he would have had the chance or why.

I set it back down and close the lid then stand and put the last dress with the others I have already unpacked.

Kitty lifts herself up on her elbows. "No, I mean all of this? Can you believe I was able to secure such a wonderful match?"

It is strange that such a well-off family would allow their son to be seen with someone from our family. We were low even within our own social circle to begin with. The little money I had saved would have been decent for someone of a lower class and she still would have been better off than we were. Though I don't voice these thoughts. Instead, I lift my face and smile.

"It is everything I've ever wanted for you, and everything you deserve." It seems impossible, but my words and wishes for her came true.

Kitty stands and pulls me into a hug once more. "I am so glad you could come visit for the wedding." She takes both of my hands in hers and squeezes gently. "I can't imagine what you've been through."

I smile at her. *Again*. If I keep this up, she will think I have lost my mind.

For the first time in my life, I feel like a stranger to my sister. I am lost for words. It's as if I woke up from a dream that had been so real, so consuming... and now I am trying to remember the reality I have somehow forgotten.

"I thought that monster killed you..." Kitty doesn't have to say, "*like mother*." We are both thinking it. Then her eyes brighten. "But you look better than I have ever seen you."

"Thank you," I say.

Demons and saints! How did holding a conversation with my sister become so difficult?

"Clara?" her voice is soft and careful. "Are you all right? You don't seem yourself."

As if her touch could allow her to read my thoughts, I pull my hands away and busy them by smoothing down my skirt. "I'm just tired. We traveled as fast as we could. I was anxious to see you again."

She takes a step closer, her light brown eyes narrowed... looking for the lie. "He... that monster didn't hurt you or..." Kitty's words trail off, but I grasp the meaning of what remains unsaid.

I feel the prickle of heat crawl up my chest and my neck. "No," I say, louder than intended. "He didn't do anything to me."

"Good," she says.

I want to change the subject to anything other than Alaric.

"Enough about me," I say, grabbing her by the shoulders and spinning her. "Let's talk about your wedding. One month, and you will be a married woman. Before we know it you will have three adorable little children..." I press a finger to my cheek, pretending to think. "One boy and two girls. One of whom you will obviously name after me."

"You are already planning my future!" She swats playfully at my arm, laughing, and I laugh with her.

"Is he good to you?" I ask.

"Yes, he and his whole family are so wonderful."

"Do you love him?"

She blinks at me, and I freeze. I don't know what possessed me to ask that. Kitty wrinkles her nose. "You know that love doesn't matter when it comes to marriage."

I *do* know. It has never concerned either of us before.

We sit on the edge of the bed. Kitty leans into my side and rests her head on my shoulder.

"That is very unlike you to ask, sister." She pokes my nose with a finger, then sighs. "But... I think in time I will. I don't see how I couldn't. They are nothing like Father. And he's so kind and handsome."

Love has never mattered... though with Xander, we have always been an exception. His family is beyond our reach, but he believed we could circumvent his parent's expectations if we just waited until his brothers married.

Perhaps now, with Kitty marrying into such a prominent family, it will be easier for Xander and I to finally marry.

I tug on the edges of my sleeves, conscious of the thin wraps that cover my arms. "Have you heard anything from Xander Callowell?" I ask.

Kitty straightens and looks at me, entirely bewildered. I suppose it makes sense. My relationship with Xander was the one secret I kept from her.

"Callowell? Why would you ask about the Callowell boy? You mentioned him in your letters, but I assumed it was some sort of coded message I wasn't able to decipher." Kitty scrunches up her mouth, but there's more to her tone than her words imply.

My heart skips. I can't be angry with her because I have not been entirely honest with her either. But this is about Xander... and my future.

I have only been away for a month and a half, not much could have changed... then again. Sitting in the Morgan's manor, with Kitty engaged to their eldest son, is as far as we could be from the life we had before I was claimed.

Kitty gasps. "Was it code? You must tell me, I must know what you meant." She claps a hand over her mouth as if finally realizing. I like this version of her —energetic and animated. "Oh! I bet it was one of your market friends? Why didn't you just say so?"

Market friends... she and Father both knew most days I hunted and sold the pelts of what little I caught to the butchers and clothiers in the market, but they both talked about it as though I worked for a reputable business. I suspect at least Father knew I picked pockets as well.

I open my mouth to explain my relationship with Xander to her, to explain that it wasn't code and that we have a relationship, but a knock on the door interrupts the moment.

The older woman from earlier, Mrs. Smithe, who I have since learned is the head housekeeper, opens the door and pokes her head in.

"Pardon my intrusion young Miss, but the guests will be arriving in an hour."

"Thank you," Kitty says energetically. Her excitement at being treated as if she always belonged here is apparent.

She jumps to her feet, facing me, and I know our conversation is at an end.

"We must get you ready!"

And just like that, I am swept up in a whirlwind of silks and accessories as Kitty goes about picking out our clothes.

CHAPTER TEN

CLARA

"Clara," Kitty says. "You must wear this one to the party tonight."

I lower the dress I hold up for her to examine. She has the rich olive material pinched between two fingers of one hand and is stroking it with her other.

"Why didn't you tell me earlier about the fine dresses he sent you with?" she lifts the material and strokes it against her cheek, then murmurs, "Perhaps being taken by a vampire might not be as bad as we thought…"

My heart nearly stops in my chest. While it's true that Alaric is not as we always thought vampires to be, his guests are proof that he is a rare exception.

"No," I snap. "Vampires are dangerous. Do not let

pretty dresses and trinkets fool you into thinking otherwise."

She drops the hem of the gown, hurt and annoyance warring in her expression. "How can you say that? You are well fed, and I doubt he would send you with these things if he was not taking care of you."

"Yes, he did. And yes, I am alive but A—Mr. Devereaux is not like other vampires... Did you forget about the one that took Mother?"

I say *took*, but we both know I mean claimed and killed.

"Maybe something else caused her death?" she offers. "He looked terribly mean and violent when he took you, but... look at you. You're fine. You're more than fine."

I don't know why I'm arguing with her or how this became a fight so quickly. Alaric is not a bad man, and it twists my heart to even talk of him as if he were. But it is far more disconcerting to think that sweet, innocent Kitty could have her opinion changed by material possessions.

I worry she will be careless in town, that she will leave her home during a claiming and cross paths with one, only to suffer the same fate as Mother. After all, marriage doesn't protect anyone. If anything, it's more likely to doom them faster. And women, especially beautiful ones like Kitty, are more likely to be claimed.

"I am," I say calmly. "But I have come across other vampires, ones that wouldn't hesitate to kill you to quench their thirst for blood and violence."

Kitty's face pales, and the bitter taste of guilt coats my tongue. She nods, accepting.

I lay the dress out in her arms and quickly untie the dress I've worn for the last two days.

"Do you think I have time for a bath before I get ready?" I ask, trying to ease away from the argument. I don't want to fight with her. I want to spend time with her. I want to share smiles and laugh with her again like we used to. As glad as I am that I made it here so fast, I do wish I had had the chance to stop at an inn. Though I'm not sure how I would have paid for it...

I suppose that in itself is another problem I will need to solve eventually. Now that Alaric has broken our bargain and freed me, that leaves me where I started. Though perhaps I can stay with Kitty while i look for a job to work until Xander and I can marry.

I will write him first thing in the morning to let him know I am back.

She giggles and I eye her over my shoulder. "By the time they finish boiling the water for you the party will have already started! Besides the only rooms that have working plumbing are Abraham's parents."

"I suppose that was a ridiculous question," I say, peeling my dress off and letting it fall to the floor.

"Clara!" Kitty gasps. "What has happened?" She grips my shoulder and spins me around.

My dress falls to a heap on the floor, and I quickly bend down to pick it up to cover myself so that it doesn't wrinkle.

"You said he wasn't hurting you... but *look*," she hisses. "Both of your arms are bandaged. Why did you lie?"

"No, Kitty, please. It wasn't him. I swear it. I wouldn't lie about this." Except... even if her assumptions had been correct, I think I might choose to lie. Because the truth would only distress her at a time when she deserves to be happy.

"You can tell me the truth," she whispers as if there was a chance we could be overheard. "He can't get to you here. If it's him I will have Abe—"

"Kitty, it wasn't him," I repeat this time, I keep my words slow and calm. "It was an accident. I was in a part of the manor I shouldn't have been in. I did this through my own carelessness. He was the one who found me and bandaged my wounds."

There. Nothing about that is a lie, though it is not entirely the truth. Still, a strange part of me hates talking about Alaric to her, I don't want her to know anything about him.

She presses her lips and arches a brow.

A dull throb starts behind my eyes. "Let's not talk about such things now. I am here for your wedding, and we have an engagement party to dress for."

Kitty holds onto her doubt for another second before I can see it visibly melt away, and her mood brighten.

After helping me dress, we walk arm-in-arm through the hall. Since she saw the bandages, the quiet between us has been heavy with unspoken words.

I clear my throat. "You are looking well, Kitty."

"You've said that already," she says. Lifting her chin a fraction, she adds, "You keep calling me Kitty. I prefer Kathrine now. I'm too old to be Kitty and besides, I will soon be a married woman of status."

"Kathrine it is then." Her full name feels strange on my tongue. "You must be getting the best medicine money can buy. I'm glad to see that they are taking such good care of you."

She is silent, and when I look at her, she blushes and averts her eyes, then offers me a sheepish smile. "I will tell you a secret… but you have to promise not to be upset with me."

I list my head to the side. What kind of secret

could she have to share with me now? And one that might be upsetting…

I nod.

"No, you have to promise," she insists.

I don't like making such agreements without knowing more about the situation, but this is my Kitty—my *Kathrine*. "I promise."

She stops in her tracks and pulls on my elbow, turning me to face her. "I never meant to make life harder for you, but… I'm not strong like you are. I don't have the skills you do…"

"Kit-Kathrine, out with it already," I admonish.

"All that hard work would have calloused my hands and made them rough and then I never would have been able to secure an engagement with Abraham. It's all right though, because it's all worked out in the end. I have Abraham and his family, and you have a nice… Lord to take care of you."

My mouth parts as I struggle to put everything together.

"I was never sick. I didn't need the medicine, and with me being weak… Father would leave me alone."

She watches me, waiting for a response. But I have none.

Life would have been easier if I'd had her help. We might have had more food on the table and maybe even a little extra money. I wouldn't have spent precious extra coins on medicine she never needed.

"Remember you promised you wouldn't be angry with me…" she says in a small voice.

And then I look at her. She is small, nearly half a head shorter. And even with as well fed as she is now, she is still willowy. I suppose she wouldn't have survived having to do those things.

"I'm not upset," I say. What surprises me more is that I think I believe it too. I am not angry, though there is a splinter of hurt that has wedged itself into my heart.

I give her the best smile I can manage, and it seems to be good enough to appease her. Tension melts from her shoulders, and we hurry down the hall and head down the stairs to meet her guests as they arrive.

I suppose I was not the only one keeping secrets. But there is something calculating and devious about this secret she kept all these years. It makes me wonder if either of us really knows the other at all.

CHAPTER ELEVEN

ALARIC

Black clouds block out the moon and stars, blanketing the world in a nearly impenetrable darkness. Mr. Steward closes the door behind us as my foot lands on the gravel drive.

A low rumble emanates from Victor's chest. His hunger lends desperation to his movements as he steps forward.

I block his way with my arm, forcing him to come up short. He glares at me as if he's debating ripping the limb off to get by.

"Remember, we are *all* to conduct ourselves in the way I instructed." I glance at Victor from the corner of my eye. "This is my town, *my* territory, and I will not have my arrangement with the humans damaged in anyway. Any you feed on must agree of their own free will, so compulsion is forbidden. Do not harm or frighten them."

I pause and look at each of the others in turn. Lawrence and Della stand side by side, taking in my words. This is not their first time here.

Cassius crosses his arms as if my orders mean little to him. But Victor struggles to pay attention.

"Above all, these humans are to be treated with respect." I lower my voice and focus on Victor. "I do not want a repeat of what happened a month ago."

Victor's gaze finally snaps to mine, wide eyes narrowing into a glower at the mention of his action during their second night here. Being held accountable for his actions seems to be a new situation for him, but that doesn't mean I'll go easy.

"You caused me a great deal of trouble cleaning up your mess—and not only having to dispose of that poor girl's body."

That lie, all those humans compelled... the situation still leaves a bitter taste on my tongue.

Victor huffs but doesn't move to defy me.

"How are the people out at night for us to feed on? We hunted during the day, the last time we were here," Della mutters.

I turn on her. My patience grows short, and know

I must feed soon, or my inner demon will take over. "In exchange for their willingness to be fed upon, I keep the demons from coming within several miles of their town."

"You work as a slave for these humans," Cassius snorts under his breath.

I ignore him and run. I stand at the edge of town within a minute. A bustling noise comes from the central square, lit gas lamps line the streets, and the clack of hooves on the cobblestone all mix to create an atmosphere that most humans only hear in the day.

Keeping the demons back and changing so many lives was a point of pride for Rosalie. This is the life she had wanted before I took that possibility from her.

"We leave our demons here," I say.

"But how—" Victor starts.

"You do not need your demon to feed. They stay or you will return to the manor."

Cherno leaps off my shoulder and takes flight. Arinah squeaks and leaps off Lawrence, landing with a soft thump in the half-frozen grass. I don't hear Asmod slither from Cassius, but I know he wouldn't dare defy me on this. He might want to be Elizabeth's first, but he will never be more than her second.

A moment later, Zegan croaks once before

hopping from Victor's outstretched hand. Cherno circles above, chittering as he keeps watch.

"Remember the rules," I say.

Lawrence and Della run off toward the center square. Victor is only a second behind them. I reach out and grip Cassius's forearm.

"Watch him," I order.

His lip curls. He wants to argue, but they are in my territory. After a moment, he averts his gaze unable to meet my silent challenge.

Swallowing the dread that crawls its way up my spine, I walk into town.

I have barely made it several blocks when a loud gasp draws my attention. A woman, perhaps only a year or two older than Clara, has stopped in front of me. Recognition sparks in her eyes, a large smile spreading across her mouth. Her hat sits askew atop her head, and her dress tells me she is off to see a play or the local opera.

The woman walks up to me. Her boldness reminds me again of Clara. She looks nothing like her, but I see fierce brown eyes in her green ones, and messy, dark brown hair worn loose in this one's tightly pinned flaxen curls. Her corset is tied so tight that her waist seems too narrow for even her delicate build.

"Are you hungry, my Lord?" she asks in a sweet

voice. Everything about her says she has been groomed to attract the most desirable match. The woman tilts her head to the side to expose her neck.

I want to refuse her, to find another—someone who doesn't remind me of Clara. But I see her in everyone and everything.

"Are you willing?" I ask.

She straightens and blinks her large eyes. "Well, yes," she says, humor in her tone. "Of course. I am offering."

Even without her exposing her neck, I knew. The eagerness with which she approached was enough to tell me that she was willing. One of the many reasons I prefer not to feed in town.

"Very well," I say.

She slips her arm through mine and walks with me down a deserted side street. The glow from the gas lamps shines, gilding the damp cobblestones.

"Will you be late?" I ask.

"Late?" she bats her eyelashes.

"You are going out tonight."

"Oh yes," she says. "But I can spare a little time for you, my Lord. An hour or two if need be."

This woman is expecting far more than a simple feeding. However, other than her blood, I have no interest in anything she has to offer.

I stop her and press her back against the stone

facade of a building. Her gaze goes from questioning to excited. She tilts her head to the side, her hands roaming across my chest, gripping my shoulders as she presses her body into mine.

I despise those who wish to use me as their fantasy. Unfortunately, I need to feed, I am too close to losing control of my bloodlust.

I sink my teeth into her neck and drink, thinking about Clara.

She writhes and moans. Her hands roam, reaching between us. Disengaging, I back out of her reach and give her a halfhearted bow. "Thank you, Lady," I say and turn away.

Otherworld damn that woman, she is like a demon with their claws latched deep into my brain. I feed on others as I would feed on Clara.

"But... I thought..." she says.

I stop but don't face her. "I don't know what you've heard, but I do not bed my meals."

Before she can say another word, I hurry away. I have never been so cold toward a donor before. No doubt she is currently pouting. She has no idea how lucky she is that nothing more than her pride was injured this night.

A long time ago, I would have given in to such baser urges and combined the two. Back then I didn't care if humans used me to fulfill their fantasies. I didn't care about anything. So long as I didn't kill them for Rosalie's sake, I thought nothing more of them.

Now, the thought of doing more than feeding is unappealing.

I shake off the unwanted thoughts and focus on finding the others.

Lawrence and Della stroll side by side down the main street toward the edge of town. I appear at their side.

"Done already?" Lawrence asks in a way that makes me wonder if he saw the woman I fed on. Della's smirk only confirms that suspicion.

"Have you seen Cassius or Victor?" I ask, pointedly ignoring their insinuation.

Lawrence nods toward a street several blocks back.

"Meet me at the edge of town," I say.

I waste no time seeking the other two out. It is them I cannot trust.

Moans echo from the darkened street. The gas lamp on the corner has been snuffed.

I turn the corner in time to witness Cassius straightening his trousers. He gives me a fiendish grin as he pulls a handkerchief from his pocket and dabs the corner of his mouth.

The woman with him has her back to me as she

scrambles to straighten her dress. Her wild, red hair is a waterfall of messy curls. I narrow my eyes. There is something…

Cassius grips her arms from behind and leans down to whisper something in her ear I cannot make out. She nods before hurrying away.

I don't care what he said to her, I am only relieved she lives. His reputation for killing during feeding has followed him for decades. I'd expected I would have to watch Cassius closely during his visit, but thus far, he has surprised me. No doubt an attempt to get on Elizabeth's good side. There is nothing he doesn't do that is not an attempt to please her.

"Wait with the others, your demon is expecting you," I say.

Then I turn my back on him and hurry through the streets of Windbury to find Victor.

I scour every dark corner and alley. Worry eats at me as I venture farther and farther into town.

As I near the southern edge of the city where the buildings give way to small farms, I catch a soft whimper coming from the tree-lined edge of one such piece of land. I follow the sound.

On the other side of a small copse of trees, Victor is with a girl under him, writhing on the ground. Her hands swat weakly at his shoulders.

"Enough… that's enough… I'm not… not feeling well," her voice is a hoarse whisper.

I step closer, only to stop short by gasping breaths from yet another girl who is huddled against a nearby tree. Blood stains the collar of her dress. She whimpers at the sight of me and curls further into herself.

These women are terrified. *Fucking demon cursed bastard.* This is a blatant disregard of my orders.

"Victor, get up. We are leaving," I bite out.

Victor pauses his movements as if he only now noticed I was here. He lifts his head and smiles. Blood coats his mouth and teeth, thick lines drip down from both corners of his mouth. Victor pushes up, leaving the girl without so much as a glance in her direction.

He wipes his mouth with the back of his hand and waits for my next command. "Apologies, my Lord, I am still getting used to the bloodlust."

"Join the others and wait for me." I dismiss him with a wave of my hand and kneel down next to the young woman.

She flinches.

"Don't worry," I croon, infusing a light compulsion into the words—just enough to settle her nerves—and offer her my hand. Reluctantly, she places her cold fingers in my grasp. "Be at ease."

I help her to sit up. Pushing her hair from her

shoulder, I examine the overzealous bite marks that are already bruising her flesh. I place my palm over the wound, still oozing blood.

The girl hisses but doesn't try to move away. I close my eyes and push my power through my hand and into her.

When I'm finished, I remove my hand and appraise her. The color returns to her cheeks.

Gingerly she reaches up and touches the spot where the bite marks had been. Her eyes widen.

"T-thank you," she stammers and throws her arms around my neck in an embrace that nearly knocks me over. She withdraws almost as quickly. "I'm so sorry. I shouldn't have—"

I place a hand on the top of her head and laugh. "It's all right."

Relief settles over me. Victor's actions tonight have not made her fear me. But I still cannot allow them to remember the fear they felt.

Turning to the other girl I gesture for her to join us. She hesitates, but one glance at her friend, and she is up, walking over to us on shaky legs, then kneels. I repeat the healing process on her wounds.

After using my power to heal two mortals, I will need to feed again sooner than anticipated. But I can manage for another week or two.

I swallow the guilt prickling at my conscience.

Altering a human's state of mind… taking away their will, their thoughts, histories, experiences, their opinions—it's never sat well with me.

"We had a wonderful time tonight," I say, infusing power into my voice.

Their eyes widen, pupils growing large until they nearly swallow up the entirety of their eyes.

"Thank you, ladies, for being so patient. I do hope that you will forgive me for not being as neat as I should have." I place a palm of my hand on each of their cheeks. More power flows through me, sending them images of the night and erasing the fear and pain they experienced "Take a few days to rest and eat well."

They nod in unison.

My guilt is only slightly assuaged by the fact that this will be better for them in the end. They were not seriously injured; they were more frightened by Victor's cruelty.

"Now go, return home and get cleaned up," I say.

Again, they nod and rise as one, then walk from the field. If nothing else, they are alive.

Rising to my feet, I clench my fists at my sides. There is a young vampire who is in need of being taught a few lessons.

I race to the far end of town, where the others await me.

Once Victor is within my sights, I speed up and slam into him. We land on the ground, him on his back with my hand wrapped around his throat as I crouch over him.

I bare my fangs and lower my face close to his. "You and I are about to have a little chat."

CHAPTER TWELVE

CLARA

WE ARRIVE AT THE PARTY IN TIME FOR THE FINAL THREE carriages to pull up outside. Murmuring filters down the hall, the voices mixing with the soft lull of the string quartet.

Kathrine beams as she leans in close to whisper, "It looks like I will be fashionably late to my own party!"

I don't understand the point. *Why would anyone want to be late?* But if it makes her happy, then it makes me happy. She was always more attuned to social nuances, expectations, and other such things.

Kathrine loops an arm through mine and pulls me along to the room where everyone awaits. When we near the threshold, she releases me and pushes me forward, causing me to stumble a few steps before I catch myself.

One or two people look my way, giving me nothing more than a passing glance before turning away. I am not the face they want to see.

There are several people I recognize here, many of whom I have helped myself to their coin a time or two. Unsurprisingly, they all seem to be doing well.

A moment later, heads turn, and murmurs fill the room as Kitty strides in, smiling and beaming at everyone who has come to celebrate her upcoming nuptials. She pauses to greet everyone she passes.

I feel like a fish out of water, though Kathrine looks as though she's been the guest of honor at parties all her life.

Abraham crosses the room in a few strides and takes her hands, leading her back to where he was standing moments before. The two of them laugh and talk excitedly with another couple, a few years older.

I keep close to the wall, taking in the throng of people milling about. Couples are spread throughout the space, while groups of singles have gathered together. The eligible bachelors chat and posture, obviously intending to impress. While young women whisper among themselves, openly gazing at the men with flirtatious smiles.

The room is similar to the music room at Alaric's manor, though it is smaller and brighter. Instead of dark mahogany and crimson, this room is decorated with creams and golds with various shades of green for accents.

Alaric... I can't seem to stop thinking about his name... comparing everything I see or experience to my brief time in Windbury. Even during the drive here, I couldn't stop thinking his name—mostly cursing him for not instructing the driver to stop for the night.

It hasn't even been a full day yet and I have lost count of how many times I thought of him—comparing everyone to him, everything to Windbury since my return to Littlemire.

I need to stop.

That is no longer my life.

I am no longer beholden or indebted to him.

He is no longer *in* my life.

Demons take me for this sickening twinge stabbing at my heart when I remember the finality of our inadequate goodbye.

Now isn't the time for thoughts that need long, quiet hours to sort through. This is my sister's engagement party. She is the reason I am here, the reason I was able to return.

I exhale a long breath and shake away everything that threatens to take me away from this moment—away from Kitty.

Attempting to be more social, I search the faces near me for someone who looks amiable. A familiar laugh breaks through the steady din of voices. The warmth of the sound overwhelms me with a wave of memories.

It can't be. I am imagining things.

Slowly, I turn my head and look over my shoulder.

The blood drains from my face. Xander stands near the entrance of the room with a bright-eyed blonde woman attached to his arm. She's not his sister—he is one of four boys... Perhaps she is a cousin? It's hard to tell from this distance, but she appears several years younger.

She responds to something he says, her voice sweet and delicate, is followed by bell-like laughter.

I hadn't expected to see him here, let alone with a woman on his arm.

My pulse thunders in my veins, and I want to hide. I had a plan. I'm not ready to face him yet. But Xander's eye snags on mine before I can look away. His smile slips a fraction before reforming, larger this time, as confusion transforms into recognition, then surprise.

He takes a step in my direction, and I take a step back. This is not how I wanted our first meeting to go after all this time. It's far too crowded.

I feel like a caged animal… the need to get away is overpowering. But then the woman with him points to another part of the room and pulls on his arm until he follows.

My shoulders sag in relief.

If I thought for half a second that I could sneak away and hide for the rest of the night without Kathrine noticing, I would. So much has changed in the last two days.

Surrounded by people I don't know, I feel as though I am in the eye of the storm, surrounded by too much all at once and unable to handle any part of it without being pulled into the maelstrom. All I can do is wait for it to die down so I can breathe again.

I skirt the edge of the room, keeping an eye on Xander as I move. He has managed to separate himself from those he arrived with, and as I move deeper into the room, he makes his way toward me.

When I'm only a few feet away from a long table with filled glasses of various colored liquids, two girls step into my path. Somehow I just barely avoid running into them. They wear pastel colored gowns, one a creamy, butter yellow, the other a summer sky blue. Their hairstyles match—pinned up with short cascades of curls falling over opposite shoulders.

"I don't believe we've met," says the one on the left.

"Isn't this party fantastic?" the other gushes. "Hugo and Mina Morgan have spared no expense!"

"I am Tessa Fontaine, and this is my sister, Malory," the one in yellow says.

I peek around them, searching for Xander, but I can't see through the crowd.

"Why haven't we seen you at one of these parties before?" Malory asks. "Are you from Durford?"

Their chatter draws my attention back to them. I have never had to interact with others in such a formal situation. Anything I've learned about such situations, I learned in the few short weeks I spent with Alaric, and most of that was in the last seven days.

I plaster a practiced smile across my mouth I say, "No, I'm Kathrine's sister, Clara Valmont."

The blood drains from their pale faces, making them look ill. Their eyes dart to my neck before returning to my face. It is not the first time people have stared at that particular patch of skin since I entered this room, but none were quite so obvious.

"Oh… oh! I—" Malory starts.

"We were on our way to get refreshments," Tessa interrupts. "You'll excuse us. We will see you around." She takes her slack-jawed sister by the arm and practically drags her into the crowd—away from the drinks.

That was… peculiar.

I catch the eye of anyone I can. Though a few pause to meet my gaze, it is never for long. I understand them looking for bite marks. In all honesty, if I were in their place, I would do the same. But there is something else in the expressions that I can't identify.

And right now, understanding what a room full of strangers think about me is the least important thing on my mind. I push the strangeness aside and continue toward the back.

When I make it to the table, I grab a flute filled with a bubbly golden drink and take a sip.

"It's been a while," Xander's familiar voice croons at my side.

Tension tightens my shoulders. I take another sip from my glass, then turn to him. My nerves spike.

Xander is more handsome than I remember. His face is clean-shaven, and dressed as he is, he seems like a different person than the boy I've known for years. Of course, we have only ever spent time together in town and the surrounding areas. Never a formal occasion such as this.

His eyes go wide as he takes me in slowly from head to foot. "You look beautiful," he says.

And just like that, the warmth and familiarity

between us has returned. I don't need to be flawless and he doesn't need to conform to expectations.

"Thank you."

I feel at ease in his presence, but there is so much that remains unsaid. As though he has the exact same thought, our gazes travel to the woman he'd arrived with. I open my mouth to ask, but I don't get the chance.

"There you are, Clara! I see you've found Xander." Kathrine's voice rings out behind me.

The short moment Xander and I shared is shattered.

Kathrine joins us, and seconds later, the woman, who has spent the evening attached to Xander's arm, joins us. With each passing second, her presence becomes more and more unnerving. I want to know who she is, but a part of me fears her innocent face and large doe eyes.

"Xander?" she asks with her voice is sweet. She links her arm in his and leans in, blinking with wide, innocent eyes. "Do you know this woman?"

Xander looks me in the eye. I will him to explain who we are to each other—to explain who we will be —but he remains silent.

Kathrine wraps her arms around my waist, resting her cheek on my shoulder. "They are old friends, they used to work near each other in the market."

Xander still doesn't speak. My brows crease. Why isn't he telling them the truth? My pride stings at his refusal to acknowledge me—*to acknowledge us*. But then… I'm not speaking up either, and I hadn't told Kathrine the truth when I had the opportunity.

"Oh!" the blonde exclaims, bouncing on her toes. "You're the one who was taken by the vampire." Then she scrunches up her face. "Everyone thought you were dead."

I'm taken aback by her bluntness. I can't blame anyone for assuming I would be dead that day or soon after, I would have assumed the same.

Kathrine releases me and moves so the two of them are close. They grasp each other's hands and chatter about vampires and my assumed death.

I stand frozen, unsure of what to do. I suppose this can't be any easier for me than for anyone else. After all, it is unheard of for someone who's been claimed to return, especially unaccompanied by their vampire master.

Xander clears his throat quietly, drawing me out of my shock.

He jerks his head, motioning for me to find a way out of this crowded room. It seems I'm not the only one desperate to talk.

"It's warm in here," I announce a little too loud. "If you will excuse me, Kathrine, I need some air."

No one responds. Kitty and the woman, who seems to be her friend, are too consumed in their conversation.

I take two steps before Kathrine's words send a jolt thought me, so sharp my vision blurs with the violent pulse of my heart.

"Can you believe it? First you and Xander are married and now I am to be married in less than a month!"

My mouth goes dry. I force myself to keep walking even though my legs shake with each step until I'm in the hall.

I look around desperately, searching for an empty room or some dark corner to hide in. Xander's footfalls hurry after me, but I keep going.

Near the end of the hall is a dark room with the door ajar. No lights are lit from within, no fire burns in the hearth.

I push my way into the room, my breath coming out in short bursts.

Of course he didn't wait for me. They all thought I was dead... but I had sent him letters, how could he not know? My racing thoughts pound at my temples, and I massage them with my fingers.

The door clicks shut, cutting off the small amount of light from the hall. I drop my hands and look up. Xander stands in the shadows near the doorway. Only pale moonbeams filter in from the window, giving shape to his form.

For a long moment the two of us face each other in heavy silence. There are so many unspoken words between us.

"You're married?" I finally blurt. The words echo painfully off the walls.

CHAPTER THIRTEEN

CLARA

"Clara," Xander starts. He lifts both his hands and approaches cautiously. "It's not what you think…"

Married… Xander is married. I can barely keep the thoughts and questions straight in my head.

"And what is it that I think?" I snap. "Because it seems rather simple. Either you're married or you're not. There is *nothing* complicated about it." He grimaces but says nothing as he inches closer. "Did you get married almost as soon as I was taken? Did you get my letters? Did you even know or care that I had been claimed?" My questions burst forth in a rush.

He stops in front of me and places his hands on my shoulders. I shrug him off taking a step back.

"I got your letters," he says quietly.

I lick my lips. I don't want to know the answer, but I can't keep from asking, "How long did you wait?"

Xander drops his gaze to the floor. Even in the dim light I can see color fill his face.

"A few days," he finally admits.

A few... *days*—not even a week—but *days*.

I had waited for him for years. Even if Alaric had never claimed me, our engagement would have been nearly a year off if not more.

"I wanted to wait..." he says trying to close the distance between us once more. "But my parents pushed for it."

I take another step back. "Demon shit," I hiss. "All you had to do was read my letters to know I would return."

Xander gives me a doleful expression. "I didn't have a choice."

"You always have a choice, Xander." I turn my back to him and gaze out the window. The moon seems to look in, watching us. "You told me you could make your choice once all your brothers married... was that ever a possibility?"

"Once you were claimed, I didn't see the point in fighting it any longer," he says flatly.

My shoulders slump. I wait for the wave of hurt, for tears to well up... but they never come. Not even the prickle of emotions that precede them, or the gut-twisting hurt of loss.

I am not angry or furious with him. There is nothing, at least nothing but disappointment directed at Xander.

My pride stings. For the first time since I was eight years old, I don't have a plan to work toward.

I only feel aimless.

Everything I thought I always wanted has evaporated and ground to a halt. It's strange. Abrupt. Like running for miles only to stop suddenly at the edge of a precipice.

The truth hits me with an uncomfortable force. I don't want to be here. I don't want to have this conversation. I don't even care if all of Xander's promises were childhood wishes or intentional lies. I feel nothing for the loss of the future we had planned.

Was I so desperate to escape Father, I convinced myself that what I had with this boy was love?

It has to be shock. Because losing the one you love to someone else hurts. Learning someone never loved you hurts. People don't agree to marry someone else if they are in love, and have plans.

Xander circles around and wraps me up in his familiar embrace.

"You know I've only ever wanted you," he says.

He trails a finger along my jaw, then presses his

mouth against mine. My mind takes entirely too long to catch up to what's happening. The kiss is awkward… it feels… *wrong*.

I shove against his chest, pushing him away. "You're *married*," I hiss.

"I never wanted to marry Charisma." He tries to wrap his arms around me again, but I resist.

"Do you love her?" I don't know what possesses me to ask, but I think if he cared for her, even a little bit, it might soften the blow to my pride. It would mean h

Xander releases me, finally realizing I won't give in to his advances. He dips his head. "No," he finally admits.

He reaches for me again. I step away, crossing the room to the fireplace, and rest my hand on the stone mantle.

"It can still work between us," he says.

I don't feel relieved at his words, I feel pity for the poor girl. But marrying for love is a luxury only the poor who have no chance to improve their situation can afford. I shouldn't expect him to love her, but he should have some spark of loyalty.

I shake my head. "No, Xander… it can't."

My heart should ache. Xander was the man I wanted to marry. Instead, it feels like a weight has lifted from my shoulders. Learning of his marriage to

Charisma was surprising and my first instinct was to panic.

"Why?" he demands, his voice harsh and jarring.

I spin to face him. He towers over me with a scowl, his hands balled into fists. Xander's sudden anger and hurt smolder in his hazel eyes. I don't want to hurt him. But he's married—he should understand.

The idea of being hidden, of being someone's dirty little secret, of living my life on the side without love or acknowledgment or hope of a future is not something I can be for anyone. Even considering it forms an empty pit in my heart.

I don't know what will become of me now. I won't stay with Kitty, she has her own life to live. Alaric sent me away and the future I always imagined with Xander is impossible, and returning to that shack I spent most of my life in is something I will never do.

"Why?" Xander demands again. I flinch when his hand slaps the wooden mantle next to my head. "Because you're in love with that monster that stole you from me? Is that all it takes, Clara? Fancy clothes… and you fall at his feet."

I recoil at the venomous words.

The harshness is almost like a slap to the face. He's never been aggressive like this before. My mouth opens and closes several times—too stunned to form words.

"Why would you say that?"

"Answer me, Clara."

"He's not like other vampires—" The second the words leave my mouth, I know it's a mistake.

Xander scoffs. "You disgust me."

I pull in a slow breath, trying to tamp down my anger. He's lashing out from hurt. Pain can cause people to do things they wouldn't normally do, but I don't have to take this.

"Xander, you are married—your wife is waiting for you down that hall," I point vaguely in the direction of the party as I take a step forward into his space. "I won't live my life as your paramour, I deserve better than that. We have to let go of our past… you need to let me go."

Xander crosses his arms across his chest and narrows his eyes. I don't miss how his gaze lingers around my neck. He can look all he wants, but what he's searching for isn't there.

I turn and stare distantly into the night. Moonlight lines the trees and land in silver, casting thick shadows everywhere it cannot touch.

"What did you have to give him in return for letting you live in his manor? To get such a fine dress? I bet you have many more of them upstairs."

My gaze snaps to his. He's gone too far.

"You don't get to judge me. Alaric has nothing to

do with this," I say. "Just because you are disappointed in the outcome, doesn't mean you are allowed to treat me this way. You made your choice, and now we both must live with the consequences."

Xander grabs my shoulders, his fingers digging in. "So you did let that thing touch you."

My face heats—but not from shame. Because I cannot deny it, even if what happened is different from Xander's meaning. Because I *had* wanted Alaric... and because I was a fool to think I could come back here and expect everything to be as it was before. It was naive to think everyone and everything I left behind would remain the same.

Time marches on, never wavering. Life doesn't stand still because of a single person's hopes or wishes.

But this level of hostility from Xander—the sweet boy I've known almost all my life—I never would have expected this.

"Xander, please," I say. I keep my voice soft, hoping it will ease his temper.

"Look at me," he grinds out.

My heart aches. I feel my friend slipping away as he grasps at every sliver of anger.

Slowly I raise my eyes.

"How could you?" his face contorts in a sneer. "You betrayed what we had."

I frown. "Xander I—"

His fingers dig painfully into my skin. "I bet you fucked that beast and then begged for more just so he would give you everything you wanted."

My jaw drops. I scramble to think of something to say—how cruel he is, how untrue his statements are…

He knows me better than this.

He *knows* me…

And still, he thinks so little of me.

I should say that I am not the one who married a stranger at the first opportunity. I'm not the one who vowed their life to another.

But I don't.

There is already enough pain between us. Causing more won't do either of us any favors.

When I don't say anything, Xander tsks and releases me with a weak shove.

I back up against the wall, putting space between us. He glares for a long moment before turning on his heel and striding from the room.

I don't go after him. If this is what he needs to let go, then he can have it.

CHAPTER FOURTEEN

CLARA

I LIE AWAKE IN THE PREDAWN LIGHT OF MORNING. Outside the window, a dreary gray swallows the entire sky.

Exhaustion weighs heavy on my shoulders, unrelenting after a countless number of parties. I have attended a lifetime's worth—at least one each night that I've been here. Though, I've managed to get out of a few by feigning fainting spells or illness. With every passing day, I find that I fit in less and less here, surrounded by countless people—people I don't know and don't care to know. It's lonely in a way I've never experienced before.

I've found peace on those few free nights, sitting in the meager library and reading by the light of a tallow candle. The flickering light allows me to transport to another, more familiar place.

Though guilt pricks at me for not spending more time with Kathrine, I know it is for the best. Since that first party, I became attuned to how the people of Littlemire view me. Before Alaric claimed me, I was unseen. Invisible. Now, my life has been touched by that of a vampire, and in their eyes, I am tainted.

Which should bother me, but it doesn't. I don't care about the simpering idiots in this town.

This is the life I once fought to have, and I have hated every minute of it.

I blink at the suddenly blurry ceiling and roll to my side.

The window of this room looks out to the northwest, toward the edges of the Shade forest. I've only ever ventured into the eastern edge. These trees don't make me think of the countless days and hours I have spent wandering there, learning to lay traps and shoot an arrow well enough to kill only the occasional animal.

Instead, the purples and reds bruising the sky peeking through the spaces between branches remind me of a different forest. One full of higher demons...

A single hot tear rolls down the side of my cheek and seeps into the pillow.

A loud series of knocks pulls me from my

darkening mood and signals the third wolf hunt in as many days. While the hunts are a break from the incessant parties, they are also a sickening ritual.

I don't understand how hunting *baby* wolves—or any other animal—with contraptions tied to their feet to slow it down is supposed to bring good fortune and fertility to the married couple.

My stomach rolls from repulsion. At least when I hunted, it was out of necessity and not sport.

On the first day, the pup managed to get away. Kathrine sulked, convinced it was a bad omen for her marriage. Yesterday, the wolf was caught and killed. The pelt was carried away to make a gift for the couple's wedding night. I don't want to imagine what it will be.

Today is the final hunt and the day before the wedding. If I could get out of this, I would. The month-long affair has only reinforced how much I don't belong.

I rise from the bed and dress. My fingers are cold and shake as I button up the bright yellow hunting jacket. The swallow tail hangs down to the back of my knees. The tan leather breeches fit snugly but allow me to move. Finally, I slip my feet into the knee-high, black riding boots.

After tomorrow, these parties and hunts will be

over, and I will be able to begin my search for a new future.

By the time I get to the stables, all twelve of them are already on horseback—Kathrine, Abraham, his brother Watson, the Lord Byron of Progsdale and his wife, the mayor of Durford, and several others whose names I didn't bother to learn.

I take the reins from the stable hand, mount my mare, and guide her to where everyone is waiting. We all walk to the edge of the forest and line up.

Two of the men are laughing and making a wager on which of them will be the one to kill it.

Ahead, the stable hand sets down a metal wire cage, quiet whimpers come from within.

"Are you sure you don't want a pistol?" Watson asks from beside me.

I smile wanly and shake my head. "No… No. I'm still getting used to staying in the saddle with both my hands. I don't think I can manage to stay seated while holding anything."

"That's all right," Abraham says, reaching over to pat me on the shoulder. "Gives me more of a chance to catch the thing for my lovely bride."

He says *thing*, as being born a wolf makes it less than a living creature. It's an old fear, from a time, hundreds of years ago when people feared shifters, blaming them for the horrible acts of demons.

Though everyone knows better, they are still seen as less than animals.

Oblivious to my disgust, Abraham and Kathrine share a sweet look. He is obviously smitten with her, and despite how many times she has insisted otherwise, I think she is falling for him.

The stable hand brings a whistle to his mouth, then releases the latch of the cage. A shrill noise sounds and a wolf pup with ruddy brown fur limps out of the cage. The poor thing cowers into a pile of damp leaves as soon as it spots us.

The man swings his foot and kicks the pup into motion, running into the edge of the forest with an uneven gate.

The stable hand's eyes are glued to a pocket watch while we wait for his signal atop horses that shift in place.

Time ticks on. A few members of the hunting party have teamed up, while others brag about their hunting skills. Wagers are placed and written down.

The stable hand raises his arm.

My stomach churns.

The signal is given. Everyone leaps into action, running into the woods, splitting up. My horse follows without needing to be nudged. I barely manage to keep from being jostled off.

I don't want to see the senseless murder. It's one

thing to hunt an animal for food, quite another to hunt an animal that is far from fully grown as entertainment.

After some distance, my mare gradually slows to a walk. I turn her head, guiding her to the north of the hunting party.

I ride alone for a few hours, staying within hearing range of the others but out of sight. The watery gray of the morning has finally lifted, and the sun shines through the mottled branches.

I breathe in deeply and close my eyes, pretending for a moment that I am somewhere else, far away.

A small yelp catches my attention. My eyes snap open as I just barely keep myself from falling out of the saddle. Pulling the mare to a halt, I glance around, searching for the source of the cry.

Then I see it. The small wolf pup is curled up and shaking violently in a tangle of mud and branches of a dying bush.

I swing my leg over the horse and keep my eye on the pup as I slowly lower myself to the ground. The horse nickers in seeming displeasure when I tie her to a low tree branch. The wolf is barely more than a scrappy ball of fur.

"It's all right. I won't hurt you," I croon as I inch closer.

The creature freezes and takes a halting step back.

When the contraption on its leg catches, fear grows wild in its eyes. It flails and struggles to get free, yelping.

"Quiet, little one." I kneel in the loam and reach for the pup. It snaps its tiny mouthful of teeth as I take hold of it by the scruff.

The poor thing shivers in fear. Roughly the size of a medium-sized dog, it is still a baby in all ways—including strength and coordination. It can't be more than a few months old.

I make soft shushing noises as I use my free hand to roam over its back, sides, and legs, searching for injuries until I get to the booted hind leg, tangled in some dying vines.

"You never had a chance," I say in the same soothing tone.

It trembles, cowering but unable to escape my grasp. I pet the pup, hoping to communicate that I mean no harm, all the while speaking gently.

"You are a sweet little thing, aren't you?" I say.

Large brownish amber eyes blink up at me.

A growl comes from several yards ahead. I jerk my gaze up to see a much larger version of the little cub watching me.

"That must be your mama," I whisper, which earns me a small whimper of a response.

Though the large wolf doesn't come any closer,

there's a spark of intelligence in its eyes. A spark I know better than to dismiss. These wolves are larger than most in the area.

I stretch my left leg out in front of me and retrieve the night forged dagger from my boot. The larger wolf lets out a low snarl.

"It's all right, I won't hurt him," I say.

The wolf takes several loping steps forward, cutting the distance between us in half. The cub's shaking starts anew.

With unhurried movements, I reach for the vines, and slide the edge of the blade across them. The tangle falls away in a single swipe.

Before the pup can manage to get away, I press its back to my chest and hold him there, continuing to talk and shush his whimpers.

After a moment, I bring the dagger to its foot. The mother wolf growls again. Before it can react, I slip the blade between the foot and the boot and jerk the dagger, slicing the leather binds.

I hold the dagger out and set it off to the side before slipping the boot off and releasing the pup. It takes a tentative step forward, pausing to look up at me. I give one more scratch on the head, then pat its butt to encourage it on its way.

The pup gleefully bounds to the other wolf, and together, they disappear into the forest.

I sit back on my heels and sigh. I hope against hope that this will help, in some way, to make up for my part in this ritual—that it makes up for my inaction during the first two days and not trying to put a stop to it.

I stand and do my best to brush off the dirt from my light breeches. Unfortunately, the dirt is damp, and I only succeed in smearing it into the material.

Giving up on my hopeless outfit, I look for signs of the wolf's tracks—small paw prints here and there, a scuffling of leaves where his foot dragged, small broken twigs.

I crouch and dig a hole to bury the leather boot. I grab a nearby fallen branch and sweep it across the path to blur the tacks left behind and camouflage any sign of the wolves.

I toss the branch and dust off my hands as I make my way back to the horse. I stroke her nose.

"Thanks for being such a good girl," I say as I mount up. At least that part is getting easier.

I guide the mare around in circles to remove any remaining evidence before heading toward the voices of the hunting party.

Kathrine spots me and trots over. Her mouth parts as she takes in my appearance. "Oh, Clara, what happened? You're covered in dirt."

My heart stutters. "I… I got unseated." I offer but it comes out more like a question.

Katherine giggles, pulling her horse up beside me. "You really do need to learn how to ride," she teases.

I smile.

"I lost the trail!" Lord Byron of Progsdale says.

Katherine frowns.

The gaze of everyone from our hunting party lowers. I notice a paw print in the damp ground and nudge my horse to the side, tramping over the mark.

What a shame. Now, they'll never pick up the trail.

"Before I fell, I thought I saw it run that way," I say, pointing in the opposite direction from where they ran.

"Why didn't you say so, girl? Let's go—time is running short," The mayor of Durford says and kicks his horse into a trot, causing his round posterior to bounce uncomfortably in the saddle.

One by one, each member of the party takes off, hurrying to catch a wolf they will never see again. But Kathrine stays at my side.

I don't look back in the true direction the wolves ran. There is no reason to.

Hours later, the party gathers in a circle, defeated. My mare shifts impatiently beneath me. I catch someone muttering that they might have caught it if they had been told where it went a minute earlier. The comment is clearly directed at me.

"We should get back. The sun will set soon, and dinner will be ready," Abraham says in an overly loud attempt to hide the remark. He smiles, but the light in his eyes dims when he glances at Kathrine, head bowed and pout on her lips.

Lord Byron huffs. "It is a shame we didn't catch the little demon spawn. Would have had for better luck on the wedding night producing a boy."

What a demon's ass. As if the wedding night is any of his business.

"You only have to look at Kathrine and Abraham to know they don't need luck in their marriage," I say. "Fate could not have designed a more perfect pair."

Katherine beams at that and raises her head a little. Abraham lets out a relieved breath of air. They don't need superstition the day before their wedding or comments from dirty old men.

"No matter," Mayor Collins says, "it was all in good fun."

As we ride back to the Morgan's manor, everyone breaks into small groups to chat. I linger near the rear, and once more, Kathrine rides beside me.

Other than Kitty's presence, nothing about Littlemire feels familiar anymore. The sense of home I once had is gone—if it had ever been there to begin with. Something I'm starting to doubt. The time I spent away from here has lifted the veil that blinded me to the truth and has left me feeling like a stranger in my own world.

"Don't listen to that old demon fart. Boy or girl, your children will be beautiful and perfect," I say.

Her shoulders relax. "Thank you, Clara. I'm so glad you could be here for this." She pauses and sniffles, eyes shining from unshed tears. "You know," she says after a while. "When you were taken, I thought my life was over."

Her words send a stab of pain through me. I hate that she had to experience such fear and uncertainty.

"Oh, Kathrine…"

She lifts her head and gives me one of her brightest smiles. "It was as if the Otherworld sent a miracle to make up for ripping you away from me."

I tilt my head, not sure what she means.

"The money you left wouldn't have made for a decent dowery, so it is a good thing our uncle heard you were claimed. Otherwise, I don't think he would have come offering to be my benefactor—"

"What?" I blurt.

My nerves hum. Something is off… we don't have

an uncle, both our parents were only children. I swear if some demon or vampire has tricked her into some bargain, I will hunt them down and drive the blade of my dagger through the spot where their heart should be.

"Yes, Mr. Steward—oops!" Kathrine slaps a hand over her mouth and giggles. "I wasn't supposed to say anything…"

I gape. *Mr. Steward? That's...* My mind ceases to function. Kathrine continues talking, but I stop listening.

Alaric sent his butler to Kathrine and arranged this marriage… Had he compelled the family into accepting Kathrine? What exactly had he done?

Alaric had orchestrated this entire thing and had said nothing. He acted as if I were doomed to go to Nightwich with him when he had manufactured the very excuse to grant my freedom.

I think back to the letter that had been wrapped with the night forged dagger. *Why hadn't he said anything?*

CHAPTER FIFTEEN

ALARIC

"Alaric," a soft voice whispers.

My eyes flutter open. Clara stands at my bedside, hands clasped. She looks down at me with a furrowed brow.

"Clara?" I reach out to her as I sit up, but she moves just out of reach. "What are you doing here?"

She doesn't answer. Her expression changes. The frown transforms into a scowl, with eyes that accuse me of betrayal.

When she moves to leave, I am on my feet in the same instant.

"Wait," I say. The word comes out somewhere between a command and begging. It is the same thing I've said a thousand times before.

Clara looks over her shoulder at me. Black has

swallowed her irises and the whites of her eyes. "You did this to me," she whispers. "You've killed me."

And then she is gone.

I startle awake—truly awake this time. A sliver of red light pours through a thin opening of the curtains. The sun is setting.

I sit on the edge of the mattress, resting my elbows on my knees, and cradle my head in my hands. Cherno remains sleeping on the pillow next to mine.

It is the same dream each night. At first, it was just her voice in the dark, then her face started to appear. There are times when her eyes are covered in the milky white film of death, others when they are encircled with a thick line of red, or entirely human and brimming with unshed tears.

Sometimes I wake upon seeing her face, other times when I reach for her. Her face and voice haunt my nights.

She is gone, and still, I cannot rid myself of her.

I cannot help but feel as though she is sending me a message. I have betrayed her in my attempt to save her.

There is no use in trying to go back to sleep. The others will wake soon, and then I must play the part of the perfect host. I push up from the bed and take my time dressing before I head to my office for an hour.

At least I will have some time to myself before the others demand my attention.

"How long will you allow yourself mope over that human?" Lawrence mutters from the doorway of my office.

I don't look up from my desk, though I rearrange the papers, flipping the one I was writing on so it's face down.

"I am not moping," I say dryly.

"I never thought I'd see the day where Alaric Devereaux claimed a human... why did you claim her? It is so unlike you."

"Isn't that what you wanted? For me to participate in these 'festivities' as you called them."

He saunters over to me and rests a hip on the edge.

I set the quill down and cross my arms, leaning back in my chair. The fire snaps and pops in the hearth. Above, Cherno hanging from one of the support beams, observing.

I sigh and rub the back of my neck, wanting to change the subject. "What do you make of Mr. Connors?"

Lawrence frowns. This is clearly not the conversation he had intended on having when he came up here to annoy me.

He cocks his head and arches a golden brow. After a moment's hesitation, he takes the bait. "What about him?"

"The last time Elizabeth made a new vampire was almost a hundred years ago. Why him? Why now?"

Lawrence waves a hand dismissively. He stands, going to stand in front of the window. He pushes the drapes aside to stare out on the manor's grounds below. "Who knows why she does the things she does?"

I sneer at the view of the drive leading through the wrought iron fence at the edge of the property and the woods beyond—a view I once enjoyed and have kept covered for the last several days.

My fingertips graze the overturned papers.

"She must see something in Victor. She wouldn't have turned him otherwise," he adds after a moment.

"There are twelve of us all together… There have *only* ever been twelve of us made by her hand for almost a hundred years now."

There is something about this new vampire and Elizabeth's motives that bothers me. It would be one thing for her to create another vampire on a whim, it is yet another to send him to do her bidding when he is still learning to control his strength, needs, desires, and his very nature.

"We know all this," Lawrence says as he studies me from the corner of his eye. "Why are you bringing this up? It won't do any good to speculate. We can't even begin to guess at her reasoning—and attempting to do so is a waste of time."

I shake my head. "I am curious, though I suppose you are right—it doesn't matter."

"Good," he says.

"Except…"

Lawrence throws his hands up, allowing the curtains to drop back into place over the window. "Except *what*, Alaric?"

"Elizabeth is a creature of habit and Victor struggles daily to control his bloodlust. He killed a young woman that first night after I explicitly forbade any of you from harming the humans in this area. And every time we feed in town, I am almost always forced to clean up his messes."

Clara had been too nervous, too inebriated to notice that the poor girl at Victor's feet was dying a slow death and begging him for it. I don't want to think what her reaction would have been if she had realized the truth.

"It was only one—"

The excusatory behavior sets my teeth on edge.

"These humans volunteer their blood and they do so with the understanding that their lives will not be in jeopardy at the hands of *any* vampire."

"Who cares if a human dies every once in a while?"

"I care," I grind out. "Do you know how many humans I had to compel into forgetting that she volunteered? I had to concoct a story for her family about how she ran away with some boy she was infatuated with, and then compel enough of them into believing this boy existed."

I sigh and rub my forehead, using so much power to compel so many of the villagers took its toll.

"You care so much for these humans… you and your sister. I will never understand."

I scoff. "Is there a single one of you who would? I'm surprised Elizabeth hasn't forced my hand all these years to participate in her ridiculous claiming."

Lawrence swivels around so fast that the rug under his boots twists from the force. He stomps over and splays his palms on the desk to loom over me. "You know why she hasn't."

My nostrils flare, but I say nothing.

"If you were anyone else, she would have." Red encircles his irises, and somewhere on the opposite end of the room, Arinah lets out a series of high-pitched squeaks at the sudden pull of power he draws from them. "She cannot force your hand—it is the only reason she allowed you to sire Rosalie, the only reason she allowed your sister to lower herself to feed on animals and didn't kill her for the insult," he spits the words. "It is the *only* reason why she has never forced you to act like what you are. *You are her—*"

"Don't," I say lowly, but there is a threat in that single word. Enough for him to understand and bow to my authority.

Lawrence straightens and looks down on me with pity. "You will give in to her one of these days, and it will be sooner than you think, now that you have claimed a human."

He turns away and walks to the fireplace, Arinah skitters over to him, crossing the mantel. He coos an apology for taking power without warning.

I lay my hand on top of the paper I had flipped over. The hidden side bares my secret—Clara's name written across the top, followed by line after line of words I wrote and crossed out... over and over, unable to figure out what I want or should say.

Nothing. I should say nothing. Writing to her would be useless. I doubt she would waste her time writing a response, let alone bothering to read it.

The fact of the matter is I claimed Clara knowing neither of us had wanted it, and she had made it clear from the start that she did not want to be here.

She left, and all I had to do was say the words that granted her the freedom she desired.

I crumple the paper in my fist and fling it into the flames. It catches immediately. Lawrence and I watch it burn until there is no trace of it left.

"You let her go," he says as he continues to stare into the fire.

It isn't a question but a statement. One I know better than to confirm or deny.

"She will not return." He faces me again. Arinah moves from one of his shoulders to the other, their little pink nose and long white whiskers twitching. "You know it as well as I do."

"That remains to be seen," I say.

He is right. I was a fool to think otherwise, to think no one would notice. Cold resolve settles in my veins. It numbs my mind, my body, my heart.

I should have compelled that command upon her, but I didn't want my last act to be one of control. She would have hated me if I had. Though that matters little, hate was always there between us from the first moment we laid eyes on each other.

Compelling her would have been pointless. Clara made it no secret in the six weeks she spent here that she wanted nothing more than to leave and return home to her sister.

Clara would never choose to be here.

"So you think she will come back… even without your mark?" Lawrence asks derisively.

I nearly flinch at the question. The truth is that I know she will not return to Windbury or to me. Admitting that aloud, even to Lawrence, would mean a fate worse than death for her.

I remain silent for several long minutes.

"Vampires cannot simply claim a human and then release them. That isn't how this works. She might be the first you've bothered to claim, but even you know Elizabeth would never allow such a thing. If not by your hand, then by another's… that human will die, and it will not be a good death."

If Clara lives, then she will be taken by a vampire, and her life will be long and painful. She is better off if she is put out of her misery.

I meet his gaze, unflinching. "Then perhaps I will hunt her down before we are to leave, and kill her. I will bring Clara's lifeless body to Nightwich and lay her at Elizabeth's feet. Do you think that will satisfy her?"

I gave Clara back her freedom, and now I mean to take her life.

It is silent for a minute. And then he laughs, throwing his head back.

"You do not mean that, my friend," he says when he finally calms.

My blood pulses at the notion of hunting her down, finding her… feeding on her. Even if I must deceive her in the end.

If death will come for her, then I can at least give her peace in her final moments. I can give her a clean death—one without pain or fear.

I place my palms flat on the desk, push myself up to stand, and look him dead in the eye. "Oh, my friend, *but I do.*"

CHAPTER SIXTEEN

CLARA

Kathrine is a vision in her wedding dress. The bell skirt flows down past her feet. The cream-colored material covers her from her wrists to halfway up her neck, with silk gloves on her hands. Shimmering gold thread with small pearl beads in strategic places adds a soft touch. On her head is a crown of white rose buds pinned in her hair to hold the veil in place.

The amount of material used in the dress combined with the extravagance of this wedding is a sign of the Morgan's wealth. The money they spent on the parties and refreshments over the past month was beyond anything ever heard of before in Littlemire. I wonder how much of it Alaric funded.

But why go to such lengths? He could have easily

married her off to someone of lesser status. Was this all generosity, or what was required for everyone to turn a blind eye to our background?

Kathrine stands before everyone with Abraham, their hands clasped as the officiant speaks.

Once it begins, the ceremony is short. Soon the two of them walk by, racing through the halls. I hurry through the doors leading outside and run around to the front, where their carriage is waiting for them.

Kathrine waves when she sees me and hurries over, leaving her new husband. She gathers me up into a hug. She will be gone for a week.

"I'm so glad you are back," she says. She places a kiss on each of my cheeks, then leans in close to whisper in my ear, "Perhaps Uncle Steward will find you an equally suitable match." She looks over her shoulder, then laughs and adds, "I am sure he can find someone almost as good."

I don't want your life. The words are on the tip of my tongue, but I swallow them back down.

"I am happy for you," I say. "Go, enjoy your trip."

Kathrine hurries to the carriage and climbs in with help from her new husband. I stand back, waving alongside everyone else until their carriage disappears down the road.

Nothing about this life fits who I am, though I'm

not entirely sure what does anymore. Even if Mr. Steward was our uncle, I wouldn't want this life.

With the newlyweds gone, the guests leave. Abraham's mother, Mina, squeezes my shoulder and gives me a tight-lipped smile before following her husband and remaining sons into the house. I linger a minute longer before heading inside and going to my room.

Once the bedroom door is shut tight behind me, I strip off the lacy dress Kathrine picked out and slip into a pair of fitted trousers and a loose blouse. I grab my worn and tattered book and plop down on the bed to read.

On my sister's request, the Morgan's have opened their library to me, but tonight I want to find comfort in something familiar.

I suck in a sharp breath and blink into the darkness. My book slips from my chest to the bed, closing with a soft thunk.

I wait for my eyes to adjust. The window to my right is small, the room itself is smaller than I remember... As my hazy mind fully wakens, it comes back to me. I am in Littlemire.

A branch scrapes against my window. I slump back onto my pillows. *Not a demon.*

Picking up my book I set it on the bedside table, and roll to my side. I close my eyes only to snap them open again a few minutes later when I am unable to fall back to sleep. My heart is beating too fast, and my mind is restless.

Since I've returned to Littlemire, the only time I was truly happy were those rare moments I spent alone with Kitty.

Katherine will be back in seven days, and she will expect me to be here—which I assume is the only reason the Morgan's haven't asked me to leave with everyone else. So the time being, I've accepted the hospitality of people I can't relate to.

But eventually, I will need to go somewhere.

I have no desire to check in on Father, let alone return to that shack that holds nothing but bad memories. I'd be more at home in the forest being possessed by a particularly nasty demon.

What will I do tomorrow? Or the next week, or the week after that?

The one thing I worked towards for as long as I can remember has finally come to pass. I have no more obligations.

What was it that Lawrence said?

"If you could go anywhere, be anywhere, without obligation, where would you choose?"

His words echo in my mind. *Without obligation...*

I am in the situation Lawrence described a month ago.

Kathrine is safe. She will be taken care of no matter what happens to me. And Xander? Xander and I were never going to end up together. I realize now that we were young and naïve. We lied to each other and ourselves.

Alaric has freed me from my debt to him. I can *go* anywhere I wish, *be* anyone I want to be…

With the Morgan's influence and help, it's possible I could find a match that would leave Kathrine ecstatic, but *I* don't want that life.

It's strange and freeing and terrifying all at once. I don't know who I am without those obligations. But I can't stay here—not in this house, and not in Littlemire.

I am on my own. Maybe I've always been on my own and just never realized it.

I roll over to my other side and face the window. The drapes are pulled back revealing the pure midnight sky dotted with stars made brighter by the fact that there is no moon tonight. In the distance, demons howl. They are quieter here, their cries sounding like a mournful song.

I feel a tug deep inside me, calling me to something else, something far from here. For weeks my thoughts have drifted to a face I should forget. *Should,* but no matter how hard I try, I can't.

Darkness has wrapped itself around my heart and won't let go. I want to surround myself with it until it becomes part of my very being.

No one in their right mind would entertain such thoughts.

But I do.

I bolt upright and swing my legs off the bed, my fingers digging into the mattress. My breaths come short and quick, as if I'd been running for miles.

The realization of what I want strikes me hard and swift. There is nothing left for me here, nothing left of the girl I used to be. To force myself to stay would be misery. Attempting to fit in and forcing others to pretend they didn't fear me for my connection with a vampire.

I will find a new place far away and start over with a new name, where no one knows who I am or that I've ever been claimed. I push off the bed, my legs weak with anticipation.

Striking a match, I light the tallow candle beside the bed and kneel in front of my mostly empty trunk. I reach in and pull out the crumpled letter Alaric sent with the night-forged dagger and smooth it out.

Keep this with you at all times...

I still don't understand why Alaric released me. It still stings. He took the time to write *this* and wrap the dagger as some kind of parting gift but didn't bother to say goodbye.

I clench the letter, my fingernails piercing the paper. Alaric lied to my face. When Kathrine's letter arrived at the manor, he'd feigned surprise.

I push back the sudden sting of tears. *I am an idiot.*

I thought, despite everything, we were past lying to each other.

Holding the letter over the candle's flame, I wait for it to catch. The edge glows red and turns black as the fire consumes it, destroying each word of the sentence. I shake the paper to extinguish the flame and let it drop. It flutters to the bottom of the empty trunk until there's nothing left but a few flakes of black ash.

The faint lightening of the sky that precedes dawn edges the horizon.

I blow out the candle, then cross to the armoire, pulling out a single outfit. My fingers shake with anticipation as I unfold the dark, doeskin trousers and matching blouse. I waste no time changing into them, then slip into my boots. Once I'm dressed, I slip the night-forged dagger into the side of the right one.

I look around the room. There is nothing I care about, nothing I want, except for my book.

I grab the satchel that held my food on the way here and place my book on the bottom. Next, I go to the vanity, where a tray of bread and cheese with dried meats sits. One of the servants must have brought it up while I slept. I wrap those in the cloth napkin then place them in the bag.

I don't care about the necklaces and earrings Alaric had sent with me, but I pack those too—they will come in handy for trading for food and lodging. With that, I'm ready.

I stand with my hand hovering over the doorknob. I still have only a vague idea of what I'm going to do or where I want to go besides away from Littlemire. I could go west, or south... or east toward Windbury.

Biting down on my lip, I cringe. I am free, and still, I can only think about returning to him. Alaric had even ordered me to not return.

But the anger twisting at my heart over his deception clouds my judgment. I know it does, and I don't care. I grab onto it, using it as an excuse.

I will give him a piece of my mind, then draw blood—truly earning my freedom. From there, perhaps I'll head south to Stormvale or north to Sangate.

It is a two- or three-day ride from here to

Windbury. Kathrine will be upset if I leave before she gets back. I will never see my sister again. That thought hurts, but it can't be helped.

I should leave a letter for her, but if I don't leave now, I'm afraid I might find some excuse to put it off. I will already be taking one of the horses.

Stealing in the past has never bothered me before, but now will look bad for Kathrine. Who wants to be known for having a thief in the family?

Tonight, when I stop, I'll write a letter to them and send someone to deliver it along with the horse.

It's not a good plan, but it's all I have. It's brash and risky, but my mind will never be at peace if I don't confront him.

At least, that's what I tell myself.

The room lightens around me further.

I pull open the door and stride out, moving fast and quietly through the halls until I'm outside. The first rays of morning light peek over the horizon and the smell of frost on the air.

The wailing of demons lessens, retreating along with the shadows they are bound to.

Desperation crawls over my skin as I jog toward the stables, remaining as silent as possible. They will wake soon, and I need to be gone before that happens.

I move through the stables. A few horses peek their heads out of their stalls as I pass, but I ignore them all and head for the one mare I know. I'm not an experienced rider, but the two of us are familiar with each other from spending the past month together.

My fingers fumble with the saddle, the cold numbing them made worse but sense of urgency building. Eventually, I get the tack on the mare. I lead her out of her stall and to the open door of the stable before mounting.

Once seated, I take a deep breath and go over my plan one more time. I will confront Alaric for his deception, demand answers to my questions, thank him for what he's done for Kathrine, and then… then I will go wherever my feet take me.

The rooster cries, causing my heart to jump into my throat. I nudge the mare into a walk, then urge her into a trot down the drive and toward the main road.

As we leave Littlemire behind, I look back and send a silent hope to the fates that Kathrine will live a long, happy life with her new husband.

I face forward once more and ask the mare to run.

CHAPTER SEVENTEEN

CLARA

My anger at Alaric's lies and deception only fuels my determination for so long until the ache in my rear and thighs becomes too much. I slow the horse to a walk, having pushed the brown mare as long as I could.

Several hours have passed. The fine mist that has clung to the forest all day thickens. I reach forward and stroke the mare's soft neck. Her absence has probably been noticed by now, and maybe even mine.

Hunger gnaws at my belly. I haven't eaten since yesterday. Nerves and stress kept the pangs at bay until now. I pull the satchel across my shoulder and rest it on my lap, reaching in for a chunk of break. I bite into it, munching as the horse sways beneath me.

The idea of slowing or stopping sets me on edge,

but as the edge of Durford comes into view, I relent and guide the horse toward the riverbank.

I dismount to let the mare drink her fill, then feed her the apple slices from my bag. They aren't pretty after several hours, but she doesn't seem to mind.

I kneel at the edge of the water. The mare dips her head, ripping up the space blades of grass. I cup my hands and splash water over my face.

The mare shifts anxiously, and then the steady beat of hooves disappears into the distance. I wipe my eyes with my sleeve in time to see the horse happily trotting back the way we came.

"Traitor," I mumble.

That's what I get for not holding onto the reins. She will probably make it home sooner this way, and I'm close enough to town that it doesn't matter.

I get to my feet, dusting off my legs. The walk across the bridge and into town doesn't take long.

My legs ache, more specifically, my thighs. It had taken far more muscle coordination to ride today than it had during the hunts.

I welcome the chance to stretch my muscles. The last time I was here, I never saw more than the town's inn. It's smaller than I expected. The sidewalks are narrower than those of Littlemire, but they lack the thick layer of soot that covers the buildings and streets there.

No one spares me a second glance as I move through the streets. I never thought I'd be so happy to go unnoticed.

There is a tug on the back of my shirt, and I spin to face whoever it is, but I don't meet anyone's gaze until I look down and into the smiling face of a young girl. Her long hair and shining large eyes are familiar.

It takes me a moment, but I finally place her—she's the girl I pulled from the river.

"Hello there," I say, crouching down to eye level. I rest my palm on the top of her head.

A snarling woman appears behind her. I blink and the girl is jerked away.

"Stay away from her," the mother hisses.

I straighten, dropping my hand to my side. "I didn't mean—"

"I didn't recognize you at first when you attacked her at the river, but I do now. You can't deceive me again." She roughly yanks the child behind her billowing skirt.

Attacked? What kind of demon shit—I saved her daughter after she fell in the river.

"Demon's *whore!*" she shouts and clutching the child tighter against her and pointing a gnarled finger in my face.

I stumble back at the outburst as if it were a physical blow.

This woman knows who I am. She doesn't care that I saved her child—only that she saw me with a vampire. And because I am claimed, she has twisted the facts.

Even though she had thanked me at the time, I never expected it—I never wanted it. But I don't deserve her cruelty.

There is no reasoning with someone like this. I turn from her and walk several blocks closer to the inn. The further I get from the furious woman, the more my shoulders hunch. Even keeping my head down, I can feel the gaze of townsfolk on me as I pass.

Whore... she had spat the word at me—as if she knew anything about the situation. She said it with such derision, such disrespect.

It wasn't the words "demon's whore" that hurt, but the venomous tone, the hate... the unfettered cruelty in her voice.

What a horrible person. I can only hope her wretchedness has no more reason to come out and infect that sweet girl of hers.

The mist that has hung on the air for the entirety of the morning finally becomes a soft drizzle. It's the perfect end to a demon shit day.

The damp seeps into my clothes, but I'm not soaked to the bone... not like the last time I was here.

At long last, I reach the inn. The stone facade and

crest are unchanged. A rueful smile ticks up one corner of my mouth. This might be the first thing I've come across since my return that hasn't changed.

The sign still reads The Grand Manor. Even the worn paint remains chipped in the same places.

I push open the door and blink to adjust to the dim lighting. The wallpaper and dark, polished wood are the same. Now, a thin layer of dust coats the dark wood. It appears they only keep up with that sort of detailed work during the claiming.

The innkeeper spots me at once and raises a thick, white brow in question. I am the only one in the lobby. An older gentleman reclines in the sitting room on the right, reading a paper.

I lift my chin and walk up to the counter with all the confidence I can muster. Without breaking eye contact, I dip my hand into my satchel to take out one of the jewelry pieces and plunk it down on the counter.

"I need a room and a hot meal."

The burly man leans forward, resting one arm on the counter. He takes his time sizing me up.

"I remember you," he says slowly in a low voice.

I say nothing. I won't deny who I am, but I'm not stupid enough to announce it either.

Reluctantly he drags his gaze away from me and looks down at my payment. He plucks it off the counter with two meaty fingers and brings it close to his eye to examine it.

"Did you steal this?" he barks the accusation. "You were a scrappy little thing the last time you were in here."

"Of course not." I narrow my eyes, infusing as much steel into them as I can, and unflinchingly meet his gaze.

He says nothing for a long time, then grunts. "You know there's a punishment for those who run from their masters. I hear it's almost as bad as that of a slayer."

I swallow delicately, and lifting my chin a little higher, I say, "I didn't run away."

At least, not this time.

Grumbling under his breath, the innkeeper pockets the necklace and turns around to survey the wall of keys before snatching one and smacking it down on the counter.

"Wait here," he says. He moves from behind his counter, then walks into the dining room doors, closing them behind him.

I take the key, gripping it in my hand. The warmth from my body seeps into the metal as I wait.

It's not long before he returns with a covered tray. He jerks his head as he passes and orders me to follow.

This time, we don't go to the top floor but stop on the second halfway down the hall. He opens the door, and I step inside.

"Your meal," he says and shoves the tray at me.

It nearly tips over as I take it with one hand. The soup is not even warm enough to give off a curl of steam, and a chunk of bread is a day past its prime. It looks like he ripped it off a loaf with his bare hands. The small chunk of cheese on the plate has a small patch of white mold covering half of it.

"You have two nights here with that trinket. If you want to stay longer, then you'll have to find your own meals or bring coin," he says.

"It's worth more than at least double that," I protest.

He narrows his eyes, taking me in. "Consider it payment for not reporting you." With that, he shuts the door with more force than necessary.

I take in the cramped quarters. Smaller than the room I shared with Alaric. The windowpanes are covered in a thick layer of dirt, obscuring the view outside.

Setting the tray on the bed, I set to work getting a small fire started. Once the flames catch, I strip out of my clothes and lay them out on the floor in front of the fire to dry—in the same way Alaric had.

Alaric. There is his name again.

It's only late afternoon, yet, somehow, I am already exhausted. I plop on the bed, and a cloud of dust plumes up around me. The bed is lumpy and creaks, sitting in its broken frame at a slight angle, but I can't find it in me to care.

I look at the meal as I pull my dagger from my boot and start slicing off the unappetizing bits before consuming the bland stew. I save the bread and cheese to wrap up and place in my satchel.

Sorting through my contents I still have some food I originally packed, but it's not much.

I'd given the innkeeper my most expensive piece. The bracelet and earrings I have left are not enough to buy a horse.

After setting the empty tray outside the room, I lock the door, then settle into bed, laying at an angle to keep my head above my feet.

I stare at the ceiling, drumming my fingers on the mattress. I *could* relieve some townsfolk of their coin, but I'm afraid my face might be too recognizable.

It looks like it will be another early morning at the stables.

Despite my exhaustion, I toss and turn.

What had Alaric expected me to do when he sent me away and told me to never return? Even though he was responsible for arranging Kathrine's marriage, he had to know I couldn't stay with her.

The more I think about his actions, the more I don't understand. The questions build upon themselves, multiplying.

Did he even care? I scoff into my pillow. Of course he didn't care.

At some point during the night, I manage to drift off to sleep, only to wake again and again. Every lump in the mattress feels like an elbow jutting into my back and every other muscle unfortunate enough to come into contact with it.

The drizzle gradually turns into a storm that rages, rattling the windows, and the rain leaves streaks in the dirt. Eventually, it is loud enough to drown out the howling of demons. Near dawn, the storm settles to a soft patter.

I will not be sleeping anymore, not here, not tonight. I push up and groan. Every muscle in my body is stiff and aching.

I slip into my now-dry clothes and sling my satchel over my shoulder, tossing the key onto the bed as I leave.

The inn is nearly silent in the early hour. The only sounds are the occasional snoring from behind closed doors. I make my way down the stairs, all too aware of every creak they make beneath my otherwise silent steps.

Light guilds the edges of the trees as I step outside.

The air is damp and cold, but not unpleasantly so. It takes some time to find the stables, but when I do, I am glad to find it void of other people.

I pause at each occupied stall until finally settling on a black and gray dappled horse, tall and muscular but lean. This one looks built for running.

It takes me longer to saddle this one than the mare I've grown used to, but eventually, I manage it. This one has more energy and spirit in him. I expect to cover more ground today. I made it to Littlemire in less than two days by carriage. I see no reason why I wouldn't reach Windbury before nightfall.

I open the stall door, quickly mounting, then lead the horse out of the stable.

As soon as we emerge, I spot the innkeeper making his way out here. Confusion turns to anger, his face turning a bright shade of red. He lifts a fist, shaking it and shouting as he attempts to run toward me.

I dig my heels into the horse's side and he leaps into a run. I'm almost unseated by the sheer power of the animal, but I manage to stay in the saddle.

The wind is at our backs, as though it were sent by some Otherworldly creature to aid us. The pounding hooves drown out the innkeeper's shouts.

Once on the road through the forest, I give the horse his head. He runs as if he has been held back for too long by his owner and this is the first taste of freedom he has ever had, and intends to enjoy it.

Even if I wanted to, I could never return to the place I always thought was my home. In the past month I have come to realize it never had been.

I never knew the people I thought I had, I kept them all at arm's length, letting necessity guide me. Except for Kathrine… I still love her, but I have let her go so she can be happy and loved by those who know how to love her the way she deserves.

As I leave Durford, I don't look back. I will never look back. My past self is gone, and now I can only go forward toward the unknown to find who I truly am.

CHAPTER EIGHTEEN

CLARA

The horse's long legs cover twice the ground with each stride and half the effort as the mare. Once we reach the foothills, I slow our pace. The rocky terrain and the incline make me uneasy, and I don't want him worn down before we arrive in Windbury.

The first time I'd traveled through this part, I had been unconscious—thanks to Alaric compelling me into a demon-induced sleep. When I finally woke, I felt as though I were crawling out of death's grip.

We follow the grooves in the road left by countless carriages that have passed this way before.

I tilt my head back and look to the sky. At some point in the past hour, a blanket of gray clouds has swallowed the sky, so thick they hide the sun's position. I squint, looking for any sign of rain-laden patches. There doesn't seem to be, but that could change anytime soon.

When we come across a small stream, I decide that a short break is worth the risk. After the dappled gray is watered, I keep the reins in one hand and walk alongside him as he grazes.

I make do with walking and eating with one hand. It's not ideal but being stranded this far from any town would mean certain death.

A twig snaps. Something flashes off to the side. I hold my breath and listen, scanning the area for any signs that I'm not alone. The sound of distant birds and the trickling stream appear to be our only company.

It's just a fluffy forest animal. Probably a bunny. These sounds are nothing to worry about.

Even I don't believe that.

I want to get going again soon because this forest gives me the creeps. I quickly pull myself back into the saddle and guide the horse into a relaxed trot.

A shiver crawls up my spine—the unmistakable sensation of being watched. Lingering in the forest is a bad idea.

I can't shake the feeling even after several minutes. I turn in the saddle to look behind. There's no sign of anyone having passed this way within the past week.

As if sensing my nerves, the horse breaks into a

run. We ride as if we are being chased for several minutes before slowing to a sustainable pace. An hour passes. Then another. Just when I think we lost whatever was following us, something flickers in my peripheral.

I focus on the right without turning my head. A large shape covered in ruddy fur flies past a break in the brush. It disappears in a blink. I continue to wait.

The wolf pops in and out of view, silent and ghost-like coming closer and drifting further away—only showing itself enough to let me know it's still with me.

I'm thankful the horse hasn't noticed. I have no doubt he'd be spooked enough to unseat me. I finally turn my head to watch. The animal meets my eye for a brief second before vanishing.

Warm amber. The color strikes a chord in my memory. Eyes I've seen before on the face of a handsome man with a wide smile and freckles sprinkled across his nose.

By some Otherworldly miracle, the wolf isn't attacking us. At least, not yet. I keep to the road, not daring to try a more direct route.

I adjust the reins around my aching fingers. The early winter air has chilled me to the bone, and I can barely feel my body, but I push on.

The world darkens gradually. Mournful cries echo

in my head and my mind runs wild with the fear that I am out of time.

The howling grows louder, and it's with a single high-pitched wail that I realize it's not in my head.

I look to the sky through bare tree branches. The gray clouds have cleared. What I'd thought was cloud coverage was the lowering sun leaving behind the muted bruised purples of twilight. And with it, the song of birds has faded.

Demon shit. I let myself get distracted and stopped paying attention to the light.

The sun dips lower with every passing second, and I am still in the forest.

If night comes and I am still in the forest, the demons will rise, and they will possess me. I will not live to see another sunrise.

I dig my heels into the horse's side, urging him to go faster but as night slithers in, I know I won't make it. I failed to take into account that I'd lose light faster beneath the cover of trees.

Hooves thunder beneath me, matching my pulse as it pounds inside my veins.

The road smooths out, and I push the horse as hard as I can. His sides heave, and sweat foams on his neck, but we can't slow.

"I'm sorry... just hang on a little longer," I murmur. "You can do this."

The trees thin out, but the sun already set, and darkness swallows the world faster and faster. The howling and cries of the high demons heralding the night surround me on both sides as if herding us. With every passing second, they inch closer with the speed of the growing shadows.

A break in the trees forms ahead. I can see the outline of the manor against the starry sky.

Under the voice of demons comes the sound of the wolves singing. If they belong to Oliver's pack, they are too far to do anything to help… but even if they were, they couldn't banish the demons.

I sit lower into the saddle and chance a look over my shoulder.

Lesser demons, half-formed, follow like impenetrable black fog nipping at our heels, swallowing up the road behind us. It swirls and dances, billowing in and out as they attempt to take form.

The horse swerves from side to side. I can practically feel the second the animal realizes the demons have come out.

Several pairs of glowing red eyes loom, stretching out their unnaturally long arms and gnarled fingers toward me. They rise up, slowly gaining ground. The two demons split up to flank us.

My heart leaps into my throat. *I'm not going to make it. I'm not going to make it.*

A deep howl, unlike anything I've heard before, roars from behind. I debate the merits of looking back and reluctantly turn my head to see how close they are.

Two massive eyes glowing like molten iron rise up from the black cloud of lesser demons. Their limbs are branch-like and twisted with more joints than anything should possess. They grab hold of the trees, pulling themselves up, up, up... wood splinters in their grasp. Their back arches, emaciated with a spine that juts out.

Finally, they raise their head, still forming around the eyes—skull like and some twisted mix of human and animal. The charred skin stretches across its bones and tendons, dry and painful.

Shit. Damn my luck to the Otherworld.

All my life, I've only seen the partially formed sentient masses of power that make up lesser demons.

Somehow, I have managed to catch the attention of a higher demon. Twice.

The demon looks around as if called into being by the activity of the others. They spot me and grin. Sharp pointed teeth jut out at every angle. If the demon had lips, they would have been shredded from the expression.

Their massive hands slam down on the ground sending a shudder through it. The horse stumbles.

I cry out, waiting for the impact of hitting the ground, but the horse regains his footing and keeps running.

"Deliccciousss morsssssel hooow I've missssed yoooou," the demon's voice rasps.

My eyes burn from tears forcing their way up. I would recognize the timbre of that voice anywhere.

The demon is large—so large that even crouching, and bracing on its hands, its back brushes against the branches of tall trees. Some limbs snap off and fall to the ground. The demon takes two lumbering steps closer and sniffs at the air. Newly fallen branches splinter into kindling beneath their feet.

"Iii haaaave beeeen waiiiting..." A long, black tongue licks at its nonexistent mouth. "Ssssuuuch a looong tiiiime foooor yoooou to retuuuurrrn."

My body quakes as I cling to the horse's silvery mane. Then we are out of the trees nearing the open gates of Alaric's property.

The demon lopes toward me, the foul breath churning my stomach as it gains.

Five shadowy figures stand at the front of the manor, unmoving.

I open my mouth to call out, but then my breath is ripped from my lungs, and I am flying, I can't tell which way is up. The horse has fallen out from under me without so much as a sound.

Searing pain rips through my leg. My body jerks. And then I am falling in a different direction.

I gasp in a lungful of air only to have it ripped from my lungs as I collide with the ground.

Pain. The pain is everywhere. Stars explode across my vision.

A loud crack. My leg is on fire.

So much pain.

I try to breathe but I can't. The movement of taking even half a breath feels like a thousand knives through my ribs.

Voices.

Silence, then more talking.

I can't think. I try to roll my head to see what's happening, to see where the demon is before it delivers its killing strike. Black spots waver in and out, obscuring everything.

An eternity has passed, and yet... I'm still alive. Otherworld take me, I want to die—*the pain... the pain... the pain.* It's too much.

My body goes numb, and that's more terrifying than the pain. *I can't feel anything.*

Silence—long and heavy.

A familiar voice.

Then nothing.

CHAPTER NINETEEN

ALARIC

A second hunt in town in as many nights. These are becoming far too regular for my tastes. And without my claimed human I can offer nothing in the way of an excuse to reduce the frequency, let alone avoid them entirely.

I exhale, long and slow. I am not looking forward to this. I detest going into town to feed. There is always too much unwanted attention, and with this lot, too many chances for things to go awry when it's impossible to keep track of everyone.

I have offered to send for willing humans, but Cassius, Della, and Victor insisted on hunting.

I have had my fill earlier in the evening from my reserves. I do not wish to partake in this ritual again so soon. Yet I refuse to let them go unaccompanied into my territory, lest something unfortunate happen without my supervision.

Lawrence steps up behind me and places a hand on my shoulder.

"It is a nice night for a hunt," he says. "Dark." He motions to the sky, indicating the lack of a moon tonight.

I drag my gaze to his, unamused. He shrugs in response.

Victor and Della tail Cassius, moving beyond the gates, anxious to get this hunt started. A loud roar echoes from the west.

Lesser demons are never that loud.

The five of us stop in our tracks and look to the edge of the forest just beyond the property line. Darkness pulses between the trees, power rippling out in wave after wave. The world holds its breath.

Then a horse bursts out of the forest with a rider clinging desperately to its back.

At first, my mind doesn't want to make sense of what I'm seeing. It is impossible.

No ordinary human would stumble across this property by accident. Humans would take the road directly into town, bypassing the one leading here. Whoever it is was sent here for a reason, or—

A higher demon breaks through the trees in the next moment, on the horse's heels. They swipe out with their gnarled fingers catching the horse and knocking its back legs out from under it. The mount falls to the ground as the demon swipes with the other claw swatting the rider from the saddle, sending them sailing through the air.

The rider cries out as their body hits the ground. The sound of pain grips my heart. *I know that voice.*

It is a voice that has haunted my nights for too long.

She lands, rolling on the ground before coming to a stop in a crumpled heap. I run to her side.

The demon roars up behind her, preparing to strike a blow. They could kill her, but like any other demon, they will want her alive—weakened—but alive to possess and torture her until dawn.

Clara groans at my feet. The shredded material of her trousers exposes the wounds on her leg, seeping blood.

I place my body between her and the demon. Bracing myself, I call up my power until it all but crackles at my fingertips.

I raise my hand and send out a command, drawing on my power from deep within. *Withdraw.*

A soft breeze flutters loose strands of hair at my brow. Lawrence walks up to my side, his hands raised, using his power in tandem with mine.

The higher demon pushes, fighting back as it

writhes against our powers, shrieking its fury. They slam their massive, gnarled claws onto the ground and the earth shudders.

The demon looks once at the other vampires standing back, watching impassively. The massive head, hard and crumbling like scorched bone, lowers. The maw opens wide, and they let out an ear-splitting screech.

Sweat drips down my temple. The demon is strong… Too strong. No single demon should possess such power.

Hot, foul breath reeking of sulfur and decay, washes across my face. The demon's power pulses once more in protest before it pushes off the ground and dissolves into a cloud of black mist, swirling up into the air, and sinking back into the depths of the forest.

The thick tang of sweet human blood fills the air mingling with the horse's scent. Though it is still alive, its breathing is labored. A human would put it down. But then a human wouldn't have the power to do anything for it.

I don't have time to examine the damage to the animal—not when Clara is hurt. I kneel at her side.

"You're going to heal her?" Lawrence asks, his words biting.

I nod in answer, not taking my eyes off Clara's

face. She squirms, her eyes squeezed shut, and forehead scrunched up in pain.

At least she is conscious, but I cannot tell if she can see or hear through her pain.

I run my hands over her body, starting at her head and moving down, checking for injuries. She hisses and whimpers when I get to her ribs. She is badly bruised. Thank the Otherworld, nothing seems to be broken.

Three large gashes run halfway up her lower left leg where the demon's claws slashed. They aren't too deep, but deep enough that blood beads and drips down her leg. The wounds are red and swollen from the demon's venom.

Any plans I had of hunting her down and ending her life go up in smoke. Blood—*her* blood—spilled by something else is infuriating.

"What happened to killing her?" Lawrence mutters.

I jerk my head up to meet his gaze, fangs bared. "I will kill her *if* and *when* I wish to, and not a moment before."

Lawrence steps closer. His nostrils flare as he inhales the scent of Clara's blood. Red encircles his hazel eyes, nearly taking over. He stumbles back several steps.

"Have the horse mended and cared for, then join

the others in the manor. Mr. Steward will see to it that you all receive the blood you need," I say.

Lawrence raises a brow in silent question, his hand clasped over his nose and mouth. "It's only a horse. I will put it out of its misery."

"No, it brought her here through the demon infested forest. It deserves better than that. Heal it then take it into town and give it to the first human you see." I turn to address the others. "The hunt is off."

Clara shifts and hisses through her teeth, drawing my gaze back to her. She grips her leg, fingers biting into her flesh as if she can staunch the pain, knuckles white from the strain.

The demon that attacked Clara is too powerful to exist on its own. I have no doubt they belong to another vampire. Who would have the ability to wield a demon stronger than my own... Who would dare bring them into my territory and give it free reign?

"Clara." Her name leaves my lips before I can stop it.

Lawrence clears his throat, and in a whisper, too low for anyone but me to hear, he says, "You were surprised to see her. One might think you weren't expecting her to return at all."

My head snaps up, and I rise slowly to face him. I could fend him off Clara if I had to, but if the others scent her blood, there is no way I could fight off the frenzy that would follow.

The expression he wears is something between awe and wonder. Over the past month, he had accused me of releasing her, of setting her free, but only now does he believe his own words. I don't know what gave it away—a word, an expression…

It doesn't matter.

Lawrence lifts a hand, halting the others who approach us.

"Go, now," I say. "The four of you still need to feed. I will join you in the drawing room later."

He nods and speeds to where the others wait, then leads them into the manor. His jovial voice rings out across the yard as he claps Cassius and Victor on the shoulder and turns them back inside.

I crouch and lift Clara from the ground. Her body shudders at being moved. She cries out, trying to squirm out of my arms.

"Be still." I almost compel the command into her but stop just as my power reaches the tip of my tongue. She is in enough pain.

Clara's eyes are still squeezed shut. Sweat glistens across her brow.

"Where are you hurt?" I tighten my arms around her. I know the answer, but I want her to focus—to stay aware.

She takes several long, deep breaths. Several minutes pass. I could swear she is attempting to will away the pain.

It isn't until we are halfway up the stairs to the third floor that she finally peels open one eye. The tension in her muscles begins to subside, and she looks around.

"Everywhere," she says hoarsely. "You can put me down now." Clara presses a palm against my chest and pushes weakly. She would not succeed with perfect health and strength, let alone with this pathetic attempt.

I ignore the demand and stride into my personal chambers. The moment my feet come to a stop at the side of my bed, Clara stops struggling. Her slender fingers dig into my jacket. I set her down gently and straighten.

There's no gratitude in her eyes for saving her, only cold fury.

I stare at her, unable to look away. She returned. I don't understand why or how she made it all the way here by herself on horseback. I never expected to lay eyes on her again. How in the Otherworld is she here?

I suppose my declaration to kill her with Lawrence was nothing more than a lie. A weak attempt at defying Rosalie. To look upon Clara's face now, I don't think I'd have been able to follow through. I would have always found an excuse to put it off.

Clara breaks our silent standoff first, breaking eye contact. Her scowl turns into a bemused frown as she takes in the dark mahogany walls of my quarters, the thick, equally dark materials of my bed blankets, and the burnished metal accents.

With her presence, I notice for the first time how dark everything is, right down to the nearly black, perpetually drawn drapes.

"This room is… depressing," she says.

She isn't wrong. It might as well be a cave for all the cheer it holds.

"Stay here and don't move," I say, finally breaking out of my trance.

At my order, her gaze snaps to me, jaw clenched, and eyes narrowed. Clara plants her hands on the edge of the mattress and shifts, dragging her legs off and leaning over to prepare to stand.

Demons and saints, this woman would risk further injury just out of spite.

A loud hiss escapes her lips as she bites back a whimper of pain.

"Don't," I say. "Let me heal you first."

"No," she snaps.

"Clara, you're hurt."

"I don't care," she says.

"Let me heal you," I say again, slowly, trying to keep calm.

"Don't touch me again." Her words are full of venom.

I blink at the intensity of her anger. "You can barely move. If you don't bleed to death, then infection will kill you."

She pushes up to stand, and it's all I can do to keep from stopping her.

All her weight is on her uninjured leg. Her face has gone deathly pale, damp with a fine sheen of sweat.

She opens and closes her mouth a few times before saying, "I am only here to talk to you. Then I will be on my way. But I would… like to get cleaned up first." The strain of standing has her panting by the time she finishes. This demon damned woman is too stubborn for her own good.

I point to the door on the far side of the room.

Clara limps toward it, each step causing a small whimper. And each whimper twists in my gut because I know she would refuse any offer of help.

She pauses midway. Then without bothering to look back, she says, "I will be leaving first thing in the morning."

My feet move on their own accord. She just arrived, and she expects to leave at first light—as if it would be so easy.

I halt inches away, my fingers itching to reach out to her. My hands hover over her shoulders for a moment before dropping down to my sides once more.

When she still doesn't move I position myself in front of her. She turns her face away, refusing to look at me. I wrap my arms around her shoulders and pull her into a hug, careful not to hurt her.

She raises her hands and pushes against me, not putting any force behind it.

She heaves a heavy sigh and leans her head against my chest. Her fingers weakly grip the sides of my shirt.

"I hate you," she whispers, but like her efforts to push me away, there is no force behind the words. I don't begin to understand.

We stay like this a moment longer. I don't want to let her go. But when she finally pulls away, I relinquish my hold.

Clara keeps her head down until she reaches the door to the bathing room. She lifts her head and looks over her shoulder. Her expression is unreadable. There is something different in her, something that wasn't there the last time I saw her.

"Clara." Her name falls from my lips unbidden. I hadn't meant to speak. "Please talk to me."

She stands in the doorway with a hand resting on the frame. "Why?"

A single word has never been filled with more meaning. She isn't asking why I want her to talk—she's saying so much more than that.

I have no answer.

She dips her chin, then goes into the bathing room, closing the door behind her.

CHAPTER TWENTY

CLARA

Tears burn the backs of my eyes as I close the door. Tears from the pain in my muscles and bones, tears from the turmoil of warring emotions I felt looking into Alaric's eyes—so overwhelming I want to cling to him and run away as fast as I can, and everything in between.

I massage circles into my temples with my fingers and lean back against the door to lessen the weight on my aching left leg.

My feelings are nothing more than anger.

They aren't. It's only pain and exhaustion that makes it seem like more.

Every inch of my body hurts, but my leg is the worst. The burning has lessened to a dull roar—more spread out. Rather than searing, white-hot pain, it feels as though under my skin sits a bed of hot coals. I must have struck a rock when I landed.

My clothes are covered in mud and grass stains and… blood. The leg of my trousers is ripped—my blood has dried, plastering the material to my skin.

I release a shuddering sigh and limp toward the bathtub. I turn the faucets on and adjust until it's the perfect temperature. Placing the plug at the bottom, I allow it to fill as I straighten up.

I take stock of my body, focusing on each area in turn, moving and flexing my joints. Each movement sends a stabbing pain ricocheting through my nerves. But nothing is out of place, and everything works as it ought to.

I was lucky nothing broke when I was thrown.

It's only once I peel off my trousers that I see why my leg hurts more than anything else. Three gashes run down the side of my lower left leg. The wounds are angry and swollen. My skin burns like it's on fire.

Alaric could heal me… but anger and pride won't let me accept. Not when he lied. Mother used to tell me I was a prideful child. It seems little has changed since then.

I cross the room, feeling the burning ache more with each step, and grab a thin cloth from a corner cabinet. I slice it with Alaric's shaving blade—I'm sure he will forgive me for dulling it.

Taking a seat on the cold tail floor, I set to wrapping it. The process seems to take an eternity and I have to pause to breathe through the pain several times. My fingers shake and fumble as I work my way up my leg. The pressure I apply makes my stomach roil.

I sit back against the wall. The tight bandage gives me some relief from the relentless pain.

Gazing at the giant bathtub, I watch the curls of steam rise from the hot water as it continues to fill the tub. This is a luxury I never dreamed about before I first came to Alaric's manor. One I'm happy to take advantage of tonight, considering I'll be lucky if I have a way to boil water for future baths once I leave Windbury.

Soap bubbles up under the running facet, covering the entire surface of the water. Even from across the room, I can feel the steam curling the loose wisps of my hair.

I lift the hem of my top and suck in a sharp breath. I have to slow my movements and eventually, I manage to remove the last of my clothing. Scrapes and cuts cover my body. My skin is mottled with bruises—an exceptionally large patch is already forming over the right side of my ribs. Well, that explains why it hurts to breathe.

I grab a towel and limp to the bath. Turning off

the water, I dip a hand in to test the temperature and sigh. This is exactly what my aching muscles need.

Dropping the towel on the floor, I grip the edge of the tub. Then, slowly, I lift my injured leg and rest the ankle on the rim. It takes more maneuvering than I'd like to admit, and a too-quick movement leaves me wincing in pain for the millionth time. Steam condenses and beads up along my skin.

I eventually manage to get one leg in as I sit on the edge, bracing before trying to lower the rest of my body while keeping my bandaged leg from getting wet.

Not even halfway in, my hand slips on the damp porcelain and my next breath is full of water.

Clawing at the smooth surface I try to find purchase, to grab hold of something, *anything,* and fail. Every move sets my injuries ablaze.

I've been claimed by a vampire, outraced a higher demon through the woods, and lived—but now I'm going to die in less than three feet of water. My heart skips several beats as the reality of that truth sets in.

Darkness blots out the light of the room, or maybe it's my consciousness slipping away. Then two hands grip my shoulder and help me to sit.

I cough and sputter, clinging to strong arms as my breath comes in deep, raspy gulps.

Alaric stands before me, shirtless and barefoot,

water dripping from his scared arms and chest. We stare at each other for a long moment before the reality of the situation hits me hard.

I'm completely naked and he's nearly undressed. I let go of him and press my chest against the cool porcelain of the tub, nearly slipping all over again in my haste.

He takes hold of my shoulders again until I'm steady. My arms dangle over the edge and I feel like a nearly drowned cat. Then he does something that threatens to send me sliding back into the water all over again.

Alaric sticks one leg in the water as if—as if *he's going to join me.*

"Wh-what are you doing?" I demand.

"You need help," he says, sliding into the tub behind me. His legs cradle my hips and force me to move so I'm sitting with my back to him. The water sloshes around us, and a small wave spills over the edge, but he doesn't seem to notice or care.

I straighten my spine and lean forward trying to hide the rest of my body the best I can with one leg sticking up and out.

Ignoring my attempts to avoid touching him, Alaric gathers my hair, pushes it to the side, and rests it over my shoulder.

He sticks his hand out next to my face and says, "Hand me the cloth."

My face burns at being totally naked with him at my back. I keep my arms crossed over my breasts as I contemplate whether I should yell at him to leave or do as he asks. But even I have to admit that right now, he's the only thing keeping me from going under. I pick up the washcloth and pass it to him.

Not that long ago I would have bared myself to him. But injured as I am, this situation is different—things have changed—and I still haven't said what I came back here to say.

Alaric takes the bar of soap and lathers it, then begins to scrub in slow, rhythmic circles. He starts at my neck then moves over my shoulders, and finally my arms. When he gets to the bruises on my sides, he brushes over them with extra care, forgoing the cloth and using his bare hand. His fingers glide over the sensitive skin with the softest pressure.

Not once does he try to turn this moment into something else, nor does he try to heal me. Alaric takes his time, carefully moving over every patch of skin. And against my better judgment, I relax against him.

Some strange emotion burbles up from deep within my gut. I gasp as the realization of what it is hits me with such a stumbling force, leaving me breathless.

His movements are kind. I swallow the lump in my throat that has formed at the epiphany. This is the first time in my life anyone has treated me with such care, without wanting or demanding something in return.

There has *always* been something expected from me—money, to be presentable and play a part, to do something or be someone they wanted. Even Mother was efficient and brisk when it came to lessons and chores. She was never rough, but neither was she particularly caring. She never sang songs or coddled me as she had with Kathrine.

Alaric could drain every single drop from my veins right now if he wanted—and there is nothing I could do to stop him. I am entirely at his mercy. But he doesn't make a single move hinting that he will, even though I have an open wound and I know he can scent my blood. He could heal me as he washes me, ignoring my refusal, because it would be easier. He could mark me a hundred times over…

He does none of those things. He is being kind for the sake of being kind.

And I don't know how to handle this.

My eyes sting and before I can stop it, hot tears

slide down my cheeks and my body shakes with silent sobs.

His hands go still, and he remains like that for several long moments before turning me to the side. He slides his hand under the knee of my hurt leg to adjust it into a more comfortable position. Alaric pulls me into his chest, holding me with one arm, and stoking my hair with his other hand.

He doesn't try to stop my tears or distract me from my feelings but lets me cry until I'm done, offering his presence, and his arms.

When the tears finally stop, I don't move. I think my tears surprised him as much as they had me. I never knew I'd been missing that kindness until now. And out of anyone in this world, it had come from a man I'd once considered a monster. A man I wanted to kill for what he is.

Now I'm left wondering if I had misjudged him so horribly, then what else am I wrong about?

I lift my face to glance at him. He frowns, brows drawn together. Alaric lifts his hand to brush a thumb under my eye before pushing a strand of water-soaked hair behind my ear.

I see the question in his eyes, but he's giving me room to tell him what that was all about on my own terms… or not tell him.

The weight of his eyes on me makes my face heat.

I turn my face and press my cheek into his chest. My gaze focuses on the long scars on his bicep. Reaching out I trace a finger along one of the pale, jagged lines. His muscle stiffens beneath my touch.

"What happened?" I ask quietly continuing to trace the lines with my finger. Water beads up along his skin and trails down his arm. He shifts slightly from behind me.

He swallows hard and I listen to his heartbeat, convinced he won't speak. Then, quietly, he says, "That is a story for another time." He pulls his arm away and immediately goose bumps race over my skin at the loss of his contact. "The water is getting cold, you should get out."

I sit forward no longer caring if I'm covered. Alaric steps out of the tub with one fluid motion. Water puddles at his feet as he grabs the towel and extends a hand toward me.

Hesitantly I slip my hand into his and he helps me stand, not letting go until I can do so on my own. His eyes remain locked on mine as if I were fully dressed.

CHAPTER TWENTY-ONE

CLARA

I inch the door open and peek out at an empty room. I close the door again and look around. An article of clothing is draped over the sink. I pat myself dry, doing my best to avoid the most tender spots, then drape it over the edge of the tub's edge.

I slip the clothing Alaric had left for me over my head. The material barely covers my butt. Taking a closer look, I realize… it's one of his shirts. Not that he hasn't seen me wearing one the night he claimed me. The last time I wore one of his shirts, he ended up burning it in the fire the next morning. I wonder if it's an attempt to remind me of our tumultuous beginning to soften my anger with him.

I should care, but then the two of us have never

followed what the world would deem acceptable. We've created our own rules.

Not five minutes ago, he held me, stark naked, in the tub for… demons only know how long, while I cried.

I may have let myself be comforted by him, but my reason for returning is still the same.

Limping—with far less grace than I would like—I exit the bathing room, intending to wait for Alaric to return, but he's already back, standing before the fire. He turns to face me, a bundle of what appears to be clothes in his arms.

Perhaps he hadn't meant for me to wear his shirt after all.

He takes me in slowly, his gaze is nearly tangible.

Alaric discards the bundle onto the bed and cuts the distance between us in half.

Silence sits heavy in the air. His eyes pleaded with me to talk to him. To open up and be vulnerable, but I've already been vulnerable once already today. The longer he looks at me like that, the faster my courage and angry words flee.

My mouth goes dry and my throat thickens with more unsaid words than I'm ready to voice, even after two days of riding to get here. I pull in a breath and hold it preparing to force the words out even if it kills me.

"Good night," I say and hurry past him. Except an old man with a crooked spine and an uneven gait could walk faster.

In a blink Alaric stands before me, blocking my path.

"Clara," he says hoarsely. "Please stay. You are injured and it would be safer for you to remain with me—at least for the night."

I move around him, reaching for the doorknob.

"You almost died tonight," he adds quietly.

That stills me. My hand hovers over the door handle.

I was hurt, yes, thrown from my horse—but I was lucky, and nothing was broken. Give me a few days and I'll be healed completely with nothing but a few new scars to show for it.

But almost died?

"I don't know if I can look at you right now," I say.

Coward. I am a fucking coward.

He might have helped me bathe. He might have comforted me. He might have been the first person in my life to offer me kindness without asking for or expecting anything in return—but it doesn't erase what he did.

I expect a protest from him, but he doesn't say so much as a word in response. After a few seconds, curiosity gets the better of me and I peek over my shoulder.

He doesn't appear mad or annoyed or even the slightest bit upset as I expected. His eyes are wide and the corners of his lips tug downward. He stands perfectly, deathly, still.

"Why did you return, Clara?"

Why? Because I'm angry with him. I hate him for lying… because I had nowhere else to go. Because even when I tried to kill him, he was never cruel, or unkind.

My heart thumps painfully in my chest.

Because, even if I didn't realize it until this moment, he is a friend to me.

A vampire is my friend.

Which explains why it hurt when he released me from our bargain the way he did.

I don't answer him. How can I?

He swallows—the first sign he's not a perfectly carved statue. Then his gaze drops to the floor.

"Don't leave. I won't pretend to know or understand what you're feeling…" The fingers of his right hand stretch out then curl back into his palm as if he wanted to reach for me but thought better of it. "Hate me if you must, Clara, just, don't leave tonight. Heal, and then you can go when you are ready."

If I didn't know better, I would say he is almost desperate to keep me here.

But he's not. He wouldn't have told me never to return if he gave a shit—wouldn't have lied to me.

My jaw ticks with anger that burns away all hesitation.

I spin to face him and wince at the pain erupting through my leg. But I march forward before he can offer to heal me again or say another word.

"You don't know why?" I ask. I stop before him and look up into midnight blue eyes. My fingernails bite into my palms. "You *lied* to me."

His expression goes slack, full lips parting. I expect him to brush it off. Instead, he gapes, looking entirely bewildered.

"You kept things from me, made me believe there was a purpose to our deal. You asked me to trust you, and when I did… you *lied*."

Alaric snaps his mouth closed as understanding dawns on him.

"You should have told me what you were planning. You could have told me the truth about Kathrine… that she didn't need me, but you let me believe she did as you plotted behind my back, acting as if you didn't know anything more than I did." I heave a sigh and let my shoulders slip as hurt overpowers anger. "You lied to me Alaric," I finish in a near whisper.

He looks down at his feet. The gesture is oddly youthful and so unlike him. It confirms everything I'd figured out. He knew Katherine had never been sick... and that she had never actually needed me.

"How did you find out?" he asks.

"She was never good at keeping secrets. Then she mentioned our uncle... which is strange because our parents don't have siblings..." I pause. "Then she said his name was Steward."

Alaric flinches at the Butler's name. Still, he says nothing.

"Why didn't you tell me?" I ask. My voice is quiet, soft... and full of the betrayal I feel.

I shouldn't be hurt, he's a vampire... I should expect him to hurt me. They are horrible creatures that can't be trusted to do anything. Except, to be betrayed in the first place, there must have been a foundation of trust.

I'm struck by a twinge of guilt.

Alaric isn't like that. He is kind. Honorable. Nothing like the monsters I'd always believed vampires to be.

The man I've come to know returns, confident... yet sadness clings to his eyes. "I wanted to give you the best chance at getting back your old life, if not a little better."

I wasn't expecting that.

He wanted me to return to my life as it was before he claimed me. But a few hours with Katherine made it clear to even me that it was impossible.

I could never go back. That life was a lie I've been telling myself every day since Mother was taken. It was never real.

Tears come unbidden and burn my eyes, blurring my vision. I clench my fists again and close most of the distance between us. I pound my fists against his chest. Pathetically weak, a strike that wouldn't phase a blade of grass.

"Did you honestly think I could go back to that life?"

He lifts a hand and presses it against mine until my palm is flat against his chest. He keeps it pinned there and underneath I can feel the even beat of his heart.

"What do you mean, Clara?"

I lean forward and rest my forehead against his chest. Weariness seeps into me, down to the very marrow of my bones.

"Everyone knew I had been claimed. I couldn't have gone back even if Kathrine needed me." I sigh. The rush of the last several days, being chased by a higher demon, and crying, all finally catching up to me. I am stripped down to the depths of my core, raw, and all that is left is a dull ache in my heart. "You just sent me away without talking to me first. You didn't even say goodbye," my voice cracks at the last word.

Saying it out loud, makes it feel more real. Otherworld damn it… he has become dear to me.

He wraps an arm around my waist, then lifts my chin with a knuckle. "At the time, I thought it was best. I recognize my error now. Can you ever forgive me, my dear Clara?"

My throat tightens at the endearment. At first, he used it to mock me. I'm not sure when it changed.

I nod unable to speak. I do forgive him.

After a while, I clear my throat and ask, "What happens if I leave before the winter masquerade… for good that is?"

He hums thoughtfully. "You might be hunted, unless I can fake your death."

"You would do that?"

"If that's what you wanted," he says.

"And… what would happen to you?"

"That is not for you to worry about." There's a finality to his words—a warning not to dig further. But a telling shiver rolls over him, and whatever that fate might be—it is not a good one.

"I could stay until then," I say.

"You don't have to decide now." Alaric brushes his

fingertips across my forehead to push stray wisps of hair off my face. Then he pulls back keeping his arm around me, and says, "Come, you must get some rest."

CHAPTER TWENTY-TWO

CLARA

Alaric leads me to the bed and eases me down. Walking is less painful with his help—not a lot, but enough that I can bare it.

With my weight off my leg, the ache lessens, and I am able to breathe a sigh of relief.

"Will you allow me to heal you now?" he asks.

I can see in his expression that he expects me to refuse.

"Yes, please," I say, then something between a laugh and a groan burbles up between my lips. "It really does hurt."

He kneels before me, eyes instantly focus on the task at hand. Alaric rests a hand on my knee and uses the other to lift my leg by the heel. Then, slowly, he unwinds my makeshift bandage.

I suck in a sharp breath through my teeth. The fresh air and lack of pressure make the gashes in my flesh feel newly made.

Alaric takes his time as he examines them from several angles. The skin is redder and more swollen than before.

Ever so carefully, he places a palm directly on top of the injury. The gentle touch steals my breath, and I'm unable to catch it. Spots dance before my eyes as dizziness overwhelms me. My arms give out, sending me flopping onto my back.

It cannot be more than a few seconds, but it feels like an eternity by the time the spots fade and my lungs work again.

Alaric doesn't appear to notice my reaction. His eyes close, his forehead wrinkling. I was unconscious when he healed my hand, so I am unsure what to expect now.

A small squeak comes from atop the pillows. Cherno. The demon bat crawls forward, ignoring me to crawl over to their master.

Sure, why check on the human in agony when you can comfort the vampire causing it?

A rosy glow lights his face. I prop myself up on my elbows to peer over my knees. Sparks of red dance over his hands and forearms above the glowing veins just below the surface of his skin.

A tingle of it seeps into my flesh. The sensation quickly morphs into such intensity I am immediately overwhelmed.

It hurts nearly as much as it did receiving the injury. I want to curl into a ball, to scream, to run—anything to get away from it. It's cold and burns at the same time. I swear it will suffocate me even as it soothes.

His face swims and wavers before my eyes.

"A-Alaric," I gasp his name—or... I think I do. I can't tell if my mouth is working or if my voice only escapes in an inaudible woosh of air.

Time loses all meaning, and I think I will remain trapped within this moment for eternity.

Without warning, the magic releases me. I collapse, drawing deep gulps of air that are not enough. Gradually, the world begins to right itself, returning me to the present.

I press a cold hand to my suddenly burning forehead. The mattress shifts. I blink up into Alaric's face, but he's not even looking at me.

He straddles my hips and pulls the hem of my shirt up to expose everything from just below my breasts down to my hips. I'm too worn to protest.

Before I can understand what he's doing, his palms press down my ribs, fingers splayed to cover most of my abdomen.

A look of intense focus sits on his features. Crimson circles form around the sapphire of his eyes, but unlike when he needs to feed… *they glow.* Then, his eyes slide shut again.

Bright crimson magic forms in his veins, sparking over the hands clasped to my sides. There is a fraction of a second where I think how beautiful he is, before the tingling starts anew, and I am once more overwhelmed.

The muscles in my back spasm, arching my spine. A scream scrapes up my throat, where it catches and dies before it can pass my lips.

I try to reach for him, to get his attention, and tell him it's too much, but I am unable to control my limbs.

Just as I begin to think I would rather die than suffer this agony for another moment, the red light fades, and his magic withdraws from me. Every ounce of my strength is drained. All I can do is lie on my back, letting tremors wrack my body.

Alaric moves to my side and gathers me in his arms, pulling the shirt back down. He holds me against him as he settles back against the headboard. He trails his fingers up and down my spine in soothing strokes until the after-effects fade.

"What *was* that?" I finally manage. It's an overly simplified version of the question I wish to ask.

He adjusts me to sit beside him, the tight circle of his embrace easing. "That is how my power works." He pauses and adverts his gaze. "I forgot you were unconscious the last time. I should have warned you—"

I press my fingertips to his lips, silencing the apology. I look down and gape in complete awe at my leg. In place of the three long gashes are soft pink lines over freshly mended skin. What amounts to days or weeks of healing just took place in mere moments. The skin is smooth, so the scars will be faint pale lines.

I snap my head up, meeting his worried gaze, then throw my arms around his neck and bury my face in his shoulder. "Thank you," I say quietly.

He hesitates before his arms band around me, squeezing harder than before now that I'm healed. We stay like this until a fierce yawn forces its way out of me. Alaric pulls back, disengaging from my embrace.

I grab his wrist, stopping him before he can stand. "Wait. Don't go yet." The words escape without thought. I hadn't meant to speak.

While I am beyond grateful that he healed me, it doesn't change the fact that I am still hurt and angry with him.

But the thought of him walking out the door, of being alone, leaves a hollow space in the center of my chest. I've felt alone since he sent me back to Littlemire, and right now I need… a friend.

Maybe he hears the desperation in my voice… or perhaps he doesn't wish to leave any more than I want him to.

Wordlessly, he settles himself back down and stretches his legs out. I scoot to sit at his side, our hips touching, then I rest my head on his shoulder.

"It is a good thing you bathed," he says. I stiffen, leaning away to look up into his smirking face. "You smelled like a demon's ass."

I swat at his shoulder and he laughs, tucking me back into his side.

I've never had anyone I could sit with like this—saying nothing, doing nothing. This moment holds the peace of solitude with the comfort of support.

I lean into him—this unexpected source of comfort and safety.

Safety in the arms of a vampire.

Months ago, I would have said it was impossible, and yet somehow, that is exactly what I've found in this man. It makes me wonder if this is something new for him, too.

He takes my hand and entwines our fingers. "When you leave tomorrow, please say goodbye—I know I didn't give you that courtesy, but I won't be returning to Windburry once I leave."

I freeze and swallow past the lump stuck in my throat. "I will."

His thumb traces slow, lazy circles on my wrist.

He's leaving...

When I left Littlemire, I had every intention of giving him a piece of my mind, then never seeing him again. Yet hearing him say that leaves a sour taste in my mouth.

I crane my neck to look at him, but his face is turned away. It's clear that he isn't simply moving to another city for a fresh start.

"What's wrong?"

"Where will you go when you leave?" he asks at the same time.

"I don't know," I say honestly, resting my head against his shoulder. "I hadn't thought past coming back long enough to tell you how furious I am with you."

He chuckles at that, then presses his cheek atop my head. A long moment passes. Exhaustion tugs at me, and the lull of sleep eases through my body.

"I wish you wouldn't go," he confesses, whisper soft.

"Then, I will stay," I mumble as I snuggle deeper into his side.

Alaric shifts, leaning away. I groan to protest the loss of warmth and sit up.

Contrasting with the sentiment of the moment, his face is deathly serious. "I will always welcome by my side, however, you must understand that your life will be in constant danger if you stay—even coming back was a risk."

The need to stay suddenly roots itself at the base of my spine. When only a few hours ago I was set on leaving. Yet, all it took to change my mind was his quiet admission that he wanted me to stay....

Despite the danger, I realize I am more scared of never seeing him again, of losing this strange and impossible friendship.

"I have fared well enough so far. I expected to die within hours after you claimed me—by all rights we both know I should have." He opens his mouth to protest, but I hold up a hand. "Every minute I have lived since is time I never should have had." Then reluctantly, I add, "And... I want to stay."

Demons and saints. I am really going to do this—I'm willingly choosing to stay with a vampire.

But then, I only need to look into his eyes to know everything he did was done with good intentions. For some reason, he feels loyalty toward me, and I can't leave him as if that means nothing. Especially, when everything in me demands I be loyal too.

He frowns. "Very well," he says, then places a kiss on my forehead as he pulls me tighter against him.

I nestle into his side, getting comfortable, and close my eyes.

"I have missed you, my dear Clara," he whispers into my hair.

A lazy smile spreads over my mouth. "You missed me?"

"Yes," he says, his tone serious. "There is nothing about you I haven't missed."

"Even when I try to kill you?" Another yawn.

I feel his mouth curl into a smile of his own.

"Especially then." He runs his fingers through my hair in a move that is far too relaxing. "It is unbearably dull here without a regular attempt on my life."

CHAPTER TWENTY-THREE

CLARA

Everything is exactly the same as the night I was first introduced to a room full of vampires. The same room, the same faces, the same atmosphere.

Predators lounge, their prey at their sides with downcast gazes… and I am somewhere in between. Not exactly the hunted any longer, but far from being the hunter.

Except it is different. Now I don't seek a way to escape. Now, I know this isn't a party but a gathering. Nothing more than Alaric entertaining his guests.

The first time I had naively thought it was a party, but after my short time back in Littlemire, among the upper class, I know better.

Alaric stands at the window across the room,

talking in low tones with Mr. Harkstead. The moonlight outlines his silhouette in silver.

A human man sits at the piano, playing quiet songs, filling the room with dark, subtle sounds—not enough to drown out what little talking there is.

I hold my wine glass in one hand and keep my heartbeat slow and steady. This time, I will keep my wits instead of drowning my nerves. I will be the perfect picture of calm.

Beside me, Cassius grins a smile intended to accentuate his elongated canines. "I must say, *little bird*, we were beginning to think our Alaric had no hold over you," he says. "Though, Mr. Harkstead doubted your return most of all."

The demon snake around his shoulders lifts their head, flicking a silver tongue at the air. Their metallic, dark green scales glint in the candlelight and red eyes watch me.

I do my best to ignore the demon's presence. Feigning ignorance, I list my head to the side and blink as though I have no idea what he is talking about. Everyone in this manor knows the truth, but that will not stop us from playing this game.

"I am grateful for his generosity, allowing me to visit my sister for her wedding, and at such an inconvenient time." My words are coated in honey as I speak the practiced lines.

"Mmmm," he hums in agreement.

A woman saunters by with a tray of glasses filled with a dark, red liquid. Cassius reaches out and snags one, drinking the entire thing in a single gulp. He wipes his mouth in an attempt to hide his grimace.

I raise my brows in question.

He grunts. "Prepared cannot compare with fresh from the vein."

Cassius rubs his chin, and slowly, red forms around his irises. He licks his lips and blinks several times as if breaking out of a trance, then straightens his back. The red rings in his eyes are now gone. He clears his throat and says, "Allow me to refresh your drink."

He takes my untouched glass from me and crosses the room, depositing it on the piano as he makes his way toward the man standing against the wall with a tray of wine glasses.

A snort of derision comes from behind. Startled, I whirl and find my eyes level with the knot of a cravat. I lift my chin and look into the eyes of Victor Connors towering over me.

I take a half step back so my neck will be at a more natural angle. But I don't create much space, nothing to hint at a retreat.

His eyes are muddier than I remember—darker. Lines move through his irises, almost seeming to leak into the whites. He smiles, but there is nothing friendly about it.

"Cassius has been hogging your attentions, the rest of us are starting to get a bit jealous," he says.

A frog croaks at my feet and I jump back, startled. No, not a frog—a fat, wart-covered toad. The demon croaks again and hops forward until they touch the hem of my dress. Normally, I wouldn't think twice about such a creature, but this one sends gooseflesh racing up and down my arms.

I swallow hard as I fight the urge to take several more steps back.

"There you are, Victor," Lawrence drawls, seeming to come from nowhere.

He shoves a glass of blood into Mr. Connors's hand and throws an arm around his shoulder. He looks to me and adds, "Alaric sends his regards." He tips his head toward where he stands by the window, looking at me past Cassius. "He will be a few moments more."

While his words are perfectly civil, the subtle hostility in his tone grates on my nerves. Alaric had been confident that Lawrence wouldn't be a threat to me. Except with that expression, he seems to be the one vampire in this room who would like to separate me from my blood the most.

Della slips between the two men and pouts up at

Lawrence. "I'm feeling neglected, Sire." She bats her eyes at him and sighs.

Lawrence scoffs. "You are fine, Della, there are plenty of mortal men to keep you busy."

She harrumphs, then turns her piercing eyes on me, so dark they appear almost black. Della sneers, scanning me from head to toe before returning her attention to Lawrence. "I don't know what everyone's fascination is with something so plain and…" she cuts a glance to me again, her eyes lingering on my bare arms. "*Ruined.*"

I narrow my eyes, refusing to be ashamed of the scars that run over my arms. These scars mean that I fought for my life, that I am not dead, burned on a funeral pyre and ash scattered on the wind. They mean that I am still alive.

Lawrence rolls his eyes and turns away, without bothering to acknowledge the remark.

My temper flares and I open my mouth to respond in kind, but Victor beats me to it.

"Do not worry your pretty little head, Lady Moore, you are a vampire, and she is but a human." He waves a hand. "Nothing of consequence."

I'll be damned to the Otherworld if they expect me to continue standing here, allowing myself to be insulted.

I spin on my heel and march out of the room and down the hall, fuming. The smell of flowers is thick in the air.

One of the glass doors is ajar letting the warmth and fragrance permeate the hall. I hadn't realized it had subtly filled the music room. My nerves were too frayed to notice.

I have only been in this area of the manor a handful of times. A shiver runs down my spine as the memories of my last visit come rushing back. The scars on my arms tingle with the phantom pain pulsing through them.

The creak of the unsteady staircase as it damn near fell apart under me. If I had been any higher, I would have broken something, or worse—I could have died.

"What are you doing out here alone, little bird?" Cassius asks.

I clench my jaw. I hate the nickname he deigned to bestow upon me. I am no bird. Not any longer. And no amount of beautifully woven promises can ensnare me.

I turn away from the glass doors to face him. "I won't allow myself to be insulted, not even by vampires."

He doesn't seem offended, instead, he tilts his head

and contemplates what I said. "I suppose one cannot find fault in that."

He moves to stand at my side and gestures toward the atrium.

I shake my head and put a little more distance between myself and the doors, moving back toward the music room.

"Have you given any more thought to my offer?"

My steps falter. It wasn't a dream then. Cassius had made me the offer to take me from Alaric.

Something cold brushes against my ankle, and I let out an undignified squeak, quickly leaping to the side. A snake coils, watching me, and hissing.

I look between the two of them, my palms pressed to the wall at my back.

Cassius smirks, his green eyes drinking me in and enjoying the fact that his demon startled me. He bends down and reaches out his arm. The snake wends their way up and settles around his shoulders.

I push away from the wall and stomp up to him until we are almost chest to chest, and glare. "Snakes don't bother me," I say. "I just don't walk around houses expecting them to brush against my legs."

"How well do you understand the relationship between vampires and their demons?" he asks as he strokes the demon's head with a finger.

Some things I've figured out on my own, but there is a lot I still don't know. I don't want to appear ignorant.

"I know you are demon cursed," I say with a wave of my hand as if I couldn't care less about the topic. "And I know your pet is your demon."

Cassius scoffs and rolls his eyes. "In a very basic sense, you are correct." He lists his head to the side, narrowing his gaze. "Would you like to know?"

I open my mouth to say no. But that would be a lie. I do want to know, and I believe the vampire in front of me will tell me everything because whether or not I am afraid is of no consequence to him. So, I nod.

"There are three types of vampires. Elizabeth Fairfax, our queen, was the first. She is an entity unto herself and the mother of us all, and thus she and her demon are the most powerful. Then there are the vampires—such as myself, Lawrence, and our dear Alaric. We are still quite powerful, but not compared to her."

He pauses, and I jump in. "That's interesting," I say. "But what does that have to do with being cursed by demons?"

"Patience, little bird, patience. I was just getting to that." Cassius offers me his elbow.

After a slight hesitation, I slip my arm through his. Together we walk slowly up and down the hall, not entering the atrium but also not returning to the gathering.

"To become a powerful vampire, you must be created by a powerful vampire and be strong enough to bind with a powerful higher demon—mind, body, and soul—in order to control that demon once bonded. Your soul makes the demon more powerful, and in turn, they make you more powerful. That is how higher demons become greater demons."

I chew thoughtfully on the inside of my cheek. It's hard to believe that Alaric is bound to Cherno that way. They have never seemed like a malicious being, but I wonder how much of that is Cherno's natural personality and how much of it is Alaric's control over them.

"If you cannot control your demon," he continues, "then *that* is the curse. Though some might claim being bonded in such a way to a demon is a curse in and of itself."

Something he said has been nagging at my mind and I finally realize what it is. *To become a vampire, you must be made by a vampire...* "How did Elizabeth become a vampire then, if she is the first?" I ask. "Wouldn't someone need to make her?"

"Good, you caught that." Cassius smiles warmly.

He continues to pet the demon as we walk. "No one knows for sure, and if you ask Elizabeth, she would prefer to gut you alive then reveal the story. There have been many theories and whispered rumors through the ages, but as far as anyone could tell, she was a particularly strong human who happened to find a way to bind herself to a particularly strong demon."

"How can you tell if someone is able to control a demon or not?"

Cassius stops up short and swings my arm until I stand in front of him. "There is no way to tell until a mortal is already bound."

"What happens if they can't control their demon?" My voice comes out as a near whisper as if being quiet will somehow keep me safe. Or perhaps because this information—as far as I know—has never been shared with a human before.

"The demon will control the person and they will become nothing more than a puppet, a body, for the demon to play with. It is hard to tell at first, but the longer the demon has control of them the more they will show signs of their possession."

"The third type of vampire is slightly less powerful." He smiles kindly. "but they are no less important. Like Della, she was sired by Mr. Harkstead two years after he was turned."

"Where is her demon? I've seen Lawrence's rat, your snake, Cherno, and Mr. Connor's toad, but I don't believe I've seen hers yet."

"That brings me to the final type of vampire," he says. "The kind that are created by one of us, and not Elizabeth herself, do not possess a demon, but rather have been turned by a portion of our demon's power." Cassius leans forward, bringing his mouth near my ear, and whispers, "And if you accept my offer, little bird, you will have a chance to become one of them." His voice is thick and deep, and filled with the promises he made the last time he tried to get me to accept his offer.

As if pretty words and a husky voice are all it takes to make me fall at someone's feet, I back up a step, uncomfortable with how close he has become.

I am an idiot. A fool to think he would actually share this kind of information with me. It was just a ploy to tempt me into allowing him to claim me and take me from Alaric's side.

"Thank you," I say, maneuvering back toward the music room. "I think I would make a terrible vampire."

As I turn my back on him, he calls out softly, "I will always be around, little bird, for when you change your mind."

I shiver, but my steps falter at his next words.

"It is a good thing you returned in time... there is no telling what Elizabeth would have done to Alaric had you not returned at all."

I swallow hard, forcing myself to not look back and to continue on as if his words were not a threat.

CHAPTER TWENTY-FOUR

CLARA

THE SMALL FLAME FLICKERS AND DANCES ON THE WICK of the tallow candle. I blink and look around. Night fills the hall around me.

My head aches. I didn't think I had anything to drink when I returned to the music room but maybe the conversation with Cassius had unnerved me more than I realized.

Eyes blurry from sleep I rub my eyes to clear them, but it doesn't help. Something woke me, I knew what it was when I sat up in bed and lit the candle. Try as I might, I can't seem to recall exactly *what* it was, and the harder I try to remember, the faster it slips away.

Still, something pulls at me, urging me onward.

The candles that are normally lit, even at night, have been snuffed out.

To the right is the staircase leading to the third floor. I should go to Alaric and tell him something woke me. In a house full of vampires, it would be the smart thing to do.

No... there is no need, my mind whispers.

Instead, I go left, toward the open window that looks out to the south. My bare feet pad softly over the cold, wood floor. I pull the window open wide and look out. The chilled night air hits me in the face and sucks the breath from my lungs.

A thick layer of clouds covers the sky, blotting out the stars and every bit of light from the moon. I blink and squint my eyes, but it's useless. A shadowy shape moves against the dark grounds.

Miles away, the glow of gas lamps illuminates the main town of Windbury against the night.

Something draws my attention back to the yard— the snap of a twig, a rustle of leaves, a movement, a flash of light—I'm not sure. The blur that covers my vision seems to have also made my mind hazy. Wine and nerves are a terrible combination... but again, I can't seem to remember drinking.

I should return to bed and sleep off this wine-induced nightmare. I pull back and close the window.

A whisper, no more than a breath of air, brushes past my ear. I spin around.

But no one is there.

The hall is swathed in night, save for the weak light my small candle gives off. The few candles that were lit are now dark. Probably snuffed out by the breeze.

The manor is quiet—unnaturally so with the number of night dwelling beings under one roof. My heart pounds as if I'm running, and my breaths quicken.

The temperature plummets quickly and I can't seem to force my legs to move. I exhale, my breath forming a white plume in the air. I take a single step forward, then another. and another. Each one is slow, taking all of my concentration. I swing my arms to create more momentum, but it does little good.

I nearly stumble, catching my toe on… the floor? I can't feel my legs—the cold has seeped bone deep, the pain changing from thousands of needles to finally numbing my skin and muscles.

I reach my empty hands out in front of me, wishing I had a light to guide me. I frown.

Something is off. I press the heel of my hand into my forehead. The harder I try to figure it out, the more it slips from my grasp.

Pressure sits on my chest until each breath is a struggle.

Alaric, I need to find him.

No... I don't need him.

That second thought feels strange and foreign. I grip the sides of my head with both hands.

The world shifts from under me and I can't breathe. I fall back, but it doesn't hurt... it doesn't feel like anything. There is no impact. I try to pull in a breath but I can't remember how.

Fire lances through my lungs.

I gasp and blink up into Alaric's face. Water drips from his hair. A fat drop falls, trailing down his face, past his furrowed brows to the corner of his mouth, pressed tightly into a tight line. His shirt is plastered to his sculpted body. He's soaking wet... something about that sends alarm racing through me.

I look around. We are standing in water almost as high as my neck. Trees stand black against the midnight sky like demons frozen in mid-motion.

"What are you doing, Clara?" he asks harshly.

I pull in a breath and press my hand to my head again. My pulse hammers against my skull.

Alaric wraps an arm around my lower back and lifts me up, sweeping me into his arms. We are out of the water in a few of his long strides.

"I don't... know." I trail off. I can't remember why I

came outside or when. *I was inside a moment ago.* "I can't remember anything past waking up."

Had I even woken up before Alaric touched me?

The furrow of his brow deepens.

He moves fast, the frigid night air stings against my exposed skin. We reach the manor in a blink. He kicks the door shut with his foot and strides through the halls not caring about the trail of water we leave.

Bounding up the stairs two at a time, he bypasses the second floor without a glance, and only when we reach his bedroom does he set me down.

"This isn't my room," I say dumbly.

Obviously, he knows that. I just can't seem to put my protest into words. Alaric guides me inside.

"I would feel better if you stayed with me. Your night terrors are getting worse."

I shake violently as the feeling slowly returns to my body. I am chilled down to the fiber of my being.

"All right," I agree.

"Take off your clothes," he orders.

I don't even question his motivations. I have never known any man who would say that to a woman without the intent to touch. But even in my current state, I see the logic. I need to get warm, and I can't do that while drenched in icy lake water.

Cherno flutters in, or maybe they've been here the entire time. They land on my head and lean forward to look me in the eye, blinking several times, before flittering to the hearth.

Alaric turns grabbing the folded blanket off the foot of the bed. The second my nightgown hits the floor with a sopping thud, Alaric wraps me up. I think how familiar this situation feels. But unlike last time, he doesn't leave the room. And, Otherworld take me, I can't find it in me to mind.

His hands rub up and down my arms for warmth, before leading me to the bed. Once I'm lying down, he excuses himself to change in the bathing room.

A fire roars to life. Weeks ago, I would have thought it impossible for a bat to start a fire, but Cherno isn't exactly as they seem.

Alaric emerges, walking over to sit in the chair positioned in the corner of the room. I don't know if he plans to remain there all night, but who could possibly sleep with someone watching them?

I extend a hand toward him. Alaric rises to his feet and comes to my side.

"I don't need you to stare at me as if I'm going to evaporate," I say. "Now sit." I wriggle over, making room for him, and pat the mattress.

He does, and like the night before, I sit against his side. His arms wrap around me, moving up and down mine, trying to help the heat return.

For the second time in as many nights, I curl up to

his side like we are old friends. As if we always have been. As if it is perfectly normal for an unmarked human and the vampire that claimed her to be... whatever it is we are.

I sigh. I don't know why I am plagued with such horrible night terrors, but I am glad Alaric is here to help me through them.

Eventually, the shivering lessens. I am still cold, but not painful so.

"Do you regret staying?" he asks after a while. His warmth seeps into my body. It feels good. His scent, subtle and woodsy, is comforting.

"No," I say without having to think. "Regret is useless, it changes nothing. Besides, I chose to stay because I wanted to. I'm not so fickle as to change my mind at the first sign of difficulty."

"Difficulty?" he asks with a laugh. "Is *difficult* what you're calling this?"

I shrug with one shoulder and press closer into his side. A warm glow leaks in through a break in the curtains. Dawn is coming.

"You should get some sleep while you can," he says.

I close my eyes and control my breathing, trying to force myself to sleep. What feels like hours later, I am still awake. I sigh in frustration and sit up a little further, bringing the blanket with me.

I tilt my face up and study his face. Alaric's eyes

are unfocused as he looks straight ahead. I can almost see his thoughts churning. Something weighs heavy on his mind. I want to ask him what it is, but I think he will tell me when he is ready.

I know very little about this man, yet I know he's a good man, and I trust him with my life. The deal he offered me, despite the way my crime hurt him… keeping it a secret to protect me… everything he did for Kitty—all those things and more prove he is not the monster I once believed he was.

He loved his sister, though he has hardly spoken of her to me. I don't blame him. She was important to him, and knowing the kind of man he is makes me wonder what kind of person she was.

"Tell me about your sister," I say.

I feel him stiffen at my side. He is silent for so long I don't think he will respond at all.

"Rosalie was sweet, gentle, warm… Everyone who knew her, loved her, even if she was considered weak for a vampire."

I cringe. I'd had once accused her of being weak—he had compelled the confession from me—but I had said it all the same.

"I—I—" The words stick in my throat as I twist my fingers in a corner of the blanket.

"You couldn't have known," he says, at once understanding what I want to say. After a moment he continues, "There are many kinds of strength, including the ability to stay kind and gentle in a world that would see such things destroyed."

He's right. It would be impossible for anyone weak to have this great of an impact on someone. She might not have been physically strong or had a commanding presence, but she possessed a strength that I will never know.

"I think Rosalie would have liked your spirit," Alaric says.

My face warms at that. I reach over and squeeze his hand, not having the words to respond. There's no way to know if she would have liked me, but he seems to think so, and that is enough.

"She loved humans," he says. His eyes are unfocused, and a sorrowful smile sits on his lips. "Rosalie was the first vampire to refuse to feed on humans. I tried to live as she wanted and give up mortal blood as well, but I lacked the willpower. It was my fault she was turned—I owed it to her to try. She never blamed me for not being able to live off animals."

"I'm sorry," I swallow a lump of emotions, barely able to speak. "I know it's useless and it doesn't bring her back… but I am sorry all the same."

Alaric looks down at me, tucked into his side and wrapped in nothing more than a blanket. His eyes shine from the pain I caused. He opens his mouth then closes it and gives me a single nod before pulling me closer. I shift and readjust myself.

My arm slides around his waist and I hug him as I rest my cheek against his chest listening to the steady beat of his heart. I try to comfort him even though I am the cause of his hurt. I can't tell if he accepts it, or is merely tolerating it as he keeps me warm.

Regret changes nothing, and so I try not to. But there is a seed tucked into the soil of my soul that has been planted, and I fear it will bloom and grow until one day it consumes me.

CHAPTER TWENTY-FIVE

ALARIC

It is late in the afternoon, when I wake to Clara clinging to me, our limbs tangled. At some point, while we slept, she managed to cover us both. Her long, brown hair fans out behind her, leaving her neck and shoulder bared. Her heart beats in a slow, steady rhythm. My fangs ache to pierce her skin.

Instead of giving in, I slip away, readjusting her blanket to keep her warm. I don't know how much longer I can keep putting myself in these positions with her. Clara has made it more than clear that she will never want my mark.

Most days I can pretend Rosalie didn't die at her hands. Even in all her attempts to draw a drop of blood—or flat-out kill me—she never seemed capable of it. But our conversation has ripped open the wounds and made them raw all over again.

My heart is torn between feeling as though I owe it to Rosalie to damn Clara for her crime... and forgiving her because that's what Rosalie would really have wanted.

I walk down the silent halls to the office. I need space to clear my head before I do something I will regret.

There's something unnatural about her night terrors, and I wonder if they are more than they seem... then again, I have never heard of a human attacked by a higher demon and living. Most likely it's the stress of being under the same roof as so many vampires in one place... but if that is the case, then she will not last a single night within the walls of Nightwich.

The quiet beat of Cherno's wings follows me down the halls. I sense the others in the lower layer of the manor. There's no movement throughout the house. They are in the deep stages of rest.

Since their arrival, Cherno has been doing their best to keep an eye on their demons, but that impossible task is taking its toll. I can feel the drain on our powers. Thirst gnaws at my gut. I must feed, far sooner than I would like.

I stop outside the office and they land on my shoulder.

"Blood," I say.

Feeling the need as strongly as I, Cherno launches into the air and is off to gather sustenance.

It takes twice the usual amount of blood before my hunger is sated. Still, I find it impossible to focus on my work. I set my quill down and turn to gaze out the window. Bright reds and golds are smeared across the sky.

A knock from the doorway draws my attention, and I straighten my spine. Clara peeks in, then enters without waiting for an answer, closing the door behind her. Her cheeks are flushed as her eyes roam all around the room, looking everywhere except at me.

"Clara?" I ask, rising from my chair. A flush colors her face. "What's wrong?"

Her chest rises and falls with each deep breath. She stops halfway into the room, standing behind a chair. She lifts her chin, though she still can't meet my gaze.

"I want the mark," she says after a long silence.

I am rendered speechless. Much like her willing return, I would never have expected this request. When I don't speak, she drags her eyes up to my face.

"Alaric?"

"Are you sure?" I ask.

Her shoulders slump. "Yes." She nods decisively. "I'll be going with you to Nightwich. So, if it will keep me safe, then yes." Her mouth quirks up at one corner. "It's only one bite after all."

"No," I say and her face falls into a neutral mask. "It's more complicated than that."

Clara holds onto the back of the chair and trails a finger along the damask design embroidered into the material. I can practically taste her nerves on the air.

I step up to her side so there is nothing between us. This is hard for her, but I won't let her run from the truth. She must understand everything before she commits.

"To mark someone," I say. "It takes three bites."

"Three?" Clara's face pales.

"The effects of the first bite last for a single day, the second for a month, and the final seals it forever. Each mark is valid for the duration, but there is not a vampire alive who would consider a human marked until they have received their third bite—otherwise too many humans would be marked."

I guide a lock of hair behind her ear. Her teeth scrape over her bottom lip as she takes in the information.

"And would I have to accept all of them? What

would happen if I changed my mind after the first bite?"

I shake my head. "If and when you want the marks is up to you. But without the third, there will always be a chance of another vampire being able to mark you."

She pushes her shoulders back and for the first time, looks me in the eye. "Give me the first two marks, now. I will... think on the third."

My heart stops for two whole beats before it restarts. With every bite I will want her more. I don't think either of us are ready for that yet. "I cannot give you all three at once," I lie. "There are *side effects*."

Her forehead wrinkles and her nostrils flare. She lets out a frustrated growl and places her fists on her hips. "What side effects could there possibly be? You've been trying to convince me to accept your mark since before Kitty's wedding, and now, when I finally agree to it—" She lifts her hands to the side, then lets them drop back down. "If I didn't know better, I'd say you don't want to mark me. You made it sound so simple, and now you are telling me it's a process, *with side effects*." She posts a finger at the center of my chest. "Out with the whole truth, vampire."

I brace my hands against the wall on either side of

her head, caging her in as I lean forward. There's a sharp intake of breath.

My power flares and I lower my mouth to the delicate place where her neck and shoulder meet. I scrape my teeth over her skin.

Her hands reach up, gripping my shirt. She's not sure if she wants to pull me closer or shove me away. And it is because of that I must show her the consequences of what she's asking.

"With each bite, the effects will be heightened, and by the third you will have no choice but to give into them." She swallows. "It will make us want to fuck," I say at last, brushing my lips on the shell of her ear.

I take her wrists and release them from my shirt, then step back. Her hand reaches up to brush the spot I touched with my fangs.

She clearly doesn't want my mark. I turn around wishing it were only my pride that hurt. We might have found a few moments of peace between us, but she still sees me as a monster. I don't know when her opinion of me became important, but it has.

Her fingers wrap around my wrist, and tug.

"Why are you leaving?" she demands. "I said I wanted the mark."

There is a slight tremble in her voice from fear or anticipation. Clara moves to block my path, so we stand toe to toe. She places her hands on my upper arms, fingers pressing in.

"I'm asking for your mark."

This is a dangerous path for us, but I can't deny her request. I wrap an arm around her waist, and brush her hair off her shoulder, skimming my fingertips over her skin. Clara tilts her head to the side.

I lean forward and pause to look her in the eye. "Breathe and be calm."

She nods once.

I lower my mouth, calling my power to me, and bite down.

My fangs sink into her, and the taste of her blood fills my mouth. Clara gasps and her knees go out from under her, but my arm keeps her from falling.

I can feel the mark taking hold as she responds, pressing her body tighter against mine.

Slowly I release her and place my palm over the bite marks. Red veins of power flow over my fingers, hand, and up my arm, swirling. I push the smallest amount into her. Clara hisses through her teeth.

The wound is smaller than her last and with each subsequent mark, the less she will need my power to heal. When I move my hand away the bite marks have healed completely, leaving only two small scars behind.

When she's steady, I let her go and step back. It has been so long since I have fed from anyone without compelling, so they don't look at me the way Clara is looking at me now.

Clara steps forward and wraps her arms around my neck. I know what she wants… what my mark has made her want.

It's not real.

Perhaps any other man would give in. I want her, but not like this. She needs to understand how each bite will feel. Once the effects of this first mark wear off, I don't want her to regret anything.

I cup her face with both of my hands and wait for her eyes to clear enough that I know she's ready to listen. "You should go to your rooms and rest. I will send Cherno to watch over you."

Her expression falls into one of confusion and hurt. She untangles her limbs from me, and I let go. Her brows furrow, eyes glistening and darkening as her mind and body war with one another.

It would be easy to give in, but if I took advantage of her, she would never forgive me.

As Clara opens the door to leave, she stumbles to a stop. The door opens wider.

Lawrence stands with one fist raised to knock. He lifts his face and sniffs the air. She glares openly at him, then moves past without a word.

The connection hits me harder than I thought possible. I need time alone after giving her the first mark, but it looks as if that won't be happening.

Lawrence closes the door and chuckles as he crosses the room and sits in the chair at my desk. "That one has spirit. I don't know how you do it…"

He's baiting me and I know it. I rise and take it, ready for him to get this over with and say whatever it is that he came here to say. Though, I have my suspicions about what it is.

"Do what?"

Lawrence rests his arms on the desk and leans in. "Get an unmarked human to lie for you when the truth will only get her killed once it comes to light—and it *will* come to light." He sits back, in the chair. "Does she even know the extent of the danger she's in?"

"Of course she knows," I snap.

Lawrence narrows his eyes, then scents the air. "You gave her the first mark," he says.

"Yes."

"Finish marking her or she will die."

I clench my teeth, a muscle in my jaw ticking. "Whether she is marked one or two more times is her decision. I'll not take that from her."

He throws his hands in the air, frustrated as if he's talking to a child. "You and Rosalie with your unnatural affinity to humans. They are inferior to us. They are not our equals."

I say nothing. We have debated this topic for years. We will never agree.

His eyes narrow, his mind going in the same direction as mine. "Where is Rosalie? It has been over a month, and we have not seen or heard from her. Why hasn't she been around?"

I hang my head and rub my brow. Taking a deep breath, I release it slowly. "She is dead..." I admit. "Murdered—during the claiming."

Lawrence is on his feet, palms coming down hard on the desk. The resounding slam echoes through the room.

"Why have you not reported it?" he sneers.

I drop my hands. "No, I have taken care of it."

"Who is responsible?" He stands before me now, fists grabbing my shirt, and his eyes flashing with bloodlust and rage.

There is every reason in the world for me to hate Clara. I should hate her. I should want her to die a slow and agonizing death. I should give her to Lawrence to kill. Her life is the price she owes for taking the life of a vampire.

But it's not what Rosalie would want.

Part of me hates Clara for what she has done, yet

at the same time I desire her... I have even come to care for her.

I did my best to live my life the way Rosalie wanted me to. She is the reason I fought the nature of what I am until it became dormant. A voice in the back of my mind whispers that I would still be incapable of punishing Clara, even if Rosalie had never been turned those one hundred and seventy-two years ago.

I grab his wrists and remove them from my shirt, baring my fangs. "I said, I have taken care of it."

His breaths come out in short pants as he restrains himself. I am two ranks above him. If we fought earnestly, he would lose. Something we are both aware of.

Lawrence balls his hands into fists, and for a brief moment, I think he will fight me anyway.

Then, to my relief, he turns and storms out of the office, slamming the door behind him.

CHAPTER TWENTY-SIX

CLARA

Irritation simmers in my blood. I still cannot believe Alaric gave me the first mark only to send me to my room like a child. I slept all day, I don't need or want more rest.

Alaric's power lingers in my veins, caressing every part of me, humming with energy and need.

I head downstairs, intent on doing anything other than sequestering myself. Cherno flies around me, circling my head. I pause on the bottom step.

"Bat…" I growl through clenched teeth. I close my eyes and count to three, then blow out a breath, tamping down my anger. It isn't fair to Cherno to take my frustration out on them. "Will you please land?"

Wings brush against my hair and their little feet

land on top of my head. I half sigh, half laugh. Reaching up I grab Cherno and move them to my shoulder. Leathery wings hold onto my neck as I continue toward the library. My sanctuary away from my room.

"Alaric thinks—" Cherno starts.

"I don't care what he thinks," I snap. Hearing his name twists my gut.

I'm feeling too many things and I need peace to sort through it all.

When I finally agree to accept his mark, he makes it feel cold and impersonal—like a transaction between strangers. He knew how it would affect me and sent me away, instead of…

I squeeze my eyes shut and swallow, trying to push that thought away. Already, my body reacts, and the desire to run to him is overwhelming. My injured pride is enough to keep me from giving in.

Inside the library, the room is cold and dim, as if no one. Outside the sun has just dipped below the horizon leaving the deep purples and blues of night to swallow up the last of the light.

I don't know what I had expected, or what I wanted him to do, but it wasn't to act as if I disgusted him. Somewhere between pretending to be more to each other… somewhere among his acts of kindness, I had started to see him as *more* than just an ally.

I bite my lip, thinking about the conversation we had about his sister. The realization of how foolish I've been dawns on me. I told myself we were more than vampire and claimed human until I believed this thing between us was friendship.

But we aren't friends. *We could never be friends.* How could we, when I killed his only family? He will always hate me for it.

Walking past several shelves, I grab a random book without so much as glancing at the spine. I take it to the window seat and drop down with a bone-weary sigh. Cherno snuggles into my neck tangling a wing into my hair. I would never admit it, but the little demon's presence is somewhat comforting. Even if only because his power is an echo of the power I crave.

I open the book and peer down at the pages, my eyes roll over the words, but I see none of them. All I see is Alaric's office, all I feel is his arms around me and—demons and saints—his mouth pressed to my neck.

I expected the bite to hurt or at least sting, but it was warm. I'd wanted him to kiss me, to touch me, to do so much more... Again, I have to push those thoughts down, forcing myself to focus on each and every word on the page in excruciating detail.

It's a large tome about a man's journey through the

Otherworld where he unleashes demons from their prison, allowing them to make their way into the living world. The story is completely fantastical, the language, archaic and rhythmic, like an incredibly long children's bedtime story. One meant to get them to behave and stay inside at night where they will be protected and safe.

Sometime later, Mrs. Westfield enters with a small tray of bread, cheese, and cider. She says nothing, her expression as impassive as ever. Her eyes flick to Cherno, still perched on my shoulder. She gives me a curt nod, then leaves.

"Thank you," I call out. Though she doesn't bother acknowledging me.

I adjust my position, crossing my legs and setting the book in my lap as I nibble on the food. My mouth waters at the first bite. Demons and Saints, I am starving!

I rip off a small chunk of bread and offer it to Cherno.

"I don't eat human food," they say.

I pop the piece in my mouth. And as I chew, I wonder if I dare ask, *what* a demon does eat… or if I already know the answer.

Instead, I resume eating, not looking up from my book until I reach for another bite and find nothing.

Eventually, the sky lightens, and I finally close the

book. I'm still hurt by Alaric's dismissal, but my desire to run to him, wrap myself around him, has lessened.

My mind is clear again and I can think past my upset. I didn't ask him to mark me because of any intimate reason. It wasn't out of jealousy, or lust, or lo—erm *affection*. It was purely pragmatic. If I plan to stay here with him, to go to Nightwich, then I need his mark to be safe, and I trust him.

My fingers trail over the spot where he bit me. Two small scars remain. I am one step closer to being safe... and to tying myself to Alaric for life. He and Cassius have both made sure I know another vampire could mark me, overriding Alaric's claim until I have that final mark.

I'm still not sure I want to be marked—well, I'm not sure about the final mark, anyway. The second... the second is tempting.

Not that my wants matter. Vampires rule the world and try as I might to fight against it, I will end up complying. So if I am to be claimed and marked, then I want it to be Alaric's. At least with him, I will have some semblance of autonomy. He may have pissed me the fuck off by being cold, but I still trust him.

I don't trust Lawrence. He looks at me with suspicious eyes as though my very presence is an affront to him. Cassius and Victor seem decent enough, if not a little strange, and I wouldn't want to be tied to either of them.

I jump when Cherno's head pops up, then they launch off my shoulder, and out of the library. It seems I no longer need to be watched.

Standing, I stretch my arms and legs, working out the stiffness in my muscles from sitting and reading the night away. I head to the kitchen hoping to find a hot cup of tea. The manor is silent as I make my way to the first floor, and even though the sun is not yet up, there are no signs of vampires.

I only make it as far as the dining room doorway. Mrs. Westfield sets a plate of food before Alaric. And while she looks up to give me a tight smile, he doesn't so much as lift his eyes. I can't tell if he is too consumed by the letter he's reading or if he is intentionally avoiding me.

"Have a seat, dear," Mrs. Westfield says pulling out a chair across from her master.

It isn't until I have a plate in front of me and Mrs. Westfield has left the room, that Alaric finally looks up. He says nothing. I can't tell what he's thinking but I wish he would say something. The space between us feels strained and uncomfortable. Even when I thought I hated him, it was never like this.

When he doesn't speak, I busy my hands with a

piece of toast, spreading butter and jam over it. I break our eye contact first, keeping my head down.

Parchment crinkles and I look up into deep midnight eyes locked on me. The letter he was reading is now folded neatly beside his empty plate.

I wish he would say something because the silence between us makes me feel uneasy. Though, by some miracle, I manage to avoid squirming in my seat.

I want to know what he's thinking, and why being in the same space as him now is so strained. But I don't know what to say or do. I've never felt so unsure about another person before. Does he even want to mark me, or would he rather I go away?

"Pardon me, Master, but you have visitors," Mr. Steward announces from the doorway.

Alaric pushes back in his chair and stands. He gives me another look I cannot read, then follows the butler out of the room, leaving me alone. I eye the discarded letter, wondering if it has anything to do with his mood.

In the end, I choose to leave it. If he's going to mark me, then now isn't the time to break his trust by invading his privacy. Dropping my unfinished toast onto my plate, I push back my chair and follow.

Alaric stands in the open doorway. His fingers twitch as though fighting the urge to do something rash—he does nothing to hide the scowl on his face.

"What are you doing here, Wolverik?" he snarls at the man in front of him.

Oliver's expression and body language are much the same. A man and a woman flank him, though they stand back giving the two men room. The woman and man are dressed similarly, umber breeches with forest green jackets with buttons done up at the waist, and white shirts underneath. Dark leather boots that go to the knee complete their uniform.

"We have come to discuss the demon problem," Oliver says pointedly.

He looks older now than the first time we met. All traces of the friendly demeanor I knew are gone.

"There has been a higher demon in our woods for weeks now, and it is destroying the ecosystem and poisoning my lands with its foul magic."

Alaric holds up his hand, silencing further discussion. He lifts his arm guiding the three shifters. "As you may be aware, I have *company*. Why don't we sit in the drawing room and chat. It is still early in the morning."

I step forward with every intention of following them. Oliver looks up and when he sees me, a broad, wolfish grin spreads across his face.

He pushes past Alaric and slides over to me. I take half a step back before he grasps my hand in his. Oliver presses a kiss to my knuckles as he bows.

"Hello, my Lady. It is not every day that I get the pleasure of meeting someone as lovely as yourself," he says straightening.

Meet me? What in the Otherworld is he talking about? I'm about to point out that we've already met, but then I look over his shoulder to Alaric. His eyes widen a fraction of a second before I realize why.

Oliver slips an arm around me and pulls me against him. My face heats from having him so close with the weight of Alaric's stare burning into my back. I want to punch him in his pretty face for using me to tease him.

I press my hands against Oliver's chest, trying to put a little distance between us, but he's not paying attention, and his hold is too strong. I don't like how Alaric is looking at us.

This is an expression of his I *can* read. He looks ready to rip Oliver to shreds.

CHAPTER TWENTY-SEVEN

CLARA

"WILL YOU BE JOINING US TODAY?" OLIVER ASKS, leaning in. As his face inches closer to mine, I lean back. His eyes flick to my neck, then back to my face. His smile slips a fraction, and heat travels up to burn my cheeks.

"No," Alaric says sharply. His arm curls around my shoulder, hand sliding over my collarbone in a possessive gesture to separate Oliver and me.

Oliver releases me and steps to the side. Not quite a retreat, but enough to show that he's not going to challenge Alaric.

"Clara," Alaric says without so much as glancing my way. "If you will please excuse us."

The man and woman who came with Oliver raise their chins in a barely perceptible move. Their scrutiny sears up and down my body as they appraise me. I don't know what they find, and call me skeptical, but I doubt it's unwavering approval.

"It was a pleasure meeting you, Clara," Oliver says. And then he turns striding into the drawing room, the other shifters on his heels.

I reach for Alaric's hand. He looks down, then slowly, as if it pains him, he meets my gaze.

"I want to join you." I keep my voice calm. "There is something going on, and if..." I swallow, stumbling on my words. "If I am to stay with you, I should know what it's about. This is now my home too."

His expression softens, and for a moment I think he might actually consider it. But then he sets his jaw and shakes his head removing his hand from mine. "No. Perhaps another time."

Then he closes the door, shutting me out once more. I'm fed up with him shutting me out. We were never like this—*he* was never like this before the first mark.

The murmuring on the other side begins immediately. I tiptoe closer and press my ear to the wood, trying to make out any of the conversation. But the sound of my pulse obscures most of it.

"Higher... Worse... Urgent..."

"Eaves dropping?" a man says.

My heart leaps into my throat as I whirl to face Mr. Harkstead.

"No, I wasn't... I was..."

His lip curls. "Are you sure? Because you had your ear pressed against the door," he says holding out a hand to me. "Come, there is no use lying."

I shake my head then take a deep breath and blow it out. "What I meant to say was that I wasn't trying to intrude. I am worried. That's all."

"I'm sure Alaric will tell you what you want to know when he is ready. But for now, you need to trust him."

I trust Alaric. It's the vampire standing before me I don't trust. Then I chide myself for making an opinion of him just because he has never been warm toward me. I will give him the benefit of the doubt. After all, I was once wrong about Alaric, I might be wrong about Lawrence too.

The weight of the night forged dagger in my hidden pocket gives me a small sense of safety. A girl can never be too careful.

I slip my hand into his and walk with him until we reach the music room. Half the drapes are drawn, only the ones covering the west facing windows are open allowing soft light in and blocking out the harsh direct rays of the sun.

Once we reach the middle of the room, Lawrence

drops my hand and walks over to the piano. Lifting the lid covering the keys, he takes a seat on the bench.

"Ah, no one told me there was going to be a party."

I jump, turning to face Victor. He's standing closer than I expected. He wraps an arm around my waist and lifts my left hand with his free one.

"Care to dance?" he asks not waiting for music.

He takes a few steps, picking me up just enough that my feet barely touch the ground. I'm too startled to say anything.

A jarring sound of piano keys sounds through the room, and thankfully Victor stops dancing. I don't hesitate to put distance between us.

"It is not a party, and if you want to spend time with lady Clara, then you can come back later."

Victor's brows shoot up. His eyes seem to pulse with a darkness. Then I blink and whatever I think I see, is gone. "I didn't realize you wished for alone time with her. I do apologize," he says. "I will leave you alone."

Victor inclines his head toward me, apologizing again. He smiles sheepishly, then he turns and strides from the room.

Vampires are such territorial creatures.

Lawrence positions his hands over the keys then looks at me and dips his head, indicating the spot next to him.

Hesitantly, I walk over and sit as close to the edge as I can so our sides don't touch. Then he begins to play. The tempo is slow, quiet, and sorrowful. I've never learned to play. Father always said it was a waste of time when I should be working to help our family.

As the song picks up, he moves with it until it ends on a long, soft note. Like a breath.

Lawrence turns to me. It's like he is trying to read my mind or soul or see down to my very essence.

He slowly lowers the lid down over the keys.

"I was shocked when I first learned Alaric had finally taken part in the claiming. We all were. Did you know he has never claimed a human before?" He thoughtfully runs a hand over his chin, as if rubbing stubble that isn't there. "I was with him the day before he claimed you. Even then, he was adamant he wouldn't partake in the custom."

I hold my breath, frozen where I sit. His words are innocuous enough, he isn't saying anything cruel or untrue, but his eyes hold something deadly.

"But then he did, there was no hiding that from Elizabeth. And because he finally claimed a human, he must attend the winter masquerade. I wanted to see what kind of human managed to change his mind."

I lock my suddenly dry lips. "And?" I prompt when he doesn't continue. "What did you find?"

"A puzzle."

I raise a brow in question.

"You see, you are quite unremarkable. You are not from a notable or rich family, and you don't possess any exceptional beauty and yet... you have him bewitched."

I snort, probably proving his point about me. But saying *I* bewitched a *vampire*, is an exaggeration.

Lawrence tilts his head. "Now don't look so offended, you know the things I say are true."

He stands and walks around the bench until he's on my other side and rests one hand on the piano, the other on the edge of the bench.

I say nothing.

Neither of us move for a painfully long moment. My neck begins to ache from holding it at this angle.

"Why did he claim you, Clara?" he asks. "Why would he claim a human now, after all these years of refusing to even consider it?"

I want to lie and say I don't know, but my instincts scream not to. "If you want to know, then ask him yourself. You must think a lot of me to assume I know his mind."

Suspicion settles over his shoulders like a cloak. I see it in his eyes first. They widen and then narrow. "What do you know of the vampire that was killed during the claiming?" he asks, almost too calmly.

My stomach gutters, and I'm glad I am sitting because I don't think my legs could hold me up. I can't admit everything to him. It would mean certain death.

Focus... keep your heartbeat slow, my mind commands.

I pull in a slow breath and say, "I know there was a vampire killed around the time he claimed me." Lawrence quirks a brow at that admission. "And I know that she was his sister."

There... not a lie, but not an admission of guilt.

Lawrence bares his teeth. "I find it to be too much of a coincidence that Rosalie is murdered and Alaric just happens to claim you. What do you know of her death?"

He snarls, red rings his irises, threatening to consume the green and gold of his hazel eyes.

I shouldn't be offended by his accusation, since it's true. Nevertheless, the revenge for Rosalie's death is not his to take.

My fingers twitch and I move one hand onto the cool surface of the piano, next to his. I straighten my back and hold my chin high, moving so close, our noses nearly touch. I bare my teeth. "Do not threaten me, Mr. Harkstead. It will not end well."

He goes to speak but stops as the slightest movement of his jaw presses the point of the dagger to the underside of his chin. The slightest pressure from my hand is all it would take to drive it into his skin. It might not be a killing blow, but I don't intend it to be if he forces me to follow through.

"He gave you *her* dagger?" he speaks with venom but I don't miss the sliver of pain in his voice. "Or did you steal it?"

"If you want to know about Rosalie's death, then ask Mr. Devereaux. But don't think you can corner me with the pretense of civilized conversation and threaten me into telling you whatever you want to hear."

Lawrence backs up a step and smooths the lapel of his jacket. I stand as well now wanting to equalize the power between us as much as possible. He still towers over me. I'm also not as small and delicate as Kathrine, but I'm not what anyone would consider tall.

"I can't prove anything—yet, but I know you had something to do with Rosalie's murder. What I can't figure out is why Alaric would protect you." He turns from me and strides to leave, pausing in the doorway to look back over his shoulder. "This will not end well for you, Miss Valmont." He echoes my words. "You or Alaric. Whatever it is *you* have done, you should know he will end up paying for it as well."

And then he's gone.

I remain standing for one minute... two... three. When he doesn't return, I slip the dagger back into my pocket and drop back down on the piano bench with a heavy sigh.

How had I managed to draw on a *vampire* without him noticing?

Guilt forms knots in my stomach. Did Rosalie mean something to him, or did he simply underestimate my desire to protect myself?

A shiver crawls down my spine from the encounter. I am so used to feeling safe when I am with Alaric, I keep forgetting how dangerous vampires can be.

I still want to talk to that infuriating man, but he's probably still in the drawing room with Oliver. No doubt it was the reason Lawrence chose this moment to have a chat with me.

Resting my elbows on the closed lid, I hold my chin in my hands and chew on my bottom lip.

Lawrence seemed to have only just learned of Rosalie's death. He connected my claiming with the timing, which I suppose isn't that difficult.

Alaric is still keeping her death a secret to protect me. I just wish I knew why. Most importantly, what repercussions would Alaric face for sheltering me all this time?

It's been less than an hour. Less than half... if that.

I'm tempted to wait outside the doors to catch Alaric the second he leaves the room, but there is no telling how long their talk will take.

There is a tug in my chest, urging me to seek him out. I rub my hand over the spot trying to quell the sensation. Even if I didn't know where he was at this exact moment, I think this *feeling* would lead me straight to him.

It's lessened now to a dull hum from the blinding need that first took hold. It scares me that I want the second mark. I am not ready for the final mark yet, it seems too *permanent.* I'm not sure if I'll ever be ready for that.

For now, I need to get close to it. The moment he explained everything, I had already decided on doing two of the three marks. It will keep me safe. No one at Nightwich will be able to tell that I'm not fully marked... but now I think I might want the second for an entirely different reason.

CHAPTER TWENTY-EIGHT

CLARA

KEEPING MY HAND POISED AND READY TO GRAB THE dagger, I make my way back through the halls and into the front of the manor. It's quiet. Empty.

I don't relax until I'm standing with the door to the drawing room on my left and the entryway to the dining room to my right.

I strain my ears to listen. The sounds of dishes rattling on trays come from the kitchen. While not loud, it makes it impossible for me to understand anything being said inside. A man laughs. I scoot closer, wondering if it's Alaric's or Oliver's.

"Miss Valmont?"

I jump at Mr. Steward's voice and turn to face him.

"You can drop that contrite look," he mutters,

closing the last few steps that separate us. The teacups chime softly against their saucers on the silver tray. "Here," Mr. Steward says, pushing the tray into my hands. "You should take this in."

"But…"

"I have other duties to attend to. And perhaps once you're in, they will invite you for a cup of tea," he says as he walks back toward the kitchen.

Well, I suppose this is one way to learn what this is all about. I stand before the door, one hand poised to knock. If Alaric is put out by my intrusion, then he can just send me away. *Again*. The thought of him continuing to do so sets my teeth on edge.

Before my knuckles can make contact with the wood more than once, Alaric pulls open the door. He sucks in a breath as his eyes fall on my face. He looks around the hall as if expecting the butler to be standing nearby.

For a moment, I think he might just take this tray and dismiss me. My heart pounds against my ribs, and I wait for his anger, or at the very least, his clear displeasure at my forced intrusion. Then, to my surprise, he steps back and motions for me to come inside.

Oliver stands up, a large wolfish grin plastered on his face. All those sharp teeth should be terrifying, but somehow, he looks sweet and youthful.

"Finally," the male I don't know says under his breath as I set the tray down on the small table in the center of the room. The chaise lounge is on one side, and the leather wingback chair on the other.

I pour a cup for each of them. Cream for Oliver, cream and sugar for the woman, and nothing added for the man. The two shifters take their cups and stand back along the wall.

Finally, I pour a cup for Alaric. My hand trembles as I hand it to him, the liquid nearly sloshing over the rim.

What is wrong with me?

His hand steadies mine as he takes it with his other. His fingers linger on my skin before releasing me. I make myself a cup before I can dwell too long on what any of that meant… if anything.

"Not even sugar?" Oliver asks me, both brows raised.

"No, we didn't have milk or sugar when I was growing up," I say, sharing more than necessary. Before he can continue, I hurry to stand against the wall near the fireplace.

Oliver and Alaric take their seats. Tension fills the space between them.

Alaric takes a sip of his tea before he sets the cup down. "Why are you here, Oliver?"

"Demons," he says.

"Yes. You've said as much but I don't think that requires a formal visit." He motions to the other two shifters. "I have been hunting them and doing what I can to quell the issue. As I have told you in the past, I don't go back on my end of the agreement."

He moves to stand. Oliver sets his cup down and leans forward. Something about his expression and posture makes him appear more wolf than human.

"Then you are aware the lesser and higher demons are not the only issue. We have reason to believe there is a greater demon responsible for the recent decimation of the animal population. Their corpses litter the forest—none of them are even being fed on, only shredded and poisoned. My pack has had to go well out of our territory to hunt just to feed our children. Many have not returned because the humans hunt us."

With his flirtatious nature I had missed it before now. He is not just any wolf… he is the alpha of his pack, and the two with him are not simply pack mates —but his betas.

Alaric's gaze flicks to me, then back to Oliver before he sits back down, expression darkening. "I am. But there is only so much I can do. It is not my demon, and there is no way to determine who their master is. They refuse to take shape, intentionally making it impossible."

Oliver scoffs. "There are only so many vampires of your stature and you are currently housing, two… or is it three?"

"I am but one man," Alaric says, spreading his arms. "The bargain is with me and no other. If I had assistance, perhaps I could do more, but you will find a lack of willingness to get involved with what is seen among vampires as a *shifter* priority. They are your lands."

A growl rumbles up from Oliver's chest. "They may be our lands, but it is a vampire's greater demon —that should be more than enough for the vampires to get involved."

Holding up a hand, Alaric silences him. Though Oliver's emotions have breached the surface, Alaric remains calm. "I agree with you, I am merely explaining how the others will see things. I have agreed to do what I can, but I am afraid it is a waste time attempting to persuade the others."

Oliver straightens his back, a muscle in his jaw ticking. "There is something you can do. Just give in to—"

Alaric bares his fangs and he's up and grabbing Oliver by the lapels, bringing their faces close. The two betas take a step forward, halting in their tracks with a motion from their alpha.

"Never, make such a suggestion again." The warning is deep and low.

Alaric releases him. I blink, my jaw hanging open as they both reclaim their seats, perfectly calm like nothing happened. I don't understand Alaric's anger. Oliver hadn't even finished his thought.

"Track the demon and mark the territory it is haunting. I will see what more I can do. In the meantime, you and your pack must herd the animal population away from the demon."

The man takes another half-step forward, his fists clenched at his sides. "You presume to tell the Shade forest's alpha what to do?"

The woman places a hand on his shoulder and pulls him back.

Oliver narrows his gaze and faces the man. "Dominance is not important. I do not care if a pup is the one who comes up with the solution that works so long as there *is* a solution."

"We must find something more permanent. Clara and I will be leaving for Nightwich in two weeks."

I nearly drop my cup at the mention of my name. That's the last spoken about my future as Alaric and Oliver lean in closer and move on to discussing possible strategies, pointing out flaws in the other's ideas.

Eventually, the conversation comes to an end, and

I'm not entirely convinced they have come up with a plan at all. Perhaps it's an impossible situation.

I shift on my feet, aching from standing in the same place for so long.

"Shall we adjourn to the dining room?" Alaric asks. He and Oliver lead the way out of the drawing room and into the hall.

The light through the window is bright after spending so many hours with the drapes drawn and only a fire to light the space.

Alaric sits in his usual seat at the head of the table. The two betas take seats to his left and Oliver to his right, leaving a single seat empty between him and Alaric.

"Excuse me," I say. "I will go check on the food."

Alaric's brows furrow, but I push my way through the kitchen door before he can object.

Neither Mr. Steward nor Mrs. Westfield are here, though there are trays upon trays of food. Enough for a feast.

I blow out a breath and slump against the counter. I've never witnessed anything like that in my life. It was intense and strange.

Pushing away from the wall, I reach for the closest tray. The soft thump of the door swings open and then closed.

"I was just—" I start to say, but the words die on my tongue.

Oliver blocks the door with his body, arms crossed. He looks me up and down, a frown that looks out of place on him.

"Are you all right?"

I shake my head. "What do you mean?"

He takes several steps closer, then takes the tray from my hands and sets it back down. "You were running away that day, were you not?"

That night feels like a lifetime ago. "Yes. I was."

I remember everything about that night. I can still feel the tree at my back, the press of Alaric's body against mine.

He reaches out and pushes the hair from my shoulder, exposing the mark. "I see you didn't make it far."

"Oliver—"

"Oli," he says. I let out a soft gasp as he takes hold of my head in his hands and brings our foreheads together. "My offer still stands, lady Clara, to take you from this," he adds softly.

"Thank you," I say, matching his tone. "But no."

Oliver drops his hands and leans back, lips pressed into a tight line. "For someone who had wanted to escape from the vampire who claimed her, you seem to like him."

"I don't," I snap without thinking. "We have a truce. Nothing more."

Oliver sniffs the air. "His scent is on you. He has fed on you, if not marked you," he says matter-of-factly.

I can't deny it, especially when I still want to run to Alaric thanks to this demon cursed mark. I avert my eyes unable to match the power in Oliver's gaze.

"It isn't so terrible to like your vampire. As far as their kind go, Alaric is not a bad man."

I swallow. His words echo thoughts I've had for a while now.

"I did leave, I was gone for a month. I went home to see my sister get married. But my life there is gone." I shake my head, trying to hold back the surge of emotions that welling up and making my throat thick. I ramble on, unable to stop talking. "I never had anything to begin with. It was all dreams of a naive girl. And so I came back... so perhaps I'm the horrible one, using him—"

"Do not be so hard on yourself. If he didn't want you here, then you would be gone or dead." He squeezes my shoulder. "Sometimes we must lose ourselves before we can discover who we truly are. Alaric knows this."

The door swings open as Mrs. Westfield enters,

glaring, her hands on her hips. I sidestep Oliver, breaking our contact, and reach for a tray as I hurry past her.

285

CHAPTER TWENTY-NINE

ALARIC

Cherno drops down out of the air and lands on the desk. The demon crawls until they sit atop the closed book I couldn't even be bothered to open.

The letter that arrived this morning sits unopened to my left. Since the claiming, Elizabeth's letters have grown more and more frequent—even with the four vampires she sent to make sure I attended this year's solstice. Most end up in the fire, unopened. They are all the same—pleas to give in to her desires at long last and thinly veiled threats.

"I would think you would be happy," Cherno says. "But instead, you're brooding. Why?"

I push back in my chair and scrub my face with my hands, letting out a growl of frustration.

"I gave her the first mark last night," I say begrudgingly. I have wanted to touch her, to see and feel her come undone under my hands, for so long I nearly gave into the pull of the mark. And then I sent her away, knowing how my actions would make her feel.

But with the pull of the mark dimmed—who she is, who she has always been—comes back to me. I had let myself forget.

When she is around, that is all too easy to do. Avoiding her seemed best, but she sought me out again and again until I couldn't send her away again. Having her stand next to me during the meeting was like drawing breath for the first time... though she made it hard to concentrate on the issue at hand. I hadn't expected the first mark to affect me at all.

"If you despise her bearing your mark, then you should kill her as she sleeps in your bed. Drain the rest of her blood and be done with it," Cherno says coolly.

"It isn't that," I say. "It's because I want her still. I want her to have my mark, but if I do, I won't be able to resist."

I want her.

Cherno shrugs. An odd movement for a bat, then takes off into the air, flying in circles around the room. "Sex is sex. It only means more when there is something between those involved to give it meaning."

Fuck her, Cherno means. Treat her as if she means nothing.

Guilt stabs at my chest with each word they say. It was never *just* giving into the power of the mark.

"And that is the problem—I believe there is more between us than just attraction." I lean forward and rest my arms on the desk, lowering my face to Cherno's level. "I don't understand how I can want her—how I can stand her touch, how I can want anything more than her slow, painful death... knowing that she killed Rosalie."

Cherno swoops and dives in tight circles around my head. I lift a hand and halfheartedly swat at them.

"If you cannot forgive her, then kill her."

I lift my glass of brandy and take a long sip of the amber liquid.

"If only it were that easy." I set the drink down, the ice clinking musically against the glass. "She apologized the other night."

A leathery wing smacks the back of my head. I snarl at the impudence. The demon plops down right atop the unopened letter and wiggles their rear, settling in. The scolding I was about to give is immediately forgotten, and a smile pulls on my lips.

Only Cherno has ever shown disdain equal to mine for the Queen Bitch herself.

Those deep red eyes that appear almost brown, widen chasing away the humor. "You cannot keep doing this to yourself..." they say in earnest, then after a pause Cherno adds, "Or to her. There is nothing she can say or do to change the past. Unfortunately, words do not have the power to revive the dead. Nor can they take away the pain. It is something that will lessen in time, and you must learn to continue on despite it."

"I know," my words come out strangled.

"It doesn't matter whether I finish marking her or not. Claiming and marking a human was never going to be a casual affair for you, as it is the others. You *cling* to your humanity, and therefore part of your heart remains human."

My hands ball into fists. I want to protest—except that is exactly what I've spent almost two hundred years doing for Rosalie.

How can I let her go? How can I move on when she is the reason I've stayed alive as long as I have— the reason why I didn't give some human the night-forged dagger to slay me? Rosalie helped me stay true to who I was before I was turned and to become a better man in the end.

"Claiming Clara was a rash decision. Now, the two

of you must deal with the consequences of both your actions." Cherno crawls along the desk, then up my arm to my shoulder. "You cannot keep holding on to what happened. You were both wrong and both right."

I open my mouth to protest, but tiny claws dig in, and I feel his power flow through my veins, forcing me to listen.

"You are talking nonsense, bat," I manage to get out.

"Wrong, because your assumptions of each other stemmed from your prejudices of what the other is, rather than who each of you are. And *right*, because you each did what you have always known to be right to protect those you care about. The two of you have come to know each other and have become softer for it."

Softer? Yes, I have *become soft.* I scoff. Lawrence would say weaker, but I am undecided on that as of yet.

I stand and make my way to the window. The moon's light is muted behind thick, wintery gray clouds.

Reaching up, I stroke Cherno's small head. They have changed as well. The neutrality that permeated their personality has been replaced with humor, and though they would never admit it, a sort of kindness.

"How can I let her go?" I ask. "Wouldn't that make me a horrible brother?"

"You do not," they say. "You remember her. Continue to be the man she believed you to be. But also understand that Clara is human and fallible. She could not have known better. She was raised in fear of the very thing you are her entire life, and rightly so. Her reaction to seeing a vampire caught unaware was natural."

What they don't say is a painful truth even I know. Rosalie was considered weak and vulnerable by our kind, and it is a wonder she was never killed a long time ago—by a human or a vampire. And I am grateful.

Vampires take because we rule over humans. As Clara once said... they *are* a food source and little more. It has been so long since I lived under Elizabeth's oppression at Nightwich, so long since I struggled not to become like them, that I have forgotten what it was like to be at another's mercy.

"It is possible to hold on to your love for Rosalie and forgive Clara." The words are quiet and distant. Barely a whisper.

"I must go, I have wasted too much of the night," I say. I hardly dare to believe that what they suggest is a real option.

Snatching my jacket from the coat rack I head for the door.

Cherno leaps off my shoulder, leathery wings beating the air. "Think on it, Master."

Clara is in her room, waiting for the chance to talk.

I slip my jacket on and hurry downstairs as if I can run away from these thoughts when they live inside my head. As if putting distance between the two of us could solve anything.

Stopping on the edge of the woods, I turn. Clara's form darkens the window of her room and were it not for the shadows that envelop me, I'd swear she could see me.

I hold out a hand and Cherno lands on my palm. "Go, watch over her tonight, I can handle the hunt on my own, this time."

"You have changed the way she sees the world. You have never been the monster she thought. She sees vampires as individuals now, but you must make sure she does not forget the danger she is in." Cherno leaves me with that final thought.

The demon takes off.

I wonder if they are right.

I can never forget Rosalie, but I can choose to forgive Clara.

She has pushed her way into my soul regardless. Perhaps I've already forgiven her but have been too blinded by guilt to notice.

CHAPTER THIRTY

CLARA

Cool air slips across my face from the open window. It holds the unmistakable chill that brings the promise of the first snow in the coming days. Hours have passed since Oliver and his two betas left, and I still haven't spoken to Alaric. When I returned to the dining room with the tray to serve the wolves, Alaric was already gone.

I cross my arms and let my forehead thud softly against the windowpane as I glare at the spot of the nearby woods, where the shifters vanished. I have half a mind to march out there, even as the horizon swallows up the sun, and give that demons damned wolf a piece of my mind for pulling stunt like that. Whatever tensions are between Alaric and me, Oliver's flirting did nothing to help the situation.

Pressing the heel of my hand to my forehead, I push away those petty thoughts. They are a distraction from the real issue. I can't believe nearly three months have already passed since the claiming. It feels like it has been both a few days and several lifetimes.

I am not the same person I was. I don't know who I am anymore. I'm a boat set adrift in the ocean without a sail—aimless and at the mercy of the waves. But even that doesn't matter right now.

In two weeks, I will be on my way to Nightwich with Alaric. I only have one mark, but already I'm afraid that if I keep going I will lose whatever sliver remains of who I am. But I will do what I must to survive.

The final ray of light disappears below the horizon. Four figures emerge from the manor and converge in the yard. A woman and three men. They talk for a moment, then take off running at their impossibly fast speed, heading toward the main part of Windbury. Alaric is not with them.

Minutes later, he emerges from the manor and takes off into the woods at a blinding speed. I stare after him.

I've waited too long, and now I've lost my chance. I stand by the window for what feels like hours, eventually giving up and going to the library to occupy myself until he returns.

Cherno's steady wings follow me at a distance as I make my way through the hallway.

The window seat is a comfortable place to pass the time reading, with a perfect view of the woods. I quickly settle into my usual spot and open a book, forcing myself to focus on the words.

Somewhere in the manor, a door slams, jolting me awake.

I must have fallen asleep reading. The moon is still high, so not much time could have passed. Straining to listen, I stand and hover by the door. It's quiet. I don't hear voices, so I don't think it is any of the other vampires.

My pulse picks up. This is my chance.

I lift my chin and go in search of Alaric, in case I missed his return. I search in the drawing room first, then the music room, and not having found him in those places, I make my way to the third floor.

His office is just as empty as the other rooms I

checked. I lean against the door frame and press my lips into a tight line.

Disheartened, I wrap my arms around myself. It's clear that he's avoiding me. I walk back down the hall, content to go to bed and find him in the morning. But as I pass his bedroom door, I contemplate waiting inside. I lift my hand and knock, expecting nothing.

"No tea tonight, Mrs. Westfield." Alaric's voice comes through the door, soft and weary.

My heart thuds against my chest. I turn the doorknob and push it open, and slip inside. A fire burns in the hearth, but the room is still cold.

Alaric is stretched out on the couch against the far wall with an arm draped over his eyes.

"I said…" he trails off as he peeks out from under his arm.

I half expect him to tell me to leave, but instead, he reaches a hand out to me and I go to him without hesitation. As soon as I'm within reach, he grabs me by the waist and pulls me down on top of him. My head rests on his chest, and for a while, I'm content to just be in his presence, listening to the steady rhythm of his heart.

His arms tighten around me as he hugs me. All thoughts of confronting him evaporate. Alaric buries his face in the crook of my neck and inhales. It's a move that once sent my pulse racing from fear. Now it jumps for an entirely different reason.

"Why did you send me away last night?" I whisper. Though I try to keep the hurt from my voice, I'm unsuccessful. "Why have you been avoiding me?"

His fingers tighten against me before relaxing. "I'm sorry, my dear Clara." Alaric presses his cheek against the top of my head. "I wanted you to understand what could have happened between us, without regret. I couldn't risk that as much as I wanted to give in to it," he whispers the last part.

Knowing he wanted to give in but didn't want to take advantage of me hangs between us. And that fact sends my heart racing.

Alaric's fingers trail up and down my spine. I can almost imagine the feel of his hands on my bare skin.

I pull back to look him in the eye. "I want the second mark," I say.

His eyes darken with desire as his hands press my body tighter against his. "Are you sure?"

I nod, then lick my lips. "Yes—as long as you don't leave or send me away. I want you to stay with me this time."

"I wouldn't be able to fight it, even if I wanted to," he says.

I swallow thickly. We are not talking just about the

mark but what will come after. "And do you want to? Fight it that is."

"No," he says softly.

In a swift, world tilting movement, he adjusts our position so he hovers over me. "I need you to be absolutely sure, Clara." he says again even as my knees straddle his hips.

Red rings form around his brilliant blue irises. He gazes down on me as if I own the night, and he can't bear to live under the sun's harsh rays.

"Yes," I whisper.

Alaric brushes a lock of hair off my shoulder, then lowers his head, pressing his mouth to my neck. He places a series of soft, slow kisses along my skin. Then I feel the point of his fangs, but he doesn't bite down yct.

Heat sears through my veins as I hold my breath in anticipation. Alaric's hand glides down over my breast and lingers only a second before it moves down my ribs, my hip, then my leg. He inches my skirt up until he touches my bare leg. Then his palm slides up my calf to my knee to the top of my thigh.

My heart is in my throat as he reaches my core. All the while he continues to kiss along my heated skin. My breathing picks up as his thumb moves in circles.

I gasp as his fangs pierce my skin at the same

moment his fingers enter me. My body reacts to him of its own accord.

The power of his mark driving me to want him more and more, but it's not only that—the way he moves—I feel like I am being pushed to the edge as I feel myself building, as I writhe beneath him. I lift my hips, wanting so much more.

The cool room suddenly feels too warm. I clutch at his shirt, needing him closer. Needing to feel his skin on mine. My back arches, and I am falling as my orgasm lashing through me.

Alaric withdraws his hand when I come down from my high and settles back to where he was before, his hips nestled between my legs. I can feel the hardness of his desire pressing against me through his clothes.

He reaches up and presses his hand over the bite marks. Red power lights up his face and I feel the pang of my flesh knitting itself back together. I know without checking that two small scars remain.

When the glow fades, he opens his eyes and stares down at me. I wonder what he sees.

"Alaric," I say his name, pleading for more.

He sits up, pulling me with him. I straddle his lap, a leg on either side of his hips, there's no space between us. I rest my forehead against his. The power of his mark hums through our veins. I can feel his hard length beneath me. I move against him, wanting him even more than a few moments ago.

"Clara..." he groans my name, the picture of heat and torture.

I want this feeling to last, I don't want to think, I don't want to stop. I could blame it on the mark, but I know at least an equal part is what I want regardless... what I have wanted for longer than I'm willing to admit.

I run my hands up his arms and across his broad chest. My fingers find the top of his shirt and unbutton it, then down to the second. When I reach the third, he grabs my wrists, pausing my movements.

There's something in his eyes, something uncertain. I lean forward, Alaric's large sapphire eyes framed by his beautiful thick lashes, slide closed, and I press my mouth to his, kissing him long and slow.

His hands release mine and grip my hips, and I resume unbuttoning his shirt down to the very bottom. Alaric's tongue presses against mine as he deepens the kiss.

I push the cloth of his shirt to the side, sliding my hands over his warm, bare skin. I'd forgotten about the dozens of long white scars covering his chest and abdomen. Alaric stiffens, not moving or breathing, as I trace several with my fingertips. They are harsh and formed from very deep, very violent wounds.

There's more to these than what I can even begin to guess. I look up, to see that he has turned away. As if he thinks I will find him undesirable because of them… and it breaks my heart.

I lean down and press my lips to one scar. He shivers under my touch, but he doesn't stop me. Then I kiss another and another.

There's something remarkable about the lines that mark his skin, something that makes him even more stunning to look at than if his skin had been flawless.

Meeting his gaze once more, I can't seem to read the look in his eyes. It could be want, fear, surprise, or some mixture. Neither of us speaks, so I inch back slightly and let my fingers trail down his muscled stomach to the waist of his trousers, slowly undoing them.

"You don't—" he starts.

I cut him off with a kiss and whisper against his mouth, "I want this. I want you."

Alaric braces his hands on my thighs and hikes my skirt up to my hips, his fingers brushing dangerously close to my core. I slip a hand between us, and I wrap my fingers around his hard length. He sucks in a small breath, barely noticeable, but the pressure of his fingers pressing into me tells me all I need to know. I move my hand up and down.

"Clara, I—" he says, breaking off with a growl. His

hands roam over me, eventually returning to my hips. He lifts me slightly, pulling me closer and higher to position his cock at my entrance. Then slowly, he presses me down onto him. I take him in inch by inch.

My head falls back with a moan at the sensation of him filling and stretching me around him. My breathing hitches at the feel of him.

"If I could only hear one thing for the rest of my life, it would be that sound," he says almost reverently.

My head snaps up, my face burning. He's buried deep inside me, and still, he manages to make me blush from the sheer intensity of his words.

He tightens an arm around my waist, his other hand cupping the back of my neck, guiding my mouth to his as we rock against each other. He kisses me hard as I move faster. His fangs scrape along my lower lip, but not enough to break the skin.

He grasps the material of my dress and pulls. It gives without resistance. Cool air washes over my feverish skin. Then he grips my hips, guiding my movements, keeping me from speeding up as if he wants to draw this moment out forever.

Alaric's mouth moves along my jaw and down my neck to the spot he bit. His tongue flicks the tender skin, sending a sharp aching need down to my core. It builds and builds and builds until it's almost too much.

My body tightens around him, and he drives himself into me with a powerful thrust of his hips. I cry out, back arching as my climax rips through me.

He groans in response. All I can do is cling to him as he pumps into me harder and faster, drawing out my pleasure as he chases his own.

I can feel him thickening inside me, and then he finds his release. His arms wrap tightly around my waist, and he holds me tight, trailing kisses along my neck and shoulder as our movements gradually slow.

I rest my forehead against his, staring into those strange eyes of his, the blue nearly swallowed up by the red. A shudder of desire sweeps through me and the muscles around the edges of his eyes tighten slightly as a self-satisfied smirk forms on his delicious lips.

We stay like this for a long moment, our breaths mingling.

I could blame being blinded by desire as a side effect of the mark he'd warned me about... but that would be a lie.

Alaric tilts my head and trails slow, languid kisses along my jaw and down my neck. "You are even more stunning coming undone around me than I imagined. Next time," he says against my skin. "I will take my time with you and savor every second."

CHAPTER THIRTY-ONE

CLARA

I STRETCH AS THE EDGES OF SLEEP TUG ON MY MIND and body. My muscles are a little sore, but not uncomfortably so. There is something so peaceful about lingering in the space between the dream world and the waking.

Soft material glides over my skin and I feel nearly weightless. Fire crackles in the hearth, warming the air. Alaric's musky scent surrounds me.

I would be content to stay in this moment forever.

But as always, the moment fades, and my mind rouses. I blink open my eyes. Dark blankets and materials of the opulent furnishings surround me.

I sit up, clutching the sheets to my naked body as everything comes rushing back to me.

Asking for the mark. The overwhelming need it

sparked. The first mark was nothing in comparison. And though I still feel the pull of wanting to find him and have him give me the final mark. But that, too, has transformed into something different. It remains a deep need, only without desperation clawing at me.

My hand splays out on the empty spot next to me, not entirely cooled. He must have just left. I'm disappointed.

I slide my legs off the bed and stand. Yesterday's discarded dress is gone, and draped over the back of the couch in its place is a new one, deep blue in color.

I quickly slip into it. By the time I finish lacing up the back, Alaric has not returned. My stomach tightens.

I pause near the door when the glint of firelight reflecting off metal catches my eye. The night-forged dagger sits on the bedside table. I quickly pocket it, then close the door behind me. I meander down the hall to his office, but the room is empty; not even the warm light of coals sits in the fireplace.

I swear I will cut that bastard if he is back to avoiding me. The vow feels hollow even as I think it.

Night has fallen. I must have slept the entire day away. After more aimless wandering through the manor, I find that I am once again alone.

A meal waits for me on the table. I eat quickly, then return to wandering the halls until I end up in the music room. I think of the first and only dance lesson I've had in my life. If I'm to accompany him to Nightwich, it might be a good idea to resume them again.

I stop by a window and pull the heavy drapes to the side. I lean against the frame, entirely bored. If this keeps up, the mark will send me to the Otherworld by insanity. Whatever Alaric is doing right now must be enough to distract him from the effects—if he even feels them at all.

He is probably in the forest hunting the demons again. He and Oliver did not discuss the issue in detail, but he had promised to spend more time dealing with it before we leave for Nightwich.

I wonder what Nightwich will be like. If I thought four new vampires were intimidating... what would dozens be like?

A shiver runs down my spine.

"Are you cold, Lady Clara?"

I spin to find Victor once again standing close, leaning in as if he means to pick up on the dance where we left off. His toad—*demon*—croaks from the doorway, drawing my attention. His toad is waiting at the edge of the room.

"You startled me," I say, barely stopping myself from reaching for the dagger. "I'm not sure I like this new habit of yours."

He gives me a quarter smile at that. I move to the side, needing more space. I don't know if it's his habit of sneaking up on me, or if it is the lingering effects of the second mark.

"What brings you to this part of the manor alone, so late at night?"

I tilt my head, glancing at him over my shoulder. "Is it late?" I hum thoughtfully. "I hadn't realized what time it was."

Demons and saints, in all my searching for Alaric, I must have been too busy pining to bother glancing at any of the clocks around the manor.

I bite down on the inside of my cheek. *I am already losing myself.*

I trail a finger along the edge of the piano. Inhaling, I mentally shake off the melancholy that has settled over me and continue my slow walk around the room, testing the vampire's movements. Victor follows.

"It seems someone is always occupying your time. I haven't had a chance to get to know you yet," he says.

With each step away I take, he manages to close the distance. He stops any further retreat by placing his hand over mine and pining it to the top of the piano—not hard enough to hurt, but enough that I would have to struggle to get free.

"Alaric has been keeping you to himself lately. I'm a bit jealous."

"Well, he did claim me…" I tug on my hand, hoping he will take the hint.

He doesn't.

"I would so enjoy a snack right now," he adds quietly.

It takes a too long moment for me to process the words. "Didn't you just return from hunting?"

Victor smiles, wider this time—the same one he wore when he first arrived, but there is nothing sensual in the least about it.

Red rings his irises, but the color is broken up by thin, black lines that slowly extend from the center of his pupils. The veins lengthen, edging out into the whites.

"Do not worry, lady Clara, I only want to play a little."

"No thank you," I snap as I yank my arm free. "I don't feel like playing."

I turn to leave. He wouldn't dare cross the line. He would threaten and try to scare me, but he wouldn't dare—Victor cuts me off as I round the piano, effectively blocking my path.

"Stop," he says. Power vibrates in that single word.

My feet are stuck in place, and I can't move. I can feel the compulsion in his voice, though his eyes don't glow with it. Instead, the black thickens, swallowing up the brown and spreading like spilled ink over the whites. My head throbs. I press my hands to my temples to lessen the pain.

Victor lets out a delighted sound, something between a purr and a growl. He steps even closer.

"How delightful… you are not marked." He licks his lips, his eyes dart to the tiny scars on my neck. "At least not fully… you could yet belong to me."

The possessiveness in his voice promises things I don't have the ability to imagine. I can't stop the shudder that races along my spine.

Victor gathers me in his arms, holding me too tight.

"Let me go," I say.

My attempts at escaping his grasp are weak, he doesn't even seem to notice as he fists a hand in my hair and jerks my head to the side, exposing my neck.

"Don't," I warn.

I half register a single chirp and flapping of leather wings. *Cherno… Cherno was here… and they left me to fend for myself…*

Victor brings his face close, inhaling long and deep. His tongue darts across my collarbone, to my neck and jaw, and up the side of my face.

Disgusting.

"Let me go, you piece of demon shit," I demand again.

He brings his mouth to my ear. I cringe, expecting more, but instead, he says, "Fear me."

The same pounding that always follows compulsion thrums through my head. His power forces its way into me, wrapping around every muscle. It's cold and slimy. I barely understand the words, but I know them as soon as my body obeys.

My legs tremble as terror works its icy fingers through my veins.

"It always tastes better when they are afraid," he says. "It's too bad you will never understand the sweet, tang of fear in mortal blood."

I open my mouth to tell him that I am not afraid, but I never get the chance.

His fangs rip into my skin. Fiery pain envelops my neck and shoulder, white hot, burning, burning, *burning*. I hear a scream, hoarse and cracked... and belatedly, I realize it belongs to me.

Then he releases me, taking a step back. He runs his tongue over his blood stained teeth, then licks his teeth. He uses a thumb to wipe away an invisible drop from the corner of his mouth. His eyes trail up from where he fed to meet my gaze. The black has swallowed up all of his eyes, and the veins spiderweb out of the corners of his eyes and across his cheeks. It looks like poison.

"Fall to your knees human," Victor orders. He laughs, it's deep, and throaty, and filled with my blood.

My knees hit the wood floor with a hard thud. My body continues to shake—partially from the fear he compelled upon me, and now because real fear is seeping in. I struggle to think as the power of compulsion fogs my mind. I don't know what to expect from him next.

Nothing about this is natural. His eyes should be red, not black.

Something is very, very wrong.

CHAPTER THIRTY-TWO

CLARA

"WELL, WHAT DO WE HAVE HERE?" CASSIUS STRIDES through the door, straightening the sleeves of his jacket. When he spots me, a devilish grin crosses his mouth.

Victor lifts his chin and shakes his head once. The black veins recede, and his eyes return to normal— save for some lingering black past the pupils. Then he turns toward Cassius as if he wasn't attacking me only seconds ago.

The hold of his compulsion lessens. My body is mine again. I should stand and leave the room, but all I can see is red.

How dare he take my blood without permission. How dare he compel me. How dare he touch me at all.

I reach for the dagger in my pocket and swipe at the vampire as I stand. The tip of the blade cuts across the side of his leg. My movements are slow and uncoordinated. Deep, but not deep enough to kill or slow him.

Fuck.

Blood wells up immediately, soaking the material of his trousers.

Victor rounds on me, hissing and baring his teeth. He lifts a hand high, ready to strike. I flinch. I've been struck in the face before, though never by a vampire. I expect the resounding pain, but it doesn't come.

My breath escapes my lungs in a woosh. Cassius is staying Victor's hand. For now.

"Let me go. I will kill her. That little bitch drew blood," Victor snarls.

Cassius raises a single brow. His expression changes, but I don't understand. My fingers tighten further on the hilt of the dagger. I will not let either of them kill me without a fight.

"Wrap your leg," the vampire orders. He releases Victor, and for a second, I think he might ignore Cassius and attack me anyway.

Cassius approaches with slow movements, he takes my wrist and removes the dagger from my grasp. I don't want to give it up, but if I resist, he might break my hand taking it. He sets it atop the piano, never taking his eyes off me.

Any positive thoughts I once had about either of them go up in smoke. I know them for the bastards they are.

I don't know what will happen next, but I do know that I am fucked. This will end badly. I'll be lucky if I have a somewhat quick death.

He shakes his head as if he's disappointed. "I really wish you'd taken my offer, little bird."

I want to ask him what he means when two new voices enter the room. They cease as soon as they step inside. Della takes in Victor, his leg, and the sliced drapes, then drifts over to where Cassius and I stand beside the piano. Lawrence levels me with an icy glare. "It seems," Cassius starts turning to face the three other vampires. "Our dear friend Alaric has not yet fully claimed his pet." He reaches out and grabs my wrist, pulling me forward so I can't hide behind him or reach for the dagger while his back is turned.

No one speaks. No one so much as moves or twitches a muscle.

I straighten my spine and square my shoulders. I might be surrounded by predators that don't care if I live or die. I might not have Alaric's full mark to protect me from their compulsion, but I refuse to cower.

"You know that even attempting to compel another's marked human is forbidden," Lawrence says after a long moment.

I'm shocked by his defense. He hates me.

Cassius smiles. "Ah, but she is not marked." He faces me, his eyes roaming up and down my body, lingering on the flesh of my shoulder for a long moment before turning back to the others. "Not fully.

I try to think back on our previous encounters. Had he known I wasn't marked? If so, then why pretend otherwise? Is this... is this payback for rejecting his offer?

"You wouldn't know without trying to compel her," Lawrence shoots back.

Cassius presses a hand to his chest in mock offense. "It was not I who compelled her. However, that doesn't matter now. We all know the truth." He takes a deep breath and sighs. "Unfortunately, she has drawn first blood and now it is within Victor's rights to demand a fight to the death."

The world sways under me.

"Look at her neck," Della says more to Lawrence, though we can all hear. "She's bleeding."

"You know feeding doesn't count as an attack, otherwise all humans would try to kill us when we are enjoying a meal," Cassius says before Lawrence can respond.

"Then we will wait until Alaric returns and then this mess can be sorted," Lawrence says.

I don't know why he is coming to my defense, but I could almost kiss him for it.

Victor leaps up from the sofa and takes several long strides toward me. "I will kill her right now for what she has done."

I take a step back, hating myself for showing weakness.

"It *is* his right," Cassius says with a shrug. As if they are discussing something trivial, like who gets to eat the last piece of desert.

"No," I say, glad my voice is steady despite my heart thundering in my chest. "That isn't a fair fight." I'm furious at them for debating my fate. I hold on to that anger and slap Cassius's hand away. "What chance does a human have against a vampire?"

Cassius actually has the nerve to look taken aback by my slapping his hand away. His green eyes sparkle with mirth. I glower. How heartless does he have to be to find humor in this situation?

Bastard!

I take in all four vampires. I have never been around them all at once without Alaric nearby. It's all too much to be a coincidence.

But who planned this, and why? I know it wasn't

Victor—I would be dead by now if he had, and the others wouldn't have arrived in time.

I narrow my gaze at Lawrence. He said it himself; he can't prove I killed Rosalie, but he suspects I did. He could have planned this to be rid of me while keeping his hands clean.

I tamp down my theories and questions. It doesn't matter. Because finding the answers won't save me now.

"These are ancient laws set forth by our queen. They are not for any of us to decide," Cassius holds his hands palm up as if he were the one rendered helpless. He motions to Lawrence and Della. Then he turns to pat me on my uninjured shoulder. "The three of us will witness and report the result to Alaric and Elizabeth."

My mouth drops open, and I can only stare. Being slaughtered while three others—who could save me— stand and watch is no comfort, but the way he talks, he seems to think it should be.

This will not be a good death.

Cassius grips my upper arm. I try to jerk away, but his hold is too strong, and my efforts only end up leaving bruises.

"Alaric will kill you," I snap.

He drags me to the center of the room, stopping me about two yards from Victor.

My limbs grow cold as I absorb everything about my opponent. My view is broken when Cassius steps in front of me, takes me by the shoulders, and kisses each of my cheeks as if he's wishing me luck in a game without deadly consequences.

A flash of red sears my neck, with the white-hot pain blinds me. And then it's gone. I stand panting, sweat beading across my brow. I reach up and feel my neck. *He healed me.*

Cassius's mouth quirks up as he backs away.

"This is a fight to the death. Make it clean. No compulsion is to be used, and no torture."

These rules are clearly for the vampire's sake. I will fight back, but ultimately I will lose.

Cassius retreats to stand close to Lawrence and Della. All three of them block the only way out. "On my mark."

Victor takes two steps forward. The thin, black lines reappear in his eyes, seeping out over his eyes.

Even without compulsion, I don't stand a chance against his preternatural strength or speed. I will die —but not without a fight. I swallow and widen my stance.

"What the fuck is happening here?" Alaric's deep, rich voice demands.

I have never been so relieved to see him as I am now. But that feeling doesn't last.

In a blink, Victor closes the distance between us, his hand swipes out, fingers curled into claws. I throw myself back to avoid the strike. He misses my neck, but his knife-like nails slice across my left shoulder to the center of my chest. I cry out and slam into the back of a sofa.

CHAPTER THIRTY-THREE

CLARA

I press one hand to my bleeding shoulder. Demon shit—it burns. My other hand grips the back of the sofa, fingers digging in as I try to stay upright. It shouldn't hurt this bad.

"Get out of my way," Alaric demands. "Stop this, this instant."

"You cannot interfere," Lawrence's cool voice responds. "I am sorry my friend, but you know the law."

The others say nothing.

I can't think of Alaric right now. The only things that matter are staying alive and the vampire in front of me.

Victor crouches in an unnatural pose and hisses before lunging. I push off the sofa and toward a nearby chair, putting it between us. It's small and would shatter with little effort from any vampire, but it's all I have. Victor doesn't change course fast enough and runs into the sofa. His claw-like nails shred the material as he turns toward me.

With his natural speed, he should have caught me and snapped my neck before I even knew what was happening… instead, he's toying with me.

I blink, and he rips the chair from between us, flinging it into the wall. It shatters, and thousands of splinters fall to the ground.

The air is ripped from my lungs as I'm slammed against a bookcase. Victor smiles triumphantly. The black has entirely swallowed up his eyes, and the lines vein out down his cheeks to his temples. They continue to grow into his hairline and down his face.

The shelves dig into my spine. There is nowhere for me to go. I can't run. So, I do the only thing I can think of. I ram my forehead into his face, aiming for the spot right between his eyes.

The pain is nearly blinding. Black spots form and dissipate. My vision wavers for half a second, but it works. Victor stumbles back as he grabs his face.

I run, not caring what direction I go in, as long as it's away from him. My hip hits a table sending a lamp and vase crashing to the ground.

fist tangles into my hair and jerks me to a stop.

Victor swings me around, slamming me into the piano. The force knocks something off and sends it clattering to the ground. He pulls my head back, bending my spine painfully back. I claw at his hand in my hair, desperately trying to get free. I reach out, feeling around for anything to use as a weapon.

Victor trails one hand up my arm. His blackened nails dig into the freshly made cuts. I cry out, but the sound is cut off by his hand clamping around my throat.

"I will make your death slow and painful," he says. Black moves in on the edges of my vision as his hold tightens. "I will not let you die fast. I will break every bone in your weak, human body, I—"

My fingertips brush against something cool. I stretch until my fingers wrap around the metal object and swing. The candelabra strikes him in the temple. Victor arches back.

The hand in my hair is gone but his other hand is still locked on my throat. I can't breathe. I swing at him again, but he wrenches the candelabra from my hand.

I have nothing left. My nails dig into the skin of his wrist.

"You'll pay for that, you little bitch," he snarls.

"Clara," Alaric's voice grips at my heart. He's so far

away, almost a whisper. My ears are ringing so loud that the rest of what he says is drowned out.

Victor throws me to the ground. Air fills my lungs, burning on the way in. Victor's foot strikes my ribs. I clutch my side as he gets down on his knees and straddles me. The black veins cover his face and move down his neck, and this time when he bares his teeth, they are all sharpened into points. He can rip out my throat without even trying.

"Cursed," Della gasps.

Victor leans forward, placing his hands on either side of my head, caging me in, his thighs squeezing my hips and holding me into place. "I can't wait to feel your true fear, hot on my tongue. I will drain every last drop from you before I'm finished."

My hand reaches out toward Alaric. I just want to hold his hand one last time. Hot tears spill down the sides of my face. I can't hold them back any longer.

Victor drops his head and runs his blackened tongue over the three gashes on my shoulder. It feels as though he is pouring acid on the wound.

"I will tear you limb from limb, and feed your body to swamp rats."

I grasp at anything I can hold onto. Something smooth and metal brushes against the back of my hand. I wrap my fingers around it and bring my arm up, burying the sharp point into Victor's side.

He rears back with an ear-splitting howl. The black veins swallow up every inch of exposed skin. I pull the dagger from his side. He swipes at me, his fingers are black as if dipped in ink. The bones become unnaturally long and come to sharp points that remind me of a demon's skeletal claws.

I barely have time to move before his mouth opens wide, and he is diving for my neck. I grip the hilt of the dagger with both hands and shove up. There's little resistance as the blade slides through flesh and bone.

Victor slumps forward, his weight pressing down on top of me, and as still as death.

My vision blurs. I cover my mouth with one hand as the first whimper threatens to break free.

Tears blur my vision. The hilt of the dagger presses painfully into my chest, making it hard to breathe as my body forces out silent and aching sobs.

I don't know how I managed to survive.

The weight is gone, and I gasp for breath. Alaric's face comes into view, distorted by the flood of tears I can't seem to stop. He helps me to stand. It hurts, but I don't care. Alaric draws me into his chest, holding me.

I feel nothing for having killed this vampire, but his death reminds me of another.

My hands are covered in blood.

I have killed again.

The stark contrast of this time from the first is more apparent than ever before. What I've done hits me with a force so strong it sends tremors through me.

"I'm sorry," I say, pressing my face into Alaric's chest. "I'm so, so, so sorry for Ro—"

Alaric smooths a hand over my hair and makes a shushing sound, cutting me off. "We will speak later."

He leans back and cups my face with his hands. His thumbs brush under my eyes, wiping away the tears. Feeling more collected in Alaric's arms, I look down at my would-be killer.

Victor is on his back. His eyes are open and staring unseeing at the ceiling. The night forged dagger is still imbedded in his chest.

He is dead, yet the black veins continue to spread, slithering over his body until his skin resembles charred meat. Welts form and spread.

Alaric takes several steps back, pulling me with him. I can't take my eyes off the grotesque spectacle. I tighten my grip on his and press into his side.

"Elizabeth will not be pleased," Lawrence's smooth voice says from the other side of the body. He crouches down and rubs his chin. He examines Victor as his body continues to morph.

"I don't give a fuck what Elizabeth thinks," Alaric snaps. "She sent a cursed vampire into my home."

Victor's skin dries and shrivels, spreading to his clothes and transforming them in much the same way as his skin.

I gasp as the fat, wart covered toad hops up onto his chest. The demon bloats to grotesque proportions, swelling and blistering like it's being set on fire from the inside. The demon croaks. It's a distorted sound, wet like melting wax, and then the power sweeps over them as well.

The toad crumples into a pile. The movement causes fissures to form all over Victor's body. The rifts spread, cracking and crumbling, and then he too becomes nothing more than an unrecognizable mound of ash.

"She killed a vampire," Cassius says. "Demon cursed or not, there will be a price to pay."

I want to say something. I should, but I can't put together a single, coherent thought. So instead, I glare up at the man standing behind Alaric, a stoic expression on his face. For his part in organizing the fight, he doesn't seem disappointed in the outcome, nor does he express any hint of malice, but perhaps something akin to... No, I'm mistaken—it couldn't be admiration.

"And an unmarked human at that," he continues.

"It was a fight to the death," Lawrence interjects.

He puts his hands on his knees and pushes up to stand.

I inhale sharply. *Yes. That was it.*

"She won. I have never seen it before, and it's certainly not expected, but there is no law against it."

"If she had been marked..." Cassius says, trailing off. Shaking his head, he turns away.

Alaric holds on to me a little tighter.

"You're in shock," he says. He reaches into his pocket and pulls out a handkerchief, pressing it to the gashes along my shoulder. I've bled all over his shirt. His eyes darken. "Come, we need to get you cleaned up and healed."

CHAPTER THIRTY-FOUR

CLARA

"No one is to report what happened here to Elizabeth." Alaric looks each vampire in the eye as if daring each to defy him.

I press tighter into his side, ready to be far from this room.

Della lifts her chin as we pass. Her nostrils flare, and she seems to be fighting to keep her expression in check. "He was her newest consort, you don't honestly expect her to remain unaware of his absence when the rest of us return, do you?"

I can't tell if she's displeased with the outcome of the fight or if she is having trouble reconciling Alaric's orders with Elizabeth's.

Alaric stops us. His eyes slide shut, and he pinches the bridge of his nose as if he's counting internally.

"Of course I don't, Della, but *I* will be the one to tell her." His eyes flick to the vampire at her side. "As Lawrence pointed out, it was a fight to the death." Then he raises his voice to address them all. "Clara Valmont bested Victor Connors. We all witnessed the fight—it was fair," he flinches at that word but continues, his voice booming through the room. "Both parties abided by the rules her majesty set in place."

Then one by one, they each dip their chin, acknowledging his command.

I look up at him questioningly as we begin walking again. He seems to have some sort of hold over them. I wonder if there is more to it than this being his home. Whatever it is, I keep my thoughts to myself.

Keeping the handkerchief pressed to my shoulder is more effort than I would have imagined. By the time we reach the top of the stairs on the second floor, I feel lightheaded and weak.

I've lost too much blood.

I pull away from Alaric to go to my room. I don't think I can make it up another flight of stairs without passing out. Each breath feels like I'm getting half the air I need, and a cool sweat dampens the edge of my brow.

The scowl on his face fades and is replaced with a worried look.

"Stay with me," he says.

He could order me, and I would have to comply, but this isn't a demand but a request. Alaric holds out a hand and I find I don't want to leave. Not yet anyway.

I slip my hand into his. And I must look as bad as I feel because he picks me up and carries me to the third floor. I let my body go limp and rest my head on his shoulder.

Wordlessly he sets me down on his bed and then strides into the bathing room.

I wait. I can hear him moving things around, then for a long moment, there is only silence. I slide my legs off the edge of the bed and stand. My ribs hurt, and even though I move slowly, waves of hot and cold wash over my body.

His back is to me when I reach the doorway.

"Alaric?" I say, but he keeps going through various vials and things. "Alaric," I say his name again.

He stills at the sharp tone in my voice. "Clara, you shouldn't be moving around."

I pad across the room, stopping a short distance from him. I reach up, intending to press my palm to his back. But the dried blood on my fingers stops me, and I let my hand drop back to my side.

"I'm sorry—" I say again.

I meant it when he saved me from drowning in the lake. But after tonight, I feel the weight of my actions more fully. Now he has seen me murder his kind with his own eyes. And it doesn't matter that I did so, this time, out of self-defense. The end result was the same.

I have killed another vampire.

"Go sit back down, I am almost done in here. I need to clean your wounds." His tone is cool and indifferent but not unkind.

I walk back to the bed and sit on the end, my legs dangling off, and face the bathing room.

He isn't going to heal me with his power... not that he owes it to me to do so. Truthfully, I don't think I want to go through that pain tonight, even if it means healing faster. If I stay perfectly still, my wounds don't hurt nearly as much.

Alaric returns with bandages and several small glass containers, each holding a different colored liquid. He kneels down, organizing the items in a line along the bedside table.

He removes my shoes and runs his fingers up my leg, checking one and then the other. His movements are methodical and efficient. Then he moves to my arms and checks them in much the same way. His fingers meticulously glide over my body, searching for wounds, no matter how small.

"Alaric?" I say.

But damn him, he continues on with his inspection until his hand reaches the side where Victor kicked me. I hiss through my teeth, and his eyes dart to my face.

I grab his hands. "I'm trying to talk to you."

"I know." He pulls his hand from mine, reaching for my left shoulder. With a single tug, the dress rips, and he lets the scraps hang loose to inspect the wounded flesh. His frown deepens. "I don't know how to fix this situation. I never should have left you."

"This is not your fault."

Alaric doesn't respond. He uncorks a bottle with a bright, pale blue liquid and dampens the edge of a cloth. He presses it against the first cut on my shoulder. I close my eyes, trying not to react to the sting. *Demon shit that hurts.*

"You don't have to fix anything on your own... this concerns me as well." I pause, swallowing against another onslaught of stinging as he continues to clean the long gashes. "Don't shut me out."

His movements falter at that. I had said them just before he gave me the second mark.

"You have no idea the dangers you're in."

He scowls at the bite on my neck that covers his mark. He applies the blue liquid, then a green salve over each open wound before wrapping them. The one on my neck loops under my opposite arm to avoid choking me. It's hardly comfortable, but at least the bleeding has stopped.

"Then tell me, Alaric." I take his hand and press it to my chest over my heart. It hurts, but I need him to open up.

His eyes don't move from our hands. "If they find out about the circumstances of Rosalie's death, then you will be killed."

I wait for more, but he doesn't continue.

"I know," I say. "We've both known this from the beginning."

He sighs and pushes to his feet. "It's getting late. You've lost a lot of blood and need your rest. First thing in the morning we begin preparations to leave in a week." He reaches down to a larger bundle of cloth and hands it to me. "Change into this."

I carefully unfold it, trying not to move too quickly and aggravate my injuries. I set it down and stand, trying to undo the ties of my dress at the back. The wraps are too tight, and my shoulder is in too much pain.

Alaric steps up behind me. I can feel his warmth against my back. His fingers take over, unlacing the dress and letting the ruined garment fall to the floor. One hand snakes over my bruised ribs like a breath of cool air. I feel myself melting under his touch. Then he snatches up the bundle and slips it over my head.

I smile, looking down at his choice.

It's horribly indecent to wear his shirts as often as I do, especially here when I have my own generous wardrobe. But the gesture has come to mean so much more than it would appear. When I wear one of his shirts, I know I'm safe.

I adjust the material, and when I turn around, he is sitting in a plush leather chair next to the fire, with a book in hand. I crawl into his bed and settle under the blankets. I watch him for a long time… watch how his eyes roam over the words on the page before moving on to the next. He turns each page with care to avoid creasing the paper.

"Are you planning to stay there all night?" I ask.

He doesn't look up from his book. "You should be asleep."

"What about you, don't you need sleep?" I ask.

"Do you wish me to?"

I nod. We both know he'll sleep when he needs to. Still, Alaric closes the book and sets it down.

I scoot to the middle of the bed I make room for him. Rather than sitting as he usually does, he removes his shirt and shoes and climbs in to lie beside me.

I curl into his side and rest my head on his chest, listening to the slow, steady rhythm of his heart.

"I'm sorry." It's all I can think of to say. I could say it a million times and still feel I need to say it again and again. But it's never enough, and the words I need to express myself do not exist.

There's a long silence and I'm unsure if he's fallen asleep. Slowly I lift my head, and he's gazing down at me.

"There's nothing to be sorry about." He purses his mouth as if tasting his next words, feeling them. "You have become dear to me, and as my dearest friend, I will do everything in my power to keep you safe from this fate I forced upon you."

I cock a brow. "You once said you didn't force this on me. I think *that* was the truth."

Alaric shakes his head. "No, I was trying to avoid the truth. I might not have forced you to fire that arrow, but I played my part in this."

I swallow and gather my nerves, pushing up on one elbow the best I can. "That's not what I meant, I'm sorry I killed Rosalie."

"I know."

I lay back down. I don't know what I wanted him to say, but I had expected more than those two little words. Unbidden, tears sting my eyes.

He reaches up and smooths my hair away from my face. "I forgive you, my dear Clara."

My breathing hitches. Did I hear him correctly?

"How?" My voice comes out small.

He pulls in a long, deep breath, then exhales. "Because… as someone wise once told me, we all do what we must for the ones we love."

My heart thunders against my ribs, and I know he can feel it. I don't know if he means that he understands that I did it for Kitty or that he's forgiving me for his sister's sake.

Or if he means me.

"Now sleep, dear Clara, and I will heal you so you do not have to feel the pain."

I nod against him and close my eyes. Soon, the sound of his breathing and heartbeat lulls me into unconsciousness.

CHAPTER THIRTY-FIVE

CLARA

A THIN LAYER OF FROST COATS THE WORLD IN ITS glittering beauty. Fog rolls over the land in thick waves. It's like walking through a beautiful dream. Once again, I slept in Alaric's room, his bed, and in his arms every night for the past week. I didn't even hesitate after that first night when he asked if I wanted to stay. Not a single night terror has stolen a minute of my time with him. He's been perfect, holding me every night.

Thinking about the promise he made sends a shiver down my spine and goose flesh to race over my skin.

Despite the years I spent hating all vampires because one killed Mother and tore my family apart, it is a strange feeling to know the one person I trust most in this world is one of them.

I press a hand to my chest and rub at the strange feeling that's settled there. Alaric's words warmed me, and yet… they were not what I wanted to hear—not that I have any idea what would have made me happy.

The weight of the dagger sits comfortably at my hip. I don't fear for my life, though I suppose I should with three other vampires still here. In the last week, I avoided Alaric, using the others to distract him.

I needed time alone to sort through my thoughts so I can try to understand what this connection to him is but walks in the gardens and hours in the library have done nothing to help. There is the feeling of waiting for something to happen—the first clash of thunder in a brewing storm. I itch to escape my skin, to do something, to act.

I have lost so much of who I've always believed myself to be. I no longer need to care for Kitty, I have no plans with Xander, and I can no longer justify killing vampires on sight as though they are all evil. Just knowing Alaric and understanding the kind of person Rosalie had been has changed that.

This transition from who I was to who I will be feels a lot like walking on a layer of thin ice. Underneath is a rapidly flowing river that will pull me under and sweep me away if I am not careful.

It's why this mark that ties me to Alaric scares me so much. It is taking a long time to get used to. If I'm not careful, I will find myself wandering toward him. I fear it will steal away the last of who I am. I have already lost so much. I don't want to lose whatever might be left to the effects of the mark. I don't want things between us to be forced or created by some outside force. I couldn't stand to lose my friend like that.

A pebble skips across the stone walkway behind me, drawing me out of my reverie. I draw my dagger in a fluid motion as I turn.

"Stay back. I will kill you if you try anything," I say, surprised my voice is calm and steady. Not long ago, the words would have been an empty threat.

Now, I mean them.

I am no longer afraid to do what I must to stay alive.

Lawrence lifts his hands showing me his palms and stopping several yards away. "I am not here to harm you. I only wish to talk." He gestures toward a bench half hidden by perfectly manicured shrubbery. "We can stand here if you like or sit if you prefer."

I study him—His posture, his expression, and even the way he looks at me. When I find no deception or hint of malice, I nod but keep my dagger in hand.

"Standing will do," I say.

"He should have killed you." Lawrence says. I'm not sure if he means Alaric when he claimed me or…

"Are you threatening me?"

"No. But it is the truth." He shakes his head. "Victor should have killed you. He was demon cursed."

"What is your point, Mr. Harkstead? I assume you have one?"

He takes one step forward, testing me. Then another. I refuse to retreat. "My point is that he was not the first vampire you've killed."

I blink several times. "Just how in the Otherworld did you come to that conclusion?" I ask in disbelief that I hope comes across as wonder rather than admission. "I was in shock."

He is standing right in front of me now, his hand on my wrist with the dagger. He doesn't squeeze or try to take it from me but rather keeps the weapon aimed away from him.

"You were in shock over the blood loss. But your expression was not one of someone who'd seen their first kill."

I laugh and it's a harsh sound. "That doesn't prove anything."

"It does," he says in a low voice that cuts me off. "There is no human alive who doesn't fear the repercussions of killing a vampire. It is only with their second that they have come to terms with the pain they will have to endure if caught."

I say nothing. His hazel eyes search mine, and after a moment, he releases my hand but doesn't move away.

"I loved her," he says.

My breath leaves me as though I were dealt a physical blow. His suspicion, the hostility… it makes sense now. *Why is he telling me this?* To extract a confession from me, or to confront Rosalie's killer, or just to express the heartbreak he feels.

He turns away, and I sheath the dagger, reaching for his hand.

"Lawrence…" I start, but I can't find the words to comfort him without admitting that he is right about me.

"A third kill will make you a slayer. There has not been one in over a hundred and twenty-five years." Lawrence removes his hand from my grip and walks back toward the manor.

I stare dumbly after him long after he enters the house. He loved her. *He loved Rosalie.*

One day I will tell him the truth, and I will ask for his forgiveness. Though how I can make up for this act to any of the people who loved Rosalie, I don't know.

I shake my head. There is nothing in this world

that could make up for that. I would still kill the bastard that claimed my mother and killed her—so I cannot expect anyone else to forgive me.

The morning chill finally settling into my bones. I don't entertain the idea that it could be my conversation with Lawrence that has caused it.

I sit down on the metal bench and look out across the lake to the forest that lies outside the property. Frost and fog give the land the appearance of being touched by magic.

The lake should scare me after early drowning in it. I keep waiting for fear to strangle me in the dark hours of the night, to jump at every sound, to cower at every shadow.

But it never comes.

I find the gentle lap of waves soothing.

"There you are," Alaric says from behind. His hands come down to rest on my shoulders.

My eyes slide closed. The sound of his voice, like a caress, sends shivers through me.

Alaric walks around the bench and sits next to me with only a hand's width between our bodies. He looks out at the small pond.

Warmth crawls up my neck at his nearness.

"You've been avoiding me during the days."

"No I haven't," I say too quickly, my voice shrill.

Alaric slowly turns to me with a doleful

expression. "You have. But what I can't figure out is why?"

I chew on the inside of my cheek and say nothing.

"Clara, you sleep in my arms—in my bed—every night. I have marked you, twice, and I have been inside you."

Demons and saints... why does the man have to say it like that? My face grows warm, and I think I might combust into flames in this very spot.

"Don't say it like that."

"Why not? It's true, or would you prefer if I said we've fucked?"

I glare. "No."

His dark gaze bores into me. There's no way he misses my blush, which makes it worse. "You are the human I have claimed—you are already everything you should be. It's natural for us to want to be near the other."

"Am I needed for something?" I blurt, desperate to change the subject.

Alaric regards me. I've been cold and distant toward him during the past week, but still willingly climb into his bed and have him hold me during the night. I have no doubt my actions are confusing.

"Clara... you did not have to return if you wished to stay with your sister." There is hurt in his words.

Stop being a coward, I scold inwardly. *He deserves to know what is going on in my head.*

"I know… that's not it." I turn to him, but my eyes stay locked on my hands as I twist my fingers. I blow out a breath and say, "I'm afraid I will lose who I am… that I'll end up becoming nothing more than a warm body that only wants to please you. That all my thoughts will be of wanting you." I bite down hard on my lip. I can't believe I'm admitting this. "The aspect of being with you isn't what bothers me… I would just rather it be on my own terms, not be forced on me by the mark." By the time I finish speaking, my voice is barely above a whisper.

We are friends… wanting him will make everything more complicated.

Alaric hooks a knuckle under my chin and raises my head until I look him in the eyes.

Demon shit, this is so much worse out loud than it was in my head.

"The mark can only heighten emotions and feelings, not create them. Nothing will become of you that isn't already there."

"That's just it. I'm not sure there is anything of me left. I don't know who I am anymore."

I should explain more, should say that all my goals and plans I've held onto for years are suddenly gone.

That those who've always been in my life are gone. But I think he already understands that.

"It is true that you are different since you've come back," he says.

My hand immediately goes to the spot on my neck where he bit me. Alaric gently takes my hand and lowers it before my thoughts spin out of control.

He shakes his head. "I mean, you are… softer than before." He entwines our fingers.

I freeze. Worried he will reject me for being weak. I look down. "I have," I agree. "I've become… weak…" I look down at my open palms. "I feel lost." The admission comes out barely above a whisper.

"Do not mistake softness for weakness. You can be soft and strong." His thumb traces lazy circles on the back of my hand. "You had a fight to the death with a cursed vampire and won. Do not think for one second that you are weak, Clara. It takes great strength to allow your heart to be vulnerable." He pauses for a long moment, then adds, "You have also changed me."

I have changed *him*? He is a vampire—eternally unchanging—so I don't understand how that is possible. He could be saying that to make me feel better. But something between us is shifting. Though I don't understand it.

"I did?"

He lifts my chin with a knuckle until I'm looking into those midnight depths. "It is a good thing. Life is change, and when you cease to grow and change, you die."

He releases me. This time, I don't look away.

"I think we both needed it. Now we can continue to change for the better... perhaps we can even grow together." Alaric stands and holds out his hand to me. I take it and let him help me to stand. "Sometimes you need to lose yourself to find out who you really are. Do not be afraid of that."

We walk slowly through the garden, back toward the manor.

"Do you want the final mark before we leave?" The question is so sudden I nearly trip over my own feet as I come to a sudden stop.

My breath hitches, and I squeeze my thighs together as I think about what that would mean and the promise he made after the last time.

Yes.

"No. I'm not ready. I'm not—" I stammer. "You said I didn't have to have the final mark... that the second would last a month and we have two weeks."

His hands slide over my shoulders, then glide up and down my arms as if trying to chase away a chill.

"You don't have to explain," he says. Then after a moment, he adds, "I asked because my reason for seeking you out was to tell you we are to leave within the hour."

I nod. "I will be ready."

In truth, I have been ready for the last two days. My trunks are packed, and all I need are a few small items that will take less than five minutes to gather.

He suddenly looks exhausted. "Are you ready to play the game again? Everyone must believe you are fully marked. There is no room for failure." Alaric's gaze flicks toward the manor, toward his vampire guests. "We must play the game better this time."

"I understand," I say.

"No," he says sharply. "Not only do you need to make the queen and the others believe it, but you must make me believe it as well."

I nod.

He closes what little space there is between us, his hands roaming over me. His touch leaves a trail of heat—intense and immediately overwhelming. I take half a step back before stopping myself.

This is a test.

"We will make them all believe," I say.

I place my hands on his chest and slide them up around his neck as I rise up on my toes and kiss him. I don't hold back. I don't even need to try. I simply stop resisting. As his mouth moves against mine, I moan. I forget for a second what this is until he smiles and breaks the kiss, pulling away.

"Good." He pushes a lock of hair behind my ear. "You and I cannot fail."

I nod again. My throat is dry, but not from fear. Going deeper into this shadow world of vampires will be dangerous, but I am not afraid of the unknown.

And though I am uncertain about what I want and who I am, I do not need to be protected.

I do not need to be saved.

I am strong enough to do those things on my own.

I take Alaric's hand in mine. I know I can do this with him at my side.

"It is an impossible task, and if we are found out, you will be taken from me. They will kill you if you are lucky." He's trying to scare me into understanding, but I already do. "You will be prey to them."

"They will think I am nothing more than a helpless human." A crooked smile forms on my lips.

"You are anything but." One corner of Alaric's mouth ticks up into a matching smirk. "Let them underestimate you and let them live to regret it."

THANK YOU

Thank you for reading The Vampire Curse. It's always so much fun to explore new worlds and old, and to watch my characters come to life on the page.

If you enjoyed reading The Vampire Curse, then please consider leaving an honest review on Amazon, Bookbub, or Goodreads.

Reviews are so, so important for helping other readers decide whether or not to read a certain book. They don't need to be long or super descriptive. A single sentence or a few words is all that's needed. Positive, neutral, or negative feelings are all valid. All I ask is that you be mindful not to spoil the story or the ending for your fellow readers.

Stay in touch and be among the first to learn about new releases, cover reveals, character art, special offers, exclusive content (first few chapters, bonus scenes, and spontaneous shorts), and more by signing up for my newsletter!

www.aliwinters.com/newsletter

ADULT TITLES

SHADOW WORLD GOTHIC EPIC ROMANTASY:

The Vampire Debt series:

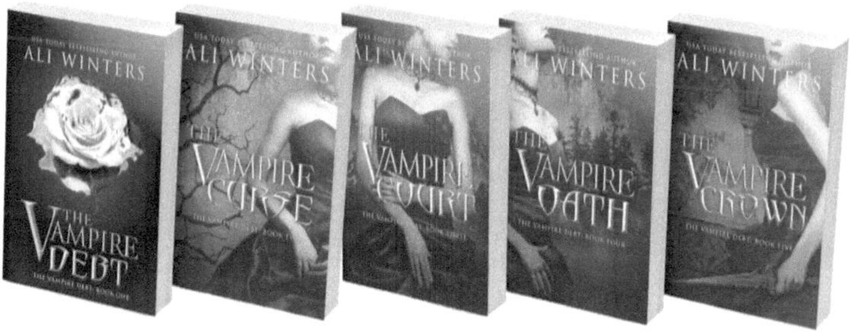

It is a truth universally acknowledged that a single

Vampire in possession of a good fortune must be in want of a mortal snack.

Learn more: **www.thevampiredebt.com**

SHADOW WORLD: STAND ALONES:

WICKED PRINCE OF FROST: an epic gothic romantasy

He promised to heal her broken heart, but if she's not careful, he may just end up taking it for himself.

Learn more: **www.aliwinters.com/shadowworld**

THE VAMPIRE TRAP: A Shadow World novella

When a series of murders breaks out across the city of Sangate, all evidence points to the most powerful vampire in the city.

Learn more: **www.aliwinters.com/shadowworld**

STAND ALONES:

HIGH STAKES: A stand alone Urban Romantasy novella

Elle Darling takes a bounty on an item retrieval job that sounds simple enough, but soon becomes deadly when the secret surrounding it is one many would kill to possess. She could end up losing her job or worse… her life.

Learn more: **www.aliwinters.com/standalones**

YOUNG ADULT TITLES

THE HUNTED SERIES:

A Reaper and her mortal enemy must team up to save the balance of life and death before all is lost. Unfortunately, to succeed, one of them must die.

Learn more: **www.aliwinters.com/the-hunted-series**

IN THE END DUOLOGY:

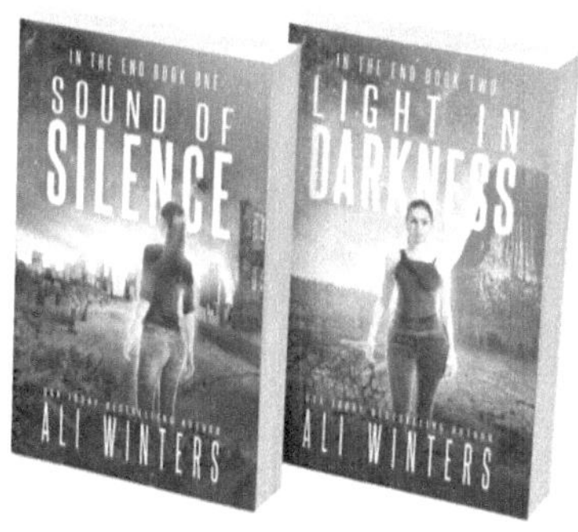

We thought we were alone in the universe. Turns out we were wrong. Dead wrong. —This book is a Romeo and Juliet retelling and contains insta-love, aliens, a virus, and zombies.

Learn more: **www.aliwinters.com/sos**

FAVOR OF THE GODS: a short story

"Like Icarus, you flew too close to the sun. Someone had to bring you back down to reality. You don't belong with princesses, heroes, or demigods."

Learn more: **www.aliwinters.com/standalones**

CAST IN MOONLIGHT

Welcome to Havenwood Falls, a small town where nobody is what you think, where truths pose as lies, and where myths blend with reality.

Cast in Moonlight is a stand alone novella in the shared world of Havenwood Falls, a multi-author collaboration.

Learn more: **www.aliwinters.com/standalones**

ABOUT THE AUTHOR

Ali Winters is the USA TODAY Bestselling author of several series filled with romance, magic, and adventure. She enjoys breaking down characters to build them up so they find their true strengths.

Her first love will always be fantasy, but she fully admits to being obsessed with coffee and T-Rex, and has a weakness for love interests that walk the line between gray and villainy.

Connect with Ali online
www.aliwinters.com

facebook.com/authoraliwinters

instagram.com/authoraliwinters

bookbub.com/authors/ali-winters

tiktok.com/@authoraliwinters

www.ingramcontent.com/pod-product-compliance
Lightning Source LLC
Chambersburg PA
CBHW031617180726
48284CB00005B/1578